INFERNO

HERITAGE OF FIRE: BOOK THREE

EMMA L. ADAMS

This book was written, produced and edited in the UK, where some spelling, grammar and word usage will vary from US English.

Copyright © 2019 Emma L. Adams
All rights reserved.

To be notified when Emma L. Adams's next novel is released and get a free prequel short story, *Adrift*, sign up to her author newsletter.

An angry dragon shifter was a dangerous thing indeed. A vengeful, grieving one, even more so. I tossed a handful of shattered fragments of Moonbeam stone across the hillside, which reflected a cloudy sky that *looked* like the one I knew well, and yet was as far from home as it was possible to be. My reflection shone back at me in fragments—bright red hair, ashy grey eyes, pale features that looked achingly similar to my sister's.

My sister, now trapped in dragon form. Because she'd given her life for mine. If my rage was a current, my grief was a tidal wave I struggled to keep in check.

A shadow fell on me from behind, and the tall, muscular form of Zeph, my fellow dragon shifter, walked up beside me. His auburn hair was longer and messier than usual, his clothes torn and stained with blood. "No luck?"

"No." I ran the heel of my shoe over the shards of

broken stone. "No magic can fix this. We're officially stuck here."

Zeph picked up a piece of the glass-like material. "The Moonbeam is a magical artefact. There's no reason we shouldn't be able to use shards of it as portals without it being whole, right?"

"Theoretically, no," I allowed. "But it's burnt out. And even if it wasn't, how can we take Ember back with us when she's stuck in her dragon form?"

Let's just say some humans' attitudes towards dragons hadn't changed much in the last thousand years. Given certain dragon shifters' predilection for plotting world domination, I supposed I couldn't really blame them after recent events. But the thought of *never* going home... of never seeing my sister's human face again...

No. I wouldn't accept it.

"We have to make a plan, said Zeph. "We have enough supplies for what, a week? Less, if you count the dragonling, but he can at least hunt for himself. We don't even know if this realm is survivable for humans."

"It must be. Dragon shifters lived in that city in both human and dragon forms." Or they had, once. Now, everything was in ruins.

Inside the cathedral-like stone structure on the hillside, Becks curled up in cat form, her amber eyes alert despite her relaxed pose. Behind her, Will and Kit sat with the dragonling, a handful of rucksacks containing our supplies heaped on the grass at their side. Tall and graceful like most half-faeries, Kit sat close to his boyfriend, who looked thin and tired, worn down by his near-miss with the virus that had almost killed all the supernaturals in London.

The dragonling, Thorn, curled up next to one of the crooked pillars inside the stone construction. He was taller than my shoulder by this point, his body more than five feet long when extended. His scales had lightened to opalescence, and his horns had grown several inches in the last few weeks. It would be a month or two at most before he reached full size.

Will stirred when I walked closer. "Any luck? Because I don't fancy my chances out there in the wilderness. A half-gargoyle is no match for a pack of dragons."

"They won't attack us." At least I hoped they didn't. "I've been to the city before. Maybe I can help them settle in."

On the other hand, I'd broken the Moonbeam and trapped us all here to begin with. The others hadn't believed the power in the stone belonged to a fire goddess who'd happily have seen us all burn… mostly because said fire goddess had used the Moonbeam's own magic to hypnotise them into obedience. I could only hope her influence had shattered along with the stone.

Zeph cast a glance at the crate of dragonling eggs lying a few feet away from Becks. Now *that* was an issue we had yet to confront: what to do when they all hatched. "Not to be a downer, but the other dragons were seconds from ripping our throats out earlier."

"Lorne had them under his thrall. Under the Moonbeam's." I waved a hand in the general direction of its shattered remains. "The hypnosis effect should have broken along with it."

"If you say so." Will ran a hand through his tangled blond hair. "I don't see them lining up to thank us."

"They just lost everything." We had, too. Even Agnes,

our witch-mage ally, was on the other side of the portal, unreachable. All we had left was a city, abandoned after the dragon clan war sixteen years ago, and it didn't take a genius to figure out it'd be nothing like London.

Out of the corner of my eye, I spotted Astor, sitting on a rock apart from the others. His brown hair was tangled, his face unshaven, and his green eyes were fixed on a point far in the distance. I followed his gaze and my chest tightened at the sight of Ember's dragon form in the sky. It wasn't unusual for the former assassin to be taciturn and antisocial, but he'd been ignoring us since Ember's spirit had become trapped in Death.

Ember stopped mid-flight, swiping at something in the fog. Several jagged shapes appeared in the gloom, descending through the clouds.

"Hey!" I shouted. "Get away from my sister."

I bounded into the air, my wings extending, scales clothing my reptilian form. Letting out a roar, I flew towards the oncoming horde of winged monsters.

Not those bastards again.

Each beast was smaller than a dragon shifter, but had similar tough scales, hard to penetrate even with claws. Red and black in colour, they had jagged wings, pit-like eyes, and clawed talons that could rip through human skin straight to the muscle. Luckily, dragon scales were a tad more resilient. One beast flew at me, our claws clashing. Its blow didn't even make a dent in my ruby red scales, and I ripped upwards, tearing its head clean off. The headless winged body fell out of the sky, but another took its place. Where in hell had the swarm come from?

Zeph rose into the air behind me, his blue-white dragon scales reflecting the weak sunlight. With three sets of claws, we tore down our assailants, creating a shower of red droplets mingling with the fog.

Despite the low visibility level, it was nice to stretch my wings over the countryside with no fear of terrifying the humans below. Maybe I understood why the dragons had chosen this realm as their home, with its rolling hills and wide-open spaces. Few such wild areas remained in the mortal realm, and even fewer where dragons could freely roam.

Ember turned to me, her ashy grey eyes shining in recognition. She knew me as her sister, even trapped in her shifter form and reduced to instinct alone. She gave a faint growl, an invitation to join her.

I shook the last droplets of the monster's blood from my claws and flew up to meet her, my wing brushing hers. *Fly with me?*

She dipped her head in understanding and adjusted her path to fly at my side. The rolling hills gave way to larger mountains in one direction, their peaks disappearing into the clouds. Below, the dragon's city spread out in an expanse of grey stone buildings and gleaming gold points which I assumed must be statues or other decorations. I skirted the city's edge to avoid being spotted, wanting to enjoy my time with Ember a little longer before I flew down to speak with the other dragons.

Behind the city were more mountains, blocking any view of what lay behind. The rolling hills continued to the east and south, marked with patches of trees. This realm didn't appear to have reached as high a technology level as earth, so it made sense there'd be more countryside and fewer cities. Yet no matter how far we flew, home wasn't reachable from the sky. Despite the feel of the wind buffeting my leathery wings, I missed the city of London like a physical ache deep within me.

Ember's wing brushed mine again as we turned back to complete our circuit of the area. As the cathedral-like stone structure came into view, I spotted Astor walking alone through the fog in the direction of the dragons' city.

As Ember continued to fly, I landed on the hill, shifting to human form again.

"Hey!" I stepped in front of Astor. "Where do you think you're going?"

"Away," he said curtly. "You might be content to fly around like you haven't a care in the world, but some of us want to get out of this shithole."

"Look, you're a former League hunter. There's a whole city full of angry dragons down there. How do you think this is going to work out?"

His mouth flattened. "They won't see me."

Right. Assassins rarely used the door, and they certainly didn't knock when they did. "At least warn the others you're leaving, or they'll worry about you."

"I sincerely doubt that."

"If not, then it's because you act like an enraged hedgehog whenever anyone except Ember tries to be nice to you."

"An enraged *what?*"

"You know, prickly." Attempting to employ my usual humour fell flat with Astor. "Ember wouldn't want you to go wandering off alone and get eaten by a monster. You can't even see where you're going in the fog."

"Neither can you."

"There are mountains that way and that way." I

pointed. "And elsewhere, a whole lot of nothing. You won't find what you're looking for out there, Astor."

"And what exactly do you think I'm looking for?"

"A way to set Ember free. And get home. In that order. You know I can see her ghost, don't you?"

He stopped mid-step. "What? She's not dead."

"No, but her spirit's imprisoned on the other side of the veil," I said. "And I have the spirit sight."

He whipped round to face me. His eyes were duller than usual, but for the first time, a spark of interest stirred. "Take me to her."

With Astor, manners were a secondary concern if at all. "I can't make you able to see and hear her. I might have the spirit sight, but I'm not a powerful enough necromancer to do more than speak to her."

His expression said, *that's not good enough.* Tough shit, Astor. I'd never viewed my ability to see and speak to ghosts as an asset—generally, they were downright annoying—but right now, my spirit sight was the one line of communication left between me and my sister.

"Don't pick on Cori," Ember said, her ghost appearing at my side. Like me, she had long curly auburn hair and ashy grey eyes, though faded and transparent in her spirit form.

"She just ordered you not to pick on me," I told Astor. "She's right... there."

I pointed through her transparent body. If I squinted, I could pretend she stood alongside me just like old times.

Astor wasn't so lucky. "She would say that. She's the one who threw herself in harm's way to save your neck."

"She's my big sister." I folded my arms. "Wouldn't you have done the same?"

He didn't say anything for a long moment. Then: "I've never had anyone I'd throw my life away for. Not until her."

I opened and closed my mouth. I mean, what was I supposed to say to that? It was the closest I'd come to hearing anything genuinely heartfelt from him, and it made me want to promise to help him get her back. But there was no repairing the Moonbeam even if I'd wanted to.

If the Moonbeam came back, so did its owner. And there was the slight issue of it being a weapon designed to turn shifters into mindless killing machines.

Ember's ghostly eyes filled with tears. "Tell him I'm here, even if he can't see me. I'm trying to find a way back."

I repeated her words. Astor's harsh expression didn't change, but he began to walk back towards the others. I spotted Zeph, who'd landed some feet away, and went to join him.

Zeph's eyes followed the ex-assassin. "He wasn't bothering you, was he?"

"Of course not. He's devastated over losing Ember."

I never thought I'd find myself defending Astor, of all people, but out of our group, the two of us had been closest to her.

"Is he leaving?" asked Zeph.

"No," I said. "Not now he knows I can see and talk to Ember in the spirit realm, even if I can't in person."

Zeph's arm came around me. "We'll get her out of that trap, Cori."

I dipped my head. Astor's eyes were averted, like he

couldn't bear to look at us happily embracing. We walked back to the others in silence.

Becks, back in human form, sat on her trench coat on the grass. "Enjoy your flight?"

"I figured we might as well make the most of all this open space."

"It's like taking a holiday," said Will. "Except instead of sun and sea, we get monsters and probable starvation."

The dragonling let out a faint whining noise. Will had a point. We had little more than the clothes on our backs. I didn't even have a change of underwear, and my flight had told me there was a marked lack of department stores here in the dragons' realm.

What did the other dragons do when they lived here, then?

"We're going to the city," I told the others. "The other dragon shifters are all there, and it's better for us to mend things with them if we're staying here for the long haul. I bet they have more supplies than we do."

"Assuming they don't chase us off for destroying the Moonbeam," added Will.

"Well, yeah," I said. "But it's them or those monsters spawning out of the sky, and I like our chances better the more dragons we have with us. Besides, if there's a way to free Ember, we're more likely to find it in the city than anywhere else."

"And we might find a way to remake the Moonbeam, too," said Zeph.

"Without setting that madwoman free," added Will. "Which sounds like a long shot."

Unfortunately, he's right. As Ignessa herself had told me, there was no freeing my sister without freeing the fire goddess along with her.

"Will, don't be a downer," Kit reprimanded him.

"Let me adjust to being stuck in a hostile world inhabited by monsters first." Will climbed to his feet. "All right, let's go. You lead the way, Cori."

I'd have rather flown, but Astor refused point-blank to ride on any dragons other than Ember, and the others might be less likely to react with hostility if we met them on the ground. We walked for a long while, Zeph and I leading the way. My fellow dragon shifter was the only member of our group who didn't look utterly exhausted.

"What are you thinking?" I asked him.

"I'm thinking that if I don't get a decent meal soon, I might have to shift and find a sheep to snack on."

"I don't know about you, but I haven't seen any sheep since we got here," I said. "Or any other living creatures, come to that. Maybe the other dragon shifters will be nice and share."

They must have seen us coming, because several dragon shifters stood waiting for us on the platform that marked the entryway into the city. On either side, a number of golden dragon statues flanked the walkway leading into the city proper. In the centre of the group stood a female dragon shifter with long auburn hair streaked with grey.

Azalea's hostile eyes met mine. "You left us here."

"I didn't mean to," I said. "We had to stop Lorne."

I didn't expect to be showered in praise, but the dozen pairs of ashy eyes facing us flared with sparks of orange— the first sign of a dragon shifter about to shift and unleash the flames.

"You destroyed the Moonbeam," she said. "Many would want me to have you executed for dooming us all."

My throat went dry. "I'm sorry. I don't know if you saw her, but Ignessa, the fire goddess—she tried to kill all of you, and the only way to stop her was to destroy the Moonbeam. I didn't mean for us to get stranded here. I did it to save all your lives, and I don't want to be your enemy."

She looked down at me, but it wasn't her eyes that watched me. Ignessa's light shone in the back of her gaze.

It can't be true. She's gone. Like Ember, Ignessa was nothing more than a ghost. Less, even, because she didn't have a real body to return to. That was why she'd tried to take Lorne's—and burned him from the inside out in the process.

So why did Azalea's stare remind me so much of hers?

"We have decided to grant you a trial," added the dragon shifters' leader. "All of you, follow me to the square."

Crap. That wasn't a good sign.

2

I'd hardly assumed we'd be welcomed with open arms, but the hostility pouring off the other dragons made me want to fly back to the relative safety of our camp. I found myself glad we'd left the dragonlings behind, though heaven knew what would happen if the eggs hatched while we weren't around.

Azalea, leader of the dragon shifters, had struggled to hold their fragile society together after Lorne's arrest, and while we'd never been the best of friends, she'd always been approachable. Then again, breaking the Moonbeam was the dragon shifter equivalent of throwing the crown jewels into an active volcano. The least I could expect was to face charges, and I had no money to my name except for a handful of coins in my pocket. *If Ignessa's influence had yet to leave Azalea's mind, to say we were screwed* was an understatement.

Our group reached the wide stone square in the centre of the dragons' city, marked by a colossal golden statue of a dragon. *Ignessa.* Generations of dragon shifters had worshipped and revered her, and nobody had known her true nature until Lorne had used her magic to destroy them. With him gone, they needed another target to blame for their misfortune, and it looked like they'd found one. Us.

The goddess stared back at me from a dozen pairs of eyes as the other dragon shifters formed a circle around our group, preventing us from fleeing.

"Shift and you die," said Azalea.

"We're your *allies*," I said. "I'm willing to make up for breaking the Moonbeam, but if you saw anything of what that fire goddess did—"

"I saw *you* destroy everything we spent our lives fighting to regain from Lorne's rule," she said. "We have lost our homes, our possessions, and too many have lost our lives to the virus he brought into our village. Now the only means of curing the virus has gone, thanks to you."

I winced inwardly. While we'd used the Moonbeam to cure every victim we could reach, if the virus returned, the dragons would have no defence against it. I understood their anger, but if I hadn't destroyed the Moonbeam, Ignessa would have vaporised every one of them.

"That was Lorne, not us," I said through dry lips. "And he's dead now. We can move on, and build a new life here together."

"We will never ally with you," said a male dragon shifter. Neil, who'd once visited our house to beg for our help. "You burned Lorne alive using unnatural magic. What's to stop you from doing the same to the rest of us?"

"Ignessa did it, not us," Zeph said from my side. "We are not your enemies."

Not a single sympathetic voice rose in our defence.

Chills raced down my back, and I turned on my spirit sight, letting grey flood my vision. Sure enough, behind the group of dragons floated the image of a woman with fiery eyes, a triumphant smile on her face.

Ignessa had poisoned their minds, and somehow, that influence had lingered even after the Moonbeam had shattered. I should have known death wouldn't be the end of her.

"Do you deny destroying the Moonbeam, Cori?" Azalea said.

There was no use in shifting and putting up a fight. Destroying my allies would serve nobody but Ignessa herself.

I shook my head. "No, I don't. But you saw what Ignessa did to Lorne. She would have done the same to all of us, given the chance. I had to do it, and I don't regret it."

"Even though your sister paid the price?" Azalea gave me a pitying look. "I have decided to show you mercy, so I will. Every one of you will be jailed indefinitely."

Disgruntled mutters passed among the other dragons.

"You're aware that's a death sentence, right?" I looked around, trying in vain to find someone who'd escaped the goddess's influence. "Can you live with that?"

"If it were up to me," said Neil, "I'd kill you myself."

The circle of dragons closed in. My claws slid out, on instinct, but even dragon shifters know when to accept defeat. For the sake of my friends, I had to give in.

Someone shoved a bag over my head. I spat out the stale-tasting cloth, my body tensing as the male dragon shifter hoisted me over his shoulder.

"I could shift right now and make things really awkward," I said through a mouthful of cloth.

"You could drop dead, too," growled the dragon shifter.

I writhed and struggled, but with the bag on my head, I couldn't see the right angle to kick him in the nuts. He didn't shift, carrying me in human form for a good five minutes through the city. I tried to count the turns—with a grid-like structure, the city was easy to memorise—but the lack of sight scrambled my sense of direction.

Then the air chilled, and my back slammed into cold, hard floor, hard enough to bruise my shoulders. I scrambled backwards, fetching up against a stone wall.

Since nobody else obliged, I yanked the bag off my head. Narrow metal bars greeted me, floor to ceiling, tall enough to accommodate a dragon. The door was bolted on the outside, while the window was too high to reach. Too high to reach as a human, that is.

The cell must be dragon-proofed, given its size, but it was worth a shot. I shifted my hands to ruby red claws, grabbing the bars on the door. An electric shock surged through my blood, sending me flying back a good five feet. My back slammed into the wall, and my spirit sight switched on as my head collided with hard stone. Fog swam before my eyes, and I swore I heard someone laughing. Maybe another dragon spying on me through the high window. I gave them the finger, whoever they were, and sat down to nurse my bruised pride.

Once my vision returned to normal, I scooted back over to the bars. Another cell lay opposite mine on the other side of a short corridor. Did I have a neighbour? Darkness filled the space within, too dark to make out any shapes on the other side. Another glance revealed my rucksack, lying in the corridor just out of reach of my cell door.

"Oh, that's just mean." I didn't have much in there, just a bottle of water and a few snack bars as far as I remembered. If the 'indefinitely' part wasn't a bluff, I was as good as dead either way, but the supplies in the rucksack would buy me a few days. Talk about a cruel and unusual punishment.

I spent the next couple of hours trying to find creative angles to wedge my hand through the bars to reach the bag without being electrocuted. My back hit the wall so many times it started to go numb, while my head pounded violently in protest at being flung against the stone so many times. I even tried shifting my feet and reaching my back claws through the bars but got only a bruised tailbone for my trouble. Minutes turned to hours, and my energy began to flag. The cell contained nothing but a dirt floor, no furniture, just a hole at the back to use as a toilet which wasn't big enough to crawl through to use as an escape route. Given the foul smell lingering around the place, I didn't want to find out what lay at the bottom. Maybe eventually I'd be skinny enough to fit through the cage bars, if I didn't implode from impatience first. I paced in circles, growling in frustration to distract myself from the hunger pangs.

Dragon shifters had been hunted by supernatural and human enemies for centuries, but I'd never thought I'd die in such an undignified manner. Starving to death in a cage. I debated summoning Ember, but imagining the sorrow on her face at my predicament stopped me short.

Eventually, sleep claimed me, only to send me cascading into dreams of holding the Moonbeam in my hands, pushing my life force into it until I felt myself beginning to fade… and then Ember threw herself in the way, and the Moonbeam shattered apart. Again and again, I saw my sister disappear in a flash of fire, until I woke with my throat dry as bone, and my rucksack right next to the door, reachable through the cage bars.

Huh? Did someone move it? A sympathetic dragon shifter, maybe. I extended a hand through the gap, pulled the open mouth of the bag closer to the bars and surveyed the contents. A couple of water bottles, a few snack bars, nothing substantial, but more than I'd thought I had.

My throat was too dry to thank my rescuer, so I guzzled the water, then tried to ration the rest. I had a guardian angel somewhere out there. Or guardian dragon. I was still trapped in the cell, but I wasn't dead yet.

I rationed the water over two days. On the third, the bag refilled itself. By now, I was sure there was something screwy going on. I emptied the bag and tried to stay awake to watch and see who came in to refill it, but nobody did.

I'd learned my lesson about trying to open the door, but that didn't stop me from shifting and attempting to reach the upper window. On the fourth day, I managed a half-shift that brought me high enough to see the sky. My wings itched to spread wide and fly over the hills, and a wild impulse seized me. Just once, I'd try the bars—

A low, rasping female voice spoke from the cell opposite mine. "You're even denser than you look."

I jumped, hitting my head on the ceiling. Stars winking before my eyes, I shifted to human and sank to the floor. "You're alive?"

"Can't you tell the difference?"

I squinted into the gloom, but the cell was too dark for me to see who spoke to me. "I guess you'd smell worse if you'd been dead for a while."

Silence. Perhaps I'd insulted her. Then she said, "I suppose. I'm Ayla."

"How long have you been here?" I asked her. "How are you still alive, if nobody's lived here in sixteen years?"

Unless…

I turned on my spirit sight. Grey light seeped into my vision, showing an outline of a female spirit. If the air of neglect around the place was anything to go by, the woman talking to me had been dead a long time.

She gave a coughing laugh. "I was once the leader of this entire city, but I suppose you won't remember it."

"You ruled this place?" I shifted into a more comfortable sitting position. "You mean, you ruled over Lorne?"

"Him." His name came out as a snarl. "He ruined us."

Ayla's words sent a deep chill into my bones. She'd lived through the war—well, not *lived*, but endured. She might even have known my parents.

A thousand questions exploded into my mind, and for the first time in days, curiosity about the realm that had become my new home roared to life inside me.

"It's his fault I'm trapped here, too," I told her. "He thought he was acting of his own volition, but it was someone else, controlling his actions. Was… was it the same with the war? I mean, I know Lorne's a scumbag, but there's someone else who's been pulling the strings here for a long time."

"You mean Ignessa."

The sound of her name lit a spark of fiery hatred

inside my chest. "The other dragons used to worship her, right?"

"Some did," she said. "You might have gathered she feeds on strife and engenders hatred and mistrust. War is her natural state of being."

"She's dead, though," I said. "Right?"

"Does it matter?"

"For most people… yes, it does." I drew my knees up to my chest. "But for a god, I guess the usual rules don't apply. So I broke the Moonbeam for no reason."

The ghost floated closer to my cell door. "You broke the Moonbeam? Is that why Lorne threw you in here?"

"Lorne's dead," I said. "If you've been here since the dragon clans' war, you've missed a lot of history. Sixteen years of it."

"Sixteen years," she murmured. "Why… for me, it's been mere weeks since the war."

Weeks? *Impossible.*

Cold dread rippled down my spine. Weeks had passed at home during my first trip here, and it had lasted an hour at most. This time, I'd been here for days. Even if I made it out of this cave, would there be anything left of Earth to go back to?

"It's been a lot longer for me." I spoke to drown out the fear threatening to steal my breath. "I was five when my parents were killed in the war."

"They weren't the only ones," Ayla said. "More died than survived. You were lucky to escape, and foolish to return."

"I didn't plan to end up stuck here," I said. "If it's only been a few weeks since the war, why does this city look so… normal?"

"A magical war leaves traces most cannot see," said the ghost. "That fog, for instance, is a side effect of the spirit lines splitting open when the gods escaped."

My heart missed a beat. "You said gods. As in, plural. There are more of them beside Ignessa?" Please, no. One mad fire goddess was quite enough for me, thanks.

"So they say," she said. "Lorne's allies locked me up long before they woke the gods. All I heard were their screams as the Ancients consumed their souls. I hoped Lorne did not survive, but I suppose he forced his witch allies to help him escape this realm."

Lovely. Lorne had described the Ancients as a race of immortal beings who predated humanity. I'd thought he was batshit crazy, but perhaps he'd been speaking from experience. I'd bet he'd fled the dragons' city the instant the gods showed up and left the others to burn.

"I thought Ignessa was the one who started the war," I said. "Through Lorne, I mean."

"She pushed the Moonbeam into his hands, yes," she said. "Through it, she poisoned Lorne's mind and led him to turn on his fellow dragon shifters. The effects of the war rippled throughout the realms, awakening beasts which never should have been disturbed."

"I don't see any other gods." Then I thought of the winged monsters who'd swarmed into the sky. "Except Ignessa, but she's a ghost."

"They destroyed one another," she said. "It takes a god to kill a god, child, including her."

"Listen, I know I look like someone's little sister, but I'm not a child." I flexed my hands, shifting them to claws. "How do you know all this, anyway? I thought—I mean, everyone thinks the dragon shifters created the Moonbeam, not *her*." Even I had, back when I'd assumed Ignessa was just a regular ghost.

"I was a scholar once," said Ayla. "Damned shame they burned all that knowledge... everything they could, anyway. Nobody believed me when I warned them of the Moonbeam's history of corruption. It lay in the mountains for hundreds of years before it was found."

"Before Ignessa made sure it was found." I rubbed my eyes, tiredness seeping straight to my bones. "Didn't anyone listen to your warnings?"

"We're talking about thousand-year-old myths, child," she said. "The Moonbeam hadn't been seen in the city for so long that everyone forgot its origins, if they ever knew them at all. Lorne popularised the current myth and kept the Moonbeam hidden. It had years to corrupt his mind before he made his play for power."

"But he gave it up." I frowned. "He gave it up as soon as he came to Earth, traded it to the Orion League in exchange for leadership over the dragon shifters. That's how we found it. If it had such a strong hold on him, how could he give it away?"

"Perhaps its influence is not as strong in your realm," said the ghost. "Before the war, travel between this realm and Earth used to be common, but the spirit lines closed when the war ended, cutting Ignessa off from her power source."

"No wonder she set Lorne on fire as soon as he gave her what she wanted." I shuddered. "Is there no way out of this realm aside from the Moonbeam? Can it be repaired?"

"The Moonbeam has never been remade. It just is."

"That's really not helpful."

Anger rose within me. I'd done my damned best to save everyone I loved and where had I ended up? Locked in a cell and forgotten. London had never felt further away. I missed every inch of it. Magic Avenue, our shelter, Will's shop... even Darcy's place. Even Tower Bridge with its resident troll. And Jake's gargoyle porn. Okay, maybe I wouldn't go that far.

"Then I guess I'll ask someone else," I said into the darkness.

I had no props, but I'd summoned Ignessa herself without the need for a summoning circle. I faced the empty cell and said clearly, "I summon you, Lorne."

"What are you doing?" yelped Ayla.

Fire flared, igniting in the dark. Then Lorne's ghostly outline appeared before me, huge, muscular, yet incapable of touching me.

I could hardly believe I'd once found this man terrifying. Ignessa had burned away all my fear, and I had none left to spare for him.

"You.' He glared at me. "Coriander, agent of my demise. It would be my delight to watch you die."

"You really need a hobby," I said. "Besides, I happen to have a guardian angel watching out for me."

"Your sister?"

My heart seized. I hadn't summoned Ember since my imprisonment, unable to bear seeing her watch me waste away in the darkness. But I wouldn't give this dickhead the satisfaction of watching me die. I raised my fist and punched Lorne in the face. My hand passed right through him, to no surprise, and I spat out a curse. Even punching my enemy brought me no joy at all.

"Even your goddess isn't coming to save you," he said.

"Why go to the trouble of reviving you from death if she planned to abandon you in your hour of need?"

"It was my sister who brought me back from death, not her." I scowled at him. "You must know she doesn't give two shits about anyone, least of all us pathetic mortals."

"Ignessa revived you from death?" said Ayla.

I turned my frown on her. I'd assumed Lorne had scared her off. "The Moonbeam did, at my sister's request. Believe me, neither of us knew we were making a bargain with the fire goddess."

"Murderer," Lorne hissed.

"I banish you," I said. "Fuck the hell off."

Lorne disappeared into the fog. Imprisonment hadn't dampened my necromantic abilities, it seemed. But summoning Ignessa herself in here might be pushing my luck. I wasn't *that* keen to hasten my inevitable demise.

Ayla studied me, looking me up and down. "I see her fire in you, yet you remain free from her influence."

"She's not bound to me." My throat tightened. "She's bound to my sister now, as long as the Moonbeam is broken. I know repairing it will work in her favour, but she already has every dragon shifter in the city under her influence. She doesn't need me, not anymore."

"They say the Moonbeam was originally forged in the flames of the goddess of fire, but her fire runs within you. Perhaps that would be enough."

My heart contracted. "Enough to what? Remake it? You said it couldn't be done."

"There is a spell," she murmured. "A spell as old as the gods themselves. If you find this spell, perhaps you have a chance of remaking the Moonbeam."

My head swam, dizzy from hunger and exhaustion. At this point, if she said a magical castle in the sky was the key to saving my sister, I'd be tempted to believe her without hesitation. A spell as old as the gods? Agnes might know of one, but she was back on Earth, while years might have passed by now.

The ghost didn't speak again. When I next woke, another water bottle stuck out of my bag, and it took all my willpower not to down the whole thing in one go.

"Thank you," I whispered. "Thank you, guardian angel."

The guardian angel meowed at me.

I dropped the bottle, which rolled to a halt at my feet. "Becks? Is that you?"

A furred head appeared beside the bars. I should have known she'd be the first to escape—these cages were designed to hold dragons, not cat shifters. I reached through the bars and stroked her. She hissed at me, and the sound brought tears to my dry eyes.

"Can you get me out?"

"Meow." She shook her head. Maybe it meant *no,* maybe *not yet.* It didn't matter. She'd kept me from starving to death, and that was enough for now.

A day or two later, I woke to the sound of a tremendous scraping sound. I looked around the cell in confusion but saw no movement at all. Then I looked up at the barred window. Or rather, where the bars *had* been. A gaping hole lay in their place, through which Zeph peered down at me. "Hey there, Cori."

I blinked, shielding my eyes from the sudden burst of light. "About damn time."

A rope flew downwards, halting at my feet. A glance

outside the cell confirmed the rucksack had vanished—Becks must have carried it outside.

"Nice getting to know you," I told the silent ghost in the opposite cell.

Then I grabbed the rope and scaled the wall. When I reached the top, Zeph pulled me out, scaling the back wall of the tower-like building. I had less patience, jumping for the ground and shifting my hands to claws to break my fall. Zeph landed beside me. His clothes were as ragged and dirty as mine and he was notably leaner than he'd been before, but he was grinning, too.

"Thanks so much," I said. "You saved my neck."

"Thank Becks," he said. "They didn't know she was a cat shifter. She managed to slip through the bars and bring the rest of us sustenance while she figured out how to get everyone free without getting caught."

"I did wonder." I held a hand over my eyes to blot out the sun. Even with the thick fog everywhere, it took some adjustment to standing in direct daylight again after so many days in darkness. "The others are out already?"

"You were under the highest security," he explained. "Becks got out first. Kit never even made it into the cell—he glamoured himself and the dragonling invisible and escaped. He's been raiding their supplies and handing them over to Becks to bring to us. Will escaped next, and then me."

"What about Astor?"

"Do you think the assassin made it into a cell?" said Zeph. "I have no idea what he did to the person who tried to lock him up, but I heard a lot of screaming. Anyway, he's been hiding with Ember. The other dragon shifters don't leave the city much, so lying low has been easier than I thought."

"Perhaps the fire goddess ordered them to stay put." I released a breath. We were here. All of us. We'd survived.

Now all we had to do was escape this realm, remake the Moonbeam—and kill the goddess of fire.

3

A dragon's cry echoed from somewhere nearby. Zeph paused, listening out. "Ah, there goes our diversion. Fly, Cori, and don't let the others catch you. Becks will be annoyed if you get dragged back into that cell after all the trouble she went through to get you out."

"But—" I broke off at the sound of several other dragons' answering roars. They must have noticed my escape. "Where to?"

"The usual spot. I'll explain later."

I assumed he meant near the Moonbeam pieces. Which was where I'd left Ember.

Ember.

I have to see her. I have to know she's okay.

I shifted to dragon form, stretching out my limbs and extending my wings. Then I leapt into flight, bidding farewell to my prison cell.

Zeph must have concocted one hell of a diversion to draw the other dragons away, but I hoped this realm had more hiding places than I'd seen. The mountains were the only place I could think of where the dragons wouldn't follow us, and they looked cold and desolate. Not a dragon shifter's paradise.

I glanced down at the hillside to get my bearings and damn near screeched to a halt in mid-air. A *person* stood below, tied to a stone statue with ropes. A dragon could snap those ropes in a heartbeat, so she must be human. But that wasn't what caught my attention. A dazzlingly bright glow shone from her forehead, piercing the fog.

Zeph had told me to find the others, but if a human had made it here, maybe she'd be able to help me get my friends home to Earth. She hadn't popped out of the sky, right?

I landed beside the dragon statue, and the woman startled. Her head tilted back as she looked me in the eyes, which showed wariness but not outright fear. From this angle, the mesmerising light on her forehead was less bright, but showed the angles of an unreadable symbol.

Is she a witch? Surely if she was, she'd have been able to slip out of the ropes with little effort.

I shifted into human form and landed beside her. "Hey. You look like you could use a hand. Or claw."

I reached for the ropes behind the statue. One slice of my claws, and she was free. The woman rubbed her wrists. "Thanks."

"That symbol on your forehead," I said. "What is it?"

She didn't say anything. If it was what I thought it was, I wouldn't trust a stranger with that information, either. But it looked like an Orion League mark. She wasn't with the League, was she? It would be just my luck if the bloody League had formed again while we'd been gone.

I let the ropes fall onto the grassy hillside. "Sorry, that was rude. It's been a while since I've talked to a living person. I'm Cori, by the way."

"I'm Ilsa," she said. "I… I know you. I've seen you before."

My mouth fell open. "Not Ilsa Lynn? I saw you at Agnes's shop not long ago. You were a child."

She looked at me as though I'd sprouted fangs. Which wasn't far from the truth.

"You haven't aged at all," she said. "How's that possible? It's been over fifteen years."

Fifteen years.

The adult Ilsa hardly resembled her child self. Gone were the cherubic features she'd shared with her sister, Hazel. Her face was more mature, her eyes a darker brown. Her hair was longer and darker, too, though tangled and matted with blood, her ankles and wrists bloody from where she'd pulled at her bonds.

"I think," I said, "time moves differently here. I've been locked in a cell for a week or so, but I'd have noticed if it'd been years. How'd you get here?"

"Through a mirror."

A mirror.

That meant one thing: the Moonbeam's portal function was working again. I could have cried. Somehow, in fifteen years, someone had achieved the impossible.

There were more questions I wanted to ask. Such as who'd tied her to a statue and left her here as dragon bait, for instance. But before I could, a second voice shouted, "Ilsa!"

I shifted to dragon form, my hackles rising at the sight of movement in the fog. A man climbed up the slope towards Ilsa. The wind caught his dark hair and blew it across his forehead. He was tall and thin with a narrow face and striking brown eyes, which widened as they spotted Ilsa standing on the hill, and the ropes coiled at her feet.

Where the bloody hell are all these people coming from?

"Morgan?" Her tone brimmed with disbelief. "What are you doing here?"

"Rescuing you." He climbed the hill, holding the reins of an animal the size of a poodle, covered in black fluff.

"What," said Ilsa, "is that?"

"A demon puppy. He helped me track you down."

Ilsa choked on a laugh. "Only you, Morgan."

Right—he was her brother. I'd seen him at Agnes's too.

Morgan stumbled over a rock when he spotted me standing there in dragon form, wings folded against my back.

"Ilsa," he said. "Don't move, but there's a dragon behind you."

"I know there's a dragon," she said. "She helped me, untied my bonds. She's a shifter."

"How do you know that?" He backed up, beckoning her to follow him. "Get behind me."

"She's not going to attack us, Morgan."

He scowled, gripping the reins of the demon puppy. "If you touch my sister, I'll slay you."

He didn't look capable of it, but he'd ended up in this realm somehow. Through the mirror. God, it seemed impossible, and yet...

Ilsa stumbled away from the statue. "I'm okay, Morgan, don't worry."

"Like hell." He glanced behind him. "Jas and the others

are handling *her*. We're gonna get out of here before she figures out you escaped. Do you have your talisman?"

"I do."

Talisman.

Ilsa had a talisman?

I readied myself to shift, and the fog lit up with magic. I recoiled from the light, and the hillside shook beneath my feet.

My wings beat against the strong current, carrying me into the air, and I lost sight of the two humans. Figures moved in the fog below, flashes of light breaking through. I flew higher, struggling to keep from being carried away by the current. I beat my wings hard, spotting the cathedral-like stone structure in the distance. *My friends are over there.*

I flew harder, wings pumping, drawing closer to the stone building. It hadn't changed in a week—or fifteen years—and most of the Moonbeam pieces lay where they'd been beforehand, scattered on the grass.

Thorn let out a cry of delight at the sight of me. I turned into my human form and landed on my feet, running to greet the others.

"*There* she is," said Will, waving at me from beside Kit and the dragonling. "You're the last to escape."

"So I've heard. I think Zeph created a diversion back in the city."

"He did," said Becks. "Nice seeing you in one piece, Cori."

"You saved my life," I told her. "All of you. Not only that, the Moonbeam is working again. We're going home."

"It's..." Becks's eyes widened. "It's still broken. Isn't it?"

"The portal function is working." I couldn't stop grinning. "There are humans here. From Earth. The portals must have recharged while we were in jail."

Will was on his feet in an instant. "It's a fucking miracle."

"I know, right?" Becks bounded upright. "Wait—humans are using the mirrors? From where?"

"Uh... good question." I stopped, my elation fading a little. "They might have ended up anywhere."

"Like under the sea?" said Astor.

The former assassin stood alone outside the cathedral, and his expression might have been carved out of stone.

"Of course not," I said. "I *saw* people who got here using the portals. Unless they've learned to breathe underwater or live in the sky while we've been in jail, they'll have come from somewhere on Earth."

Granted, it sounded like they were in trouble, but in the post-faerie invasion world, it'd be unrealistic to expect fifteen years free of drama. I'd gladly face whatever had become of Earth if it meant we got to go home again.

"Good," said Kit, beaming. "I bet Agnes looked after the mirror like you asked her to."

I slapped a hand to my forehead. "Right, of course. The Lynns know her, they're friends. They must have borrowed her mirror."

"Who?" Becks's brow furrowed.

"We met them once. Ember, Zeph and I did. What's taking him so long, anyway?"

"I think he took a detour," said Will. "Once he's back, we're outta here."

"Not all of us," said a terse voice.

I turned to Astor. "What, you're staying behind? Ember—"

"She's helping your friend create a diversion." He spoke in a dispassionate tone. "She can't live among humans in the state she's in now. Certainly not in London. I'm staying with her."

"You're staying *here?*" Will said. "You do realise those other dragons want us dead, right? If you want to go into hiding, you can go to the village instead. Nobody will be living there now."

"If there's anything left of it." My mood sobered. "Guys… it's been over fifteen years since we left home."

"What?" said Will, his eyes going wide.

"How?" Becks dropped into a sitting position on a rock. "Fifteen *years?*"

"I ran into someone on my way over here who told me." I sat down on the grass. My limbs trembled from the exertion of flight after days of deprivation. "A human. Have the other dragons been using the Moonbeam?"

"Not that I know of," said Becks. "I bet they assumed the portal stopped working, like we did."

A rumbling noise echoed across the hillside, and a vibration trembled in the earth below the grassy hill. The hum resonated through my bones, like a bell ringing, but more of a feeling than a sound. On the hillside, the Moonbeam shards quivered, some of them sliding downhill.

"Uh… is this place prone to earthquakes?" My words were lost in the sound of breaking rock, and a thunderclap that rent the sky in two.

Behind us, the cathedral-like structure trembled all over. Blinding lights shone from the pillars, and one fell into its neighbour with a teeth-clattering crash.

"Get the dragonlings out!" Kit ran to pick up the cage, and Will rushed in to help him.

"Kit, stop!" he yelled.

"I can't leave them!" Kit's frantic voice sounded beneath the clamour of falling rocks.

I think the dragon eggs will be fine. We, on the other hand, are not impervious to being crushed to death.

Becks turned into cat form and yowled a warning. Alarm blared through me when I saw the dark shapes of Kit and Will moving inside the cathedral. I shifted into a dragon, debris bouncing off my scales, and flew through the cathedral's collapsing entryway. Another pillar trembled, then fell—right towards the dragon eggs.

Fire erupted from my lungs, burning the pillar to ash. I flew above Will and Kit, shielding them from harm while they hauled the cage out of harm's way, sprinting out of the cathedral.

An instant later, the whole structure collapsed in a torrent of stone. Debris bounced off my scales, and I flew behind the others to shield them with my wings. The others didn't stop running until they reached the foot of the hill, dropping the dragonlings' cage.

"Dammit, Kit," Will burst out. "You could have died."

"I'd have shielded myself with magic," he insisted. "You shouldn't have stayed."

"Are you kidding me?" Will hugged him, burying his head in his boyfriend's shoulder. "Don't do that to me again. I can't take it."

The sound of beating wings drew my eyes to the foggy sky, and I spotted a blue-white dragon flying closer.

Zeph landed beside me, turning human. "Uh, that was more of a diversion than I planned."

"Did you do that?" I shifted into human form, too, catching my balance on the trembling earth.

"No," he said. "It sounded like… ringing. Did you hear it?"

"Either someone has the biggest dinner bell ever, or shit's going down somewhere." I tilted my head to the sky. "Where is Ember?"

"There." He pointed at the foggy horizon. Ember's red shape approached over the hillside, and I breathed out.

"Good job those Moonbeam portals are working again, because we just lost our shelter." I turned to the others, who stood at a safe distance from the rubble. "Are you guys okay?"

Will released Kit. "Yeah, but at this point, I think the bottom of the ocean would be safer than this place."

The dragonling screeched, drawing my attention to the crate of eggs.

"We can't leave them behind," Kit said. "We don't even know if the outside world is safe, let alone if the mirrors are in the same place as they used to be."

"Only one way to find out." I turned to Zeph. "Want to come with me and have a look on the other side?"

"Sure," said Zeph. "I should mention I sent a couple of humans to help Agnes and Everett escape an hour or two ago. They came here from Earth."

"Agnes and Everett were jailed, too?" Damn. Those dragons had some nerve. Agnes was part witch, part mage, and had some abilities I'd never seen anyone else use, like the power to erase a person's memories. Not to mention she carried a pendant that protected her against the flames of a dragon. How had they managed to catch her?

"They were," he said. "I didn't actually plan the diversion, but while the dragons were chasing their runaway prisoners—that Agnes woman moves fast, by the way—I came to bust you out of jail, too. Worked out pretty well. I saw those portals were back in use, so I took one of the shards over to the city so they could use it to get home."

"Wait, you *knew* about the portals?" said Will. "Why not tell us?"

"I was too busy distracting a city full of raging mad reptiles. Who can all follow us through the Moonbeam shards, by the way, so we're not out of the woods yet."

"Depends if they're willing to give up their city." Had people been hopping in and out of this realm the whole time we'd been in jail? I'd thought nobody but the dragon shifters and a few others even knew how the portals worked, but a lot might have changed in fifteen years. "Okay, we should move. We'll have a look at whatever's the other side and come back if it isn't safe."

"I'll come, too," said Becks. "Kit, Will—please be careful."

"If anything worse happens, follow us." I paced over to the Moonbeam pieces. "That's an order."

The shards of broken stone glowed as brightly as they had when they were whole. My heart climbed into my throat. *Does that mean Ignessa is stronger than before?*

Light flowed over me as I stepped closer to the Moonbeam's shards. Then Zeph gripped my arm and the two of us tumbled out into a whitewashed room. I landed on Zeph and Becks landed on me—in cat form, luckily.

I lifted my head. "You have *got* to be kidding me."

We were in the lab. Lorne's lab—or rather, the League's. An atrocious smell hit my nostrils, like something had died here. More than one something. I held my breath, climbed off Zeph, and peered through the door. Becks turned human, gagging on the stench of rot.

Sure enough, dead bodies littered the corridor outside the room. Someone had thrown salt on them, which suggested we weren't alone here. Question was, were they friends or foes?

"I thought you had friends on this side," Becks said in accusing tones.

"Um..." I hung my head. "I thought Agnes had the mirror, because Ilsa used it to get here. Maybe not."

"Ilsa," said Zeph. "That kid we saw at Agnes's place?"

"She isn't a kid. It's been fifteen years since we left." I leaned against the wall, tiredness washing over me. My allies were gone. So was our home. Nothing survived for long in this world... except, it seemed, for the Orion League's old lab.

Zeph stepped out of the room into the corridor. "Someone's been busy here."

I pushed back from the wall and followed him. The labs were a mess of dead zombies and shattered glass, covered in a layer of dust thick enough to suggest the place had only reopened recently. Question was, who'd moved the mirror, and what did they want with the League's old lab? Nothing good, I assumed.

Zeph stepped over a pair of dead bodies, leading the way. His tattered clothes looked even more worse for wear after his imprisonment and a layer of dirt caked his face, but he still looked better than he had the right to after being locked in a cell for a week. Better than me, anyway. I desperately needed a shower and a change of clothes. And deodorant. It was fortunate for all of us that dragons had a natural scent which covered human sweat.

"Are you okay, Cori?" he asked. "I should have asked earlier, but you know, circumstances."

"I am," I said. "I mean, I really need a drink and a decent meal, but I'm just glad not to be dead."

"Here." He pulled a water bottle from his bag. "Becks tried to bring supplies to all of us, but it was hard for her to avoid the other dragons even as a cat."

Becks, who'd shifted into her cat form again, meowed an affirmative.

"She saved my life," I said. "You all did. I can't believe..."

I couldn't believe the other dragons had just *left* me there to rot in the dark. Or rather, Ignessa had. She hadn't even dropped in on me in jail to have a good laugh at my expense.

Speaking of ghosts. I drank some of the water. "So, you should know... I met a ghost in jail who hinted the Moonbeam can be repaired."

Zeph stopped walking. "You're serious? Without bringing back that mad goddess?"

"She's already back." I peered into another wrecked lab. Shattered glass littered the floor, covering chalked symbols. Dark magic. A shiver raced down my spine. *Someone was definitely up to no good in here.*

"Ghosts aren't all that reliable, are they?" said Zeph. "Cori, don't get me wrong, I trust you, but..."

"The ghost was a prisoner who died in the cell near mine, and she said there was a spell that could repair the Moonbeam," I said. "I summoned Lorne's ghost to find out if he knew more, but he just yelled at me and I had to send him away."

"You summoned *Lorne?*"

"Hey, I was in jail longer than you were," I said. "I had nobody living to talk to, so I had to turn to the dead. The ghost in the cell opposite mine lived through the war and watched Ignessa take over the city. She used to be in charge of it, even." I relayed what she'd told me. "It's a long shot, but if the goddess is already running amok and influencing the other dragon shifters, I might as well find a way to free Ember. I can't live with myself if I don't try."

"I understand," he said. "She'd do the same for you."

She would. I'm the reason she's stuck the way she is. Guilt churned inside me, and the shivering grew worse. Then a pair of icy hands protruded from my chest.

I gasped, rotating on the spot. A ghost hovered behind me, shadowy around the edges with odd grey-blue eyes.

"Let me feed on your soul," he said.

"How about not?" I backed up a step, away from his chilling touch. "What are you?"

"Starving." His hands reached for me again, and cold pierced me at his touch. I'd seen something like him before… a ghost who fed on human life force. A vampire.

What was a vampire doing in the Orion League's old lab?

Zeph's claws came out. "Get away from her!"

Claws couldn't hurt a ghost. Necromancy could, but hell if I knew if it worked on vampires. "Uh… I banish you. Beyond the veil. Go." I waved both hands at him in a shooing motion. "Go. Away. Bugger off and rest in peace."

"You can't banish me," said the ghost. "I am a shade."

"No idea what that means." I took another firm step out of range of his grasping hands. "I'd be happy to give you an escort into the afterlife if I had the slightest clue what the bloody hell is going on here, but—"

Becks gave a meow of warning. A horrific screech rippled down the corridor, heralding the arrival of a huge clawed beast with red-black scales. Shadowy wings stuck out from behind its shoulder blades. With a cry, the vampire turned heel and vanished into the spirit realm.

"Cheers, ugly." I leapt at the monster, my claws gladly slicing through their prey. "Yeah, I don't think we're going to find any friends here."

"That monster didn't come from the lab." Zeph turned back the way we'd come. "It came through the mirror."

"Oh," I said. "Bollocks."

I ran back towards the room with the mirror and leapt through it, landing on the hillside in a pile of Moonbeam shards. A knife flew past my ear, burying itself in another monster's eye.

Astor cursed. "I almost hit you."

"Maybe look before you start throwing knives around," I returned. "Where'd these monsters come from?"

Astor hurled a knife at another one. "I don't know, they flew at us out of nowhere. Who's on the other side of the portal?"

"Would you believe Lorne's lab has a new owner? Didn't see them in person. And—hey!"

I pushed Zeph out of the way of another knife. He glared at Astor. "Watch it."

"Don't stand in my way, then." Astor brought another beast crashing down. "Aren't you going to help me out?"

"No, I think I'll let them eat you," said Zeph, walking away from the Moonbeam shards. Becks followed, her cat form streaking over to join the others further down the hillside. I looked around for Ember's dragon shape and instead met the eyes of her ghost, watching me through the spirit realm.

"Cori." She hovered before me. "I can't stay long. The spirit realm here… it's unstable. I'm barely hanging on."

My throat closed up. "Is there anything I can do? I can't lose you."

Ember shook her head. "I… well, I went to Earth. My dragon form did, I mean."

"What?" My voice cracked. "Recently?"

"It's worse than before," she said. "I saw zombies all over the streets and rioting everywhere. In Edinburgh, at least. I don't know about London."

"Shit." Years had passed, and the world had taken a turn for the worse in our absence. "You got out—how?"

"Someone opened a way," she said. "I think the spirit lines might be breaking down."

Crap. That had been Lorne's plan, too. But it couldn't be him this time around, right?

Ember's eyes were serious. "Cori, please, leave while you can. Take Astor with you—carry him if you have to. I'll be fine over here. The other dragons can't kill me. Ignessa won't let them."

"I don't understand." Then I got it. "You're… you're tied together. That means they can't kill you or they'll destroy her."

I wasn't bound to Ignessa anymore. My sister was, because she'd sacrificed herself in my place.

"I'm with you, Cori." Her eyes flamed. "Go. Please. For me."

A rumble of thunder pulsed beneath the earth, and behind the dragons' city, a plume of fire roared to the sky.

4

I watched, my mouth hanging open. "Whoa."

"Go!" Ember urged. "I'll watch the dragonlings, too. Do you trust me to keep them safe?"

My heart contracted. "I do. I'll come back to you and fix this."

Somehow.

Zeph caught my arm as the ground gave another heaving tremor. "Were you talking to Ember?"

"Yes. We have to leave, now. The spirit lines are breaking apart. Ember promised to watch the dragonlings. Kit—"

"I can't leave him." He looked at Thorn, his bright green eyes shining.

"We'll bring him with us, then," said Will. "If anyone complains, we'll ask him to take a bite out of them. Trust me."

Kit's whole face lit up, and he hugged Will. The dragonling tried to do the same, and his wing nearly knocked the two of them over.

Astor let out an irritated noise. "Where are we going, exactly?"

"To find Agnes." I stepped towards the Moonbeam shards. "Come on, guys. That includes you, Astor. Ember gave me permission to carry you out if I have to."

His eyes hardened. "I'd like to see you try."

"Listen to her." Zeph strode over to Astor and gave him a shove. Astor whirled on him, but the Moonbeam's light was already washing over both of them. Beckoning to the others, I ran, through the portal and into the lab.

Zeph and I crash-landed on Astor. I lifted my head, and Kit's shoe caught me in the face. Will and Becks followed, flattening us to the ground.

"Isn't this cosy?" said Will.

"Get the fuck off me," Astor said, his voice muffled at the bottom of the heap. "All of you."

The dragonling landed on top of me, letting out a distressed shriek at the sight of the zombie. Astor attempted to tug his way out from underneath the pile, knocking Becks tumbling to the floor. She swiped him on the nose, adding to the clamour.

It took a few confusing moments for everyone to get back on their feet, breathless and covered in scratches and bite marks, courtesy of Becks and the dragonling. Thank the gods he'd learned to moderate his biting, or else we'd all be missing limbs.

"I'm not all that keen on this new hotel, to tell you the truth," Will said. "Not much ambience. Smells foul, too."

"I don't like this." Kit backed away from the zombie in the doorway, trod on the dead monster's head, and jumped back with a yelp. Thorn whined and tried to use his wings to shield himself from the zombies.

"C'mon, it's only a dead body." Will beckoned to Thorn. "And we're not staying here. Cori knows the way out, right?"

"You bet," I said. "Who wants to volunteer to carry the mirror?"

"Carry it?" asked Zeph. "You want to take it to the village?"

"Ideally? Somewhere the enemy can't find it." I held my breath, wishing I could turn off my enhanced senses to block out the smell of the rotting dead. "Ilsa didn't say where the other mirror was, but considering her brother used it to rescue her, it must be with someone who's on our side."

"Ilsa?" asked Becks. "Who's Ilsa?"

Astor halted all arguments by stepping through the mirror and disappearing.

Will sighed. "Let him die, then."

Astor emerged a second later. "The other mirror is in Edinburgh's mage guild."

"How'd you figure that one out?" asked Zeph.

"I recognised the room," he said. "I think some kind of disaster hit the place. There were bodies everywhere."

I groaned. "And you walked right into the middle of it?"

"Better than wasting time snipping at one another." He scowled. "You don't have a plan, do you?"

"We're going to fix the Moonbeam."

Everyone stared at me, even Astor. "You know how to fix it?" he asked.

"Ah… no. But Agnes might."

His jaw locked. "You'd better not be bullshitting me."

"What do you take me for?" I said, insulted. "I want Ember back as much as you do."

Astor narrowed his eyes at me. Then he walked through the mirror, and this time, he didn't come back.

"Where'd he go, the other realm or Edinburgh?" I shook my head after him. "Ember told me to keep him here with us."

"I couldn't give a shit what he does," said Zeph. "Let's get out of here before that vampire brings his friends after us."

I felt an odd surge of gratitude towards Lorne for locking me up in the lab, because I'd have had a hell of a job finding the exit if I'd never been there before. Winding corridors led to ruined labs filled with rotting corpses, dead ends blocked by piles of rubble, and even a giant hole in the floor which looked as though a beast several times larger than a dragon had ripped the foundations up.

When we reached the door leading outside, I clawed it open, inhaling mouthfuls of fresh air with relief. With another swipe of my claws, I widened the doorway so Zeph could carry the mirror out onto the hillside. The dragonling bounded out next, with the others close behind him. Clouds hung over the mountains, but without the eerie fog of the other realm, it seemed much easier to breathe.

"What're the odds that the assassin's got himself arrested?" Will said.

"Not high," I said. "He's sneaky. If he tries to ask the necromancer guild to conjure up Ember's ghost for him, though, he's going to end up disappointed."

Zeph lowered the mirror. "Is she going to stay in the other realm?"

"For now." I scanned the surrounding hills, spotting an odd rippling line about a mile off. Not the Ley Line, but the visible currents of energy followed a familiar pattern. "If that's a spirit line, Ember wasn't kidding when she said it was breaking down."

Will swore. "I'd rather not be anywhere near it, then. Are you flying that mirror to Edinburgh?"

"Nah, the village." I nodded to Zeph. "Three of us can fly. Becks and Kit, you can pick who to fly with. Astor…"

"It's his own fault if he steps out of the mirror when we're a thousand feet up in the air," Zeph said. "Lead the way, Cori."

"I followed the Ley Line last time I flew to Edinburgh," I told the others. "I'll try to do the same again, but I don't like the look of that spirit line."

I shifted into my dragon form. Zeph did likewise, while Will transformed into a gargoyle. Kit climbed onto the dragonling's back, while Becks climbed to sit between Will's shoulders.

It felt good to stretch my wings again, inhaling the fresh air of the countryside. I soared above rolling hills and lakes, wishing I'd memorised the landmarks to make it easier to find the village. The only constant was the rippling line of energy on my right-hand side like a shadow above the earth. Dark shapes flew above. Monsters. My stomach lurched and I flew further to the left. *It can't be a second faerie invasion. That isn't the Ley Line.* The surging currents of energy were chillingly reminiscent of the sky when the faeries had attacked London. Relief flooded me when I spotted a familiar huddle of stone buildings. The dragon shifters' abandoned village was so distant from civilisation that even the faeries hadn't claimed it.

I descended, and Zeph followed with the mirror held firmly in his claws. An eerie quietness smothered the deserted cobbled streets, and a chill raced down my spine.

"Are you sure you want to leave the mirror here?" Zeph asked.

I dipped my head. "It's the best place for it. If we have it with us when we get to Edinburgh and the mages arrest us, we'll lose our only way of getting back to Ember."

"You mean, if the mages arrest Astor." Zeph's lips compressed. "Well, it's his loss. I doubt the other dragons want to move back here, but maybe…"

"They might," I said. "Once they're free from Ignessa's influence. The city was pretty much a ghost town after the war. Lorne left nothing behind."

Not that we'd fared much better. Now we were back home, doubts swarmed into my mind. It was all very well daydreaming of dramatic rescue missions while I'd been locked in a cell, but Ember's predicament coupled with our fifteen-year absence highlighted how utterly unprepared we were to stand up against Ignessa.

But if our positions were reversed, Ember would never think of it as an impossible task. She'd walked into the Orion League's Stronghold to rescue me; bargained with the Moonbeam to save me from death; and given me more than I could ever repay her in a lifetime. If I had to defy the gods themselves to get her back, so be it.

I took to the sky again, this time flying towards the coastline. The Ley Line's rippling currents didn't look shadowy or damaged like the other spirit line, but I flew parallel to it rather than letting myself get swept up in its flow.

Zeph took the lead, unencumbered by the mirror, as we neared the sprawling city. I'd have aimed to land on Arthur's Seat as I'd done once before, if there hadn't been a massive crater in the hillside. *Whoa. That's new.*

At least the castle looked intact, looming over the peaked roofs and winding streets. I flew lower and came into land near the foot of the hills.

Zeph landed beside me, turning human. "I think we might have landed in a war zone."

"Are you sure? It sounds quiet." It was also growing dark. I knew the way to Agnes's safe house, but if I didn't get a hot meal soon, I'd pass out. I shouldn't have pushed so hard by shifting immediately after my imprisonment, but I'd had no choice. After seven years of living in post-Faerie London, we were no strangers to hardship, but we'd never been this destitute. What would happen if we found Agnes gone, and nowhere to stay?

The cobbled streets were as silent as the village, and the faint smell of burning lingered in the air. Several roads were torn up as though an earthquake had cut through town, and piles of rubble filled the spaces where stone houses had once stood. Becks padded forwards in cat form, her hackles raised as though expecting a fight.

"This is creeping me out." I listened hard for the sound of human noise, relieved to see lights on in some of the pubs. "We should look for Astor, and then find somewhere to stay for the night."

"And there I thought you'd forgotten about me."

Everyone jumped. Astor stood behind us, for all the world as though he'd been following the whole time.

"You've learned to fly now?" I said.

"No," he said. "I sneaked out of the mages' place. Their wards are down."

"That's not a good sign," I said. "Are there still bodies everywhere? I guess we missed whatever caused this."

"They were moving the bodies when I walked through," said Astor. "Nobody gave me a second's glance."

"Honestly." I grimaced. "Only you could walk through a battlefield and look like you belonged there with nobody asking questions, Astor. Did you at least find out what killed them?"

"No."

So the mages might be dead? They couldn't all have died, otherwise there'd be rioting and looting. If I had to guess, they'd suffered casualties, but they'd survived. Still, Astor had been lucky they hadn't struck him down on the spot for breaking into their headquarters.

"Right, we're not going to the mages' place," Zeph said. "Does anyone remember where Agnes lives when she's here?"

"Yes," I said. "That is, if she's still using the same safe house."

We entered a busier area of the city. Humans gathered in tight-knit groups, hurrying from one pub to another, but the relief of seeing other living people hit me at the core. It'd have looked weird to grab and hug random humans, so I managed to restrain myself.

The enticing smell from the nearest takeout was harder to resist. "I don't know about you guys, but I need food, asap. I doubt Agnes has enough to feed all of us."

"I have cash," said Will, indicating his rucksack, which

contained all that was left of our supplies. "It's not like I had a use for it in the other realm."

"Awesome." I sniffed eagerly at the nearest window, inhaling the smell of fish and chips. "Pub or takeout?"

"Pub. We can catch up on the last decade and a half while we're at it." Zeph took my arm and steered me into a pub called the Redcap's Cave. "Look, they even allow pets."

"Pretend to be a dog, Thorn," said Will.

The dragonling made a noise that sounded more like a strangled cat.

"He needs to work on that one," said Kit, gliding through the pub doors.

Will dug through the supply bag when we'd found a table near the door. "I have some clothes here. This is just our emergency pack, so—"

"Yeah, I'll have to shower later, but I'll take clean clothes, thanks," I said. We were already attracting stares, what with Thorn sitting at the table with his tail curled around his scaly feet. "I think they might think we're traders of suspicious magical creatures."

"Where else are we supposed to go?" Will handed me a pair of jeans. "These are yours. And these."

"My dragon socks!" I cradled them to my chest, and Zeph snorted. "Come on, we lost everything else. Let me have my moment."

We scraped enough cash together to pay for our meals, by which point I'd changed into clean clothes and combed through my wild curls with my fingers. After a quick wash in the toilets, I felt almost human again. Or dragon. Either worked.

I'd expected a few stares based on our state of

dishevelment, but people seemed more annoyed with our chattering than anything. The place was oddly quiet for somewhere so crowded, and the supernatural clientele seemed to be a mixture of necromancers, witches and half-faeries. That explained why nobody looked twice at Kit. At least the world had improved in that regard in the last fifteen years, but who had the mages fought against, if not the faeries?

"Everyone here looks like someone died," Will said in an undertone. "Quickly, one of you start bawling."

Thorn whined and sank his teeth into the table leg, and Kit gave him a stern tap on the nose. There was no rule against him being here, but I sincerely hoped everyone had forgotten all about the virus. If they'd ever known the dragonlings were spreading it, that is. A lot could be forgotten in a decade and a half, and our fight with Lorne *felt* like fifteen years ago to me, not just a few weeks.

The waitresses who brought us our meals stepped back with an alarmed expression at the way I attacked the food, but I didn't have the energy to spare on manners.

"They've never had to deal with starving dragon shifters before, have they?" I said indistinctly to Zeph, half a dozen chips crammed into my mouth.

"At a guess, no." He shot me a grin. "You have ketchup on your nose."

"Eh." I resumed eating, ignoring the biting and tearing noises of the dragonling devouring a steak under the table. That alarmed the staff even more, and everyone gave us a wide berth. Given the general air of unfriendliness around the other patrons, that suited me just fine.

Astor sat apart from the rest of us, picking at his food,

eyes darting around the pub as though he expected an attack. "There was a war here earlier today. I told you. They know we're outsiders."

"Maybe the giant dragonling sitting by the table clued them in." I put down my fork, wishing I had enough cash to pay for more food to take back to Agnes's for later. I didn't have the faintest idea how we were going to survive with no money and no jobs. Fifteen years would have wiped out any traces of our lives in London. As for Edinburgh?

Maybe the necromancer guild is hiring, a cynical voice whispered in my ear. I spotted a few cloaked figures in the corner, but while my spirit sight did qualify me as a necromancer, Lady Montgomery might not be the head of the local guild any longer. Besides, if there had been a war today, the guild would be busy collecting the dead.

When someone started a fight at the bar, I took it as our cue to leave. The sound of flying punches and shattering glass pursued us outside.

"Not exactly a warm welcome, is it?" said Becks. "I miss London."

"Me too." A knot grew in my chest, thinking of Ember trapped in the other realm alone. "I hope our house is still there."

"You mean, *my* house," said Will. "Agnes had better be willing to let us stay at her safe house, because I can't afford a decent hotel for all of us."

"If there was a war here, I can't see her staying out of it." I continued along the route to the street Agnes had brought me to before. Hoping I'd got the right number, I knocked on the door.

Agnes answered a minute later. Her face was more

lined than before, but she had the same braid of silver hair and the same intelligent eyes. She wore a dressing gown patterned with dark flowers.

"Cori," she said. "You'd better come in."

I sagged with relief. "Thank the gods you're here. It's nice to see a familiar face, believe me."

We filed into the hall, except for Kit, who lingered at the door, petting Thorn's head. "He wants to go out and hunt."

"He's free to," said Agnes. "Assuming he knows not to draw attention."

"The dragonlings aren't still spreading the sickness, are they?" I asked.

Agnes pushed open a door to a living room filled with comfy-looking armchairs. "No. It hasn't been seen since Lorne left. Get in here, all of you."

"Well, that's good news." I found my way to the nearest armchair and sank into it. "We've had a day of it."

"It's been rather longer for some of us," said Agnes. "I was beginning to think I'd never see you again."

All the others, even Astor, looked too exhausted to question the wisdom of trusting Agnes with our lives here in this new, unrecognisable world.

"Likewise," I said. "After I broke the Moonbeam, the other dragons locked us in jail. I know it'll probably take you all night to tell us everything that's happened since, but why is the city in such a state?"

"Even *that* would take all night to explain," said Agnes. "The spirit lines almost came apart at the seams, and the gods are waking left and right. You chose a fine time to come back from the dead."

My jaw unhinged. "Did you say the gods are waking?"

"Yes." She eyed me. "It *is* good to see you, Cori, it's just inconvenient timing. Where's your sister?"

My throat closed up. "She's trapped in the other realm. When the Moonbeam broke, her soul was bound to Ignessa's."

Agnes listened as I ran through the events of the last week, from Ember's imprisonment to my conversations with the spirit while in jail.

"At this point, it seems there's a slim chance I can get Ember back," I said. "So, if I remake the Moonbeam—"

"No," said Agnes, sharply. "Ignessa must not return."

"She already has," said Zeph. "Believe me, I'm not keen on giving her any more advantages, but breaking the Moonbeam didn't diminish her power. She has the dragons' entire city under her influence."

"These are the gods we're speaking of," she said. "I suggest not mentioning them here for a while. The Ancients killed many people I cared for very much."

My throat went dry. "They're here? The gods?"

"Not at the moment," she said. "I'll look into the matter, but I'd suggest you rest while you can. There are three bedrooms upstairs, so some of you will have to share. We'll revisit the subject in the morning."

I opened my mouth to argue and yawned so hard my jaw cracked. Shifting had taken too much of a toll, and my body cried out for rest.

If this was a glimpse at our future, it didn't look bright, to say the least.

5

I woke to the smell of burning and Becks's yowl of alarm. My eyes cracked open at the sound of glass breaking downstairs. On my feet in an instant, I made for the window and opened it. Human screams drifted down the street, and the burning smell grew stronger.

A dragon shifter was outside.

I made for the window and opened it, launching myself out and shifting my hands to claws to break my fall. My claws hit the pavement and I prepared to shift, but Thorn got there first. The dragonling grappled with the intruder in mid-air, claws tangling, teeth tearing at scales.

"Get out of my house!" Agnes stormed out of the door, and a flash of gold light flew from her hands. The dragon shifter's wings splayed wide as Agnes's spell sent him hurtling over the rooftops. Zeph took flight in pursuit, his blue-tinged scales gleaming in the weak sunlight. Thorn flew on his tail, and I scanned the sky for other intruders.

Just the one guy—but how had he known where we were staying?

"Did he come through the mirror?" The mages would put us on their shit-list if a flood of angry dragons swarmed through right after they'd already fought a gruelling war.

"If they had, the mages would be on my doorstep, too," said Agnes. "You're attracting stares, Cori."

Oops. I wore nothing but a T-shirt and underwear, and everyone in the street had seen me fall out the window and impale the pavement on my claws. I debated shifting to follow Zeph, but he'd slowed, suggesting the other dragon had flown out of sight. I ducked back into the hallway of Agnes's house and ran upstairs to make myself decent.

By the time I returned, fully dressed, Zeph was back.

"I lost the guy over the sea." He looked as though he hadn't slept all night, his auburn hair adorably rumpled. "No idea who he was, either."

Kit appeared in the hall, from where he'd glamoured himself invisible. "Was it one of them? The other dragons?"

"Who else would it be?" Oh. "It wasn't a dragonling. I'm pretty sure the virus crisis is over, but I hope those eggs in the other realm hold off on hatching for a while."

"So do I," said Kit. "But time passes differently over there, doesn't it?"

"With any luck, it means Ember won't have to wait too long for me to set her free."

I entered the living room, finding Will sprawled in an armchair, also looking like he hadn't slept. The smell of herbs and chalk hung around him, suggesting he'd asked

Agnes for a loan of some of her books and spent the night making spells. Piles of bands covered the table next to his armchair, along with a couple of old-looking books.

"Where's the assassin?" he asked.

"Must have sneaked out." Zeph shrugged.

Astor had refused to share a room with any of us and insisted on camping downstairs, but there was no sign of him this morning. No surprise, really. He worked better alone.

A flash of light came from outside the broken window, and when it cleared, the broken glass was whole again. Will let out a low whistle. "Damn, she's good. I want to borrow some of her books."

A faint meow came from under the armchair. I crouched down beside it. "You under there, Becks? The coast's clear."

She wriggled out, transforming into her human form. "Please don't tell me the fire goddess sent that dragon."

The door slammed as Agnes re-entered, her expression suggesting that anyone who brought up the Moonbeam would find themselves subject to the same spell she'd used to blast that dragon into the sky. We *had* crash-landed in her life and brought attackers after her, so I didn't blame her for being annoyed with us.

Will cleared his throat. "Anyone want me to cook breakfast? I make awesome omelettes."

He did, too. After devouring two omelettes and taking another shower, I felt slightly more alert.

"At least one of you earns your keep," said Agnes, as Will started to clear the plates away.

"Trust me, you don't want any of us carrying crockery

around," Becks said. "Kit and I break glasses just by looking at them."

"Speaking of glasses…" I looked pointedly at her glasses-free eyes.

"I lost them somewhere in the dragons' city," she said. "Guess I'll have to get used to being short-sighted again."

So we all have fifteen-year gaps on our CVs, we're presumed dead, and one of us is too short-sighted to see her own nose. Other than that, we're amazingly employable. You never knew, though. People might still pay pennies for us to rescue cats from national monuments. I could dream.

After Zeph and I had helped Will clear the dishes away, Agnes's mood improved somewhat, though that might be down to the fresh ring of spells around the window.

"Let's see them breaking it next time," she muttered to herself. "I should have brought Everett along, but he claims travelling via the Ley Line makes him carsick."

"What is that?" Will indicated the ring of spells surrounding the window. "Water spell? You're going to spray the dragon intruders with water?"

"Hey, it works on most of us." I winked at Zeph. "Right?"

"Cats, too." Becks grabbed Will's rucksack. "How much money do we have, do you know?"

"You're in luck." Agnes gestured to a pile of bags in the corner. "I found these in the attic. It seems I was more optimistic that you'd make it back home than I remember."

"Wait, those are ours?" Will approached the heap of bags. "The stuff we brought here to Edinburgh the first time when we flew here with the mirror?"

"They've been in storage for a while, so you might want to check for dust mites," said Agnes.

It wasn't perfect, but I had some spare clothes, a toothbrush, and the necessities. "Thanks, Agnes. Can't save the world if I have nothing to wear."

Agnes grunted. "I apologise for being short with you, Cori. And for what happened to your sister. I'm sorry."

My throat closed up. "It's not your fault. I didn't know we'd lose so much time. I guess the only dragons people have seen in the last decade and a half have been under the influence of Ignessa, like the one who just attacked us."

"I'm not sure he *was* hers," said Zeph. "Might've been a rogue. Either way, I guess we're on the mages' wanted list, right?"

"I rather think they have bigger things to worry about," said Agnes. "They recently had a change of leadership."

I scrambled for the name of the last guy. "Lord Sutherland isn't in charge anymore?"

"Lord Sutherland was killed by an Ancient, after he made a pact with the gods in exchange for power."

A heartbeat passed, in which we all stared at her.

"You're joking." I sank into the nearest armchair. "The *mages* were the ones who woke the Ancients?"

"Not exactly," said Agnes. "You'll have to ask someone else for the whole story. I missed the last few months while I was in jail in the dragons' city."

"I forgot," I admitted. "Why'd they lock you up?"

"Lord Sutherland traded me to the dragons as a peace offering," she said. "Not only that, it was he who revived the Orion League's old lab in the Highlands. I don't know if you've seen the other mirror—"

"We have," said Zeph. "We flew it back to the dragon shifters' village. The place is abandoned, but we didn't know if there was anywhere safe to leave it in Edinburgh."

"It's probably for the best that you left it there," she said. "I'm still catching up on everything that happened in my absence, but this is not the world you left behind."

No kidding. "Sorry if we made it harder on you. We can leave… find somewhere else to stay."

"I've had worse than a broken window in recent months," said Agnes. "You're no bother, provided you don't bring any of *them* on my tail. The Ancients."

Uh... "Ignessa already has the other dragon shifters under her control. Every one of them. I don't know why it didn't affect Zeph…"

"Maybe she's not interested in me."

"Or she knows you're taken," Becks said, with a meaningful look at me.

I flushed crimson. "Who knows why Ignessa does anything? She's almost as powerful as she was when she was alive. Breaking the Moonbeam didn't even stall her."

"It gave us fifteen years of peace," said Agnes. "And thirteen years with no attacks from the Ancients. But I suppose with beings who cannot be killed, there is no true end."

Beings who cannot be killed.

"What is your history with Ignessa?" I asked Agnes. "You've met her before. Also, that pendant of yours…"

"I used to visit the other realm often, before I knew better," she responded. "The pendant was a gift from the dragons themselves."

Zeph turned to her. "I know you don't trust the Moonbeam. Nor do I. But Cori is right—breaking it did nothing to stop Ignessa's return. As long as the Moonbeam remains broken, she and Ember will be trapped together on the other side."

"Yeah." I willed Agnes to understand. "Ember is stuck in dragon form for the long haul until I remake it."

Agnes's expression darkened. "Cori, I appreciate your position, but the fact is, Ignessa is far from the only Ancient who rose to the surface during the recent conflict. The mages had to jail their own leader, and if they find out you're planning on aiding one of them…"

"Uh, they *have* the mirror at their headquarters," I pointed out. "Don't they worry something might walk out of it and attack them?"

"Try telling that to them, not me," said Agnes. "They claim it belongs to them and has always been at their headquarters."

"Either they have really short memories or they're being dicks," I said.

"We can set them straight," said Zeph. "We should at least warn them there's a whole city full of dragons on the other side, under the influence of an Ancient."

My chest tightened, thinking of Azalea. She'd been high-strung for good reasons the whole time I'd known her, but I refused to believe the real Azalea would thoughtlessly throw me in jail to die after everything Ember and I had done to help the other dragons recover from Lorne's tyranny. And how were her children coping with being stuck in the other realm? Were even they under Ignessa's control?

There has to be a way to destroy her. For good. Killable or not.

"I will talk to them," said Agnes. "As for saving your sister, Cori… you might want to ask Ilsa Lynn, who works at Edinburgh's necromancer guild."

"Wait, she does?" I didn't know Ilsa, but back there in the other realm, Morgan had mentioned she had a talisman of her own. It was a long shot, but perhaps she might know of the Moonbeam. "Is Lady Montgomery still in charge of the guild?"

"She survived the battle," said Agnes. "The guild's headquarters didn't, however. The necromancers relocated their survivors to the mages' headquarters."

So much for avoiding the mages. "All right. Who's coming with me, then?"

"I will," said Zeph. "Is Astor around? Where'd he go, anyway?"

"Haven't a clue." I didn't blame Astor for stalking off this time around. He might well be the only surviving ex-Orion League hunter left in the entire country, and he doubtless had his own ideas for helping Ember which he didn't intend to let the rest of us in on.

"I'm going to the market to stock up on spell ingredients," said Will. "Kit, are you coming?"

"Sure." The half-faerie glided to his feet. "Are we meeting back here?"

"If that's okay, Agnes," I said. "I think we'd better see where we stand with the mages before we ask if we can fly the mirror back to London."

We left the house as a group, splitting up when we reached a street lined with market stalls. Will and Kit headed into the witch market, while Zeph halted, scanning our surroundings. "It doesn't look as bad in daylight."

"It's not the first war in recent years," I reminded him. "Do you remember the way to the mages' place?"

Becks meowed, pointing her tail in the opposite direction. Her lithe cat form led the way through the streets, halting outside a grand old house with whitewashed walls, tall windows, balconies… and no wards.

Astor had said the mages' wards were down, so it shouldn't come as a surprise, but walking through the iron gates and not seeing so much as a salt circle made a trickle of unease run down my back. The mages *never* let their guard down, but if they'd arrested their own leader for summoning the gods, it was no wonder they'd seen better days. Becks hung back by the gate to keep watch, while Zeph and I headed down the stone path to the manor house.

Zeph frowned. "Even their doors are unlocked."

So they were. Through a gap in the oak doors, cloaked figures milled around the red-carpeted lobby. I stepped onto the doorstep and spotted a familiar face inside.

Pushing the doors open, I stepped into the lobby as though I'd been invited and approached the cloak-wearing necromancer nearby. "Hey, Morgan. Can I talk to you for a second?"

He looked startled. "How do you know my name?"

"I was there, with your sister. In the other realm."

Also, I met you when you were a kid. He likely didn't remember, though.

His jaw dropped. "You're the dragon? You really are a shifter?"

"Yeah," I said. "I am. So's he." I waved Zeph over to us.

"Jesus." He eyed Zeph. "I don't think I'm allowed to let you in."

"I know your boss. Lady Montgomery." Though come to think of it, she might not remember me either. "We need to speak to your sister, if she's around."

His expression cleared. "You know the boss? Okay. Cool. Uh, I think she's digging through the rubble of the old guild HQ and trying to see what she can salvage, but my sister was around here somewhere the last time I checked."

"Is nobody going to ward this place?" asked Zeph. "Anyone can just walk in."

"I dunno, I'm not in charge," he said. "I guess the wards blew out when the vampires swarmed in yesterday."

I remembered the dead guy in the lab. *Vampires.* Maybe that was why there was little visible damage inside the building, but I of all people knew how dangerous the spirit realm could be.

"I've never met a dragon shifter before," Morgan said to me as we made our way across the lobby. "I met a guy on a night out once who said he was a lizard shifter, but I reckon he was taking the piss. I dunno, I was pretty drunk, so I don't remember."

"Uh-huh," I said. "I take it you're a necromancer? Ilsa, too?"

"Sure." He reached a door and pushed on the handle. "Ilsa, you in there? I've got someone here who wants to talk to you."

Bookshelves lined the walls inside the room, while Ilsa stood in the middle of a circle of candles. The mages' library hadn't visibly changed in fifteen years, except the mirror wasn't here. I should have asked Astor where they were keeping it now.

"Did you have to interrupt me?" Ilsa picked up a small, square book and closed it. I glimpsed a raven on the front cover before she lowered her hands. "Wait—Cori? Is that you?"

"We need to talk to you," I said. "This is Zeph. He's a dragon shifter, too."

Ilsa stepped out of the candle circle. "I guess I owe you a favour for untying me back in the other realm. What do you need?"

"My sister's under a spell," I said, wondering how widespread the knowledge of the gods was. If they'd recently attacked the city, I'd imagine more people knew about them than a decade and a half ago. "We need help fixing a talisman."

"Did you say… a talisman?" Her gaze dropped to the book in her hand. The raven on the cover looked a little different to before, its wings tucked at its sides rather than spread behind its back. It couldn't have moved while we were talking, right? "Uh, which talisman? I don't know how much you know about recent events, but—"

"We know the Ancients are coming back," I said. "We need to fix this talisman to save my sister from one of the gods."

Ilsa sank into a seat. "*Another* god?"

Morgan groaned. "Not more of those bastards."

"Sorry to be the bearer of bad news," I said. "There's a nasty fire goddess who wants us dead, and she has my sister hostage. We need to fix the Moonbeam to free her… have you heard of it?"

"I've heard the name," she said. "I didn't know it was a talisman. I guess there might be something in here…"

She moved over to the bookshelves, and Morgan snorted. "You're just using the mages' distraction as an excuse to raid all their books, aren't you?"

"Maybe a little," said Ilsa, "but it's not like they're going to stop me. I thought the Ancients might give us a day or two before they started screwing with us again."

"She's been hassling the dragon shifters for years," said Zeph. "You haven't seen any, apart from us, have you? Because the other dragons… she has a hold on them. The goddess does. They're not on our side."

"No, I haven't seen any." Ilsa pulled a book down from the shelf. "Bloody gods… I'm not sure any magic that isn't theirs can *fix* a talisman, but the gods are better at breaking things than mending them."

"I figured," I said. "I heard there might be some kind of ancient spell that can help, but I have zero experience with talismans aside from the Moonbeam, and I didn't know it was a talisman until it broke."

"Sounds careless," remarked Morgan.

"Morgan," said Ilsa. "Do something useful or be quiet."

"Hey, I brought them to you," he said indignantly. "I dunno anything about spells. If anything, you should ask J—" He broke off as Ilsa looked stricken. "Sorry."

From the solemn air that descended, I felt awkwardly like I'd gate-crashed someone's funeral. I cast around for something else to say.

"That mark on your forehead is gone," I observed.

"Ah." Ilsa returned the book to its place on the shelf. "It's the mark of the Gatekeeper, but it's usually hidden."

"Gatekeeper?" said Zeph. "Of what?"

"Death," said Morgan.

I looked between them, then at the candles on the floor. "That's a thing?"

Ilsa picked up another book. "Don't look so worried. I'm basically a necromancer, but with a few added bonuses."

"Does that mean you can exorcise the ghost of a dead goddess?" Zeph said hopefully.

Ilsa dropped the textbook. "No. Tried it once, didn't work out. Are you saying the goddess is *dead?*"

"I don't get the impression that makes much of a difference where the gods are concerned."

"No…" Ilsa retrieved the book from under a chair. "I have to say you're right there. Where is this goddess?"

"Not here, don't worry," I said. "Ignessa's pretty active for someone who's supposed to be dead, though. She has an entire city of dragon shifters under her influence."

Ilsa's eyes rounded. "It sounds like I was lucky you were the one who found me in the other realm, then. I'll see what I can find."

6

After an hour of combing through textbooks, we left Ilsa to it, with the promise that she'd let us know via Agnes if she found anything useful.

"At least she offered to help us," I said. "Then again, I did save her from being a snack for a monster."

His brow wrinkled. "Who kidnapped her, the other dragons?"

"I didn't think to ask." I spotted Becks disappearing around the corner. "I think Becks got bored waiting for us."

"I can't believe the mages didn't notice two dragon shifters wandering around their headquarters," Zeph commented.

"They didn't notice Ilsa raiding their library, either," I reminded him. "Or doing necromancy. I guess she has a lot of freedom, being the Gatekeeper of Death."

"Is that a new thing?" Zeph said. "Do all the necromancers get fancy titles now?"

"Maybe," I said. "I notice they haven't upgraded their

uniform in the last fifteen years. They still dress like the Grim Reaper's buddies."

"You didn't tell her you have the spirit sight," he observed. "Any reason?"

"No," I said. "There's just no non-awkward way to bring it up, even with a necromancer. Besides, it's kinda irrelevant, unless the guild is looking to hire a dragon shifter who can talk to the ghost of a mad fire goddess."

It was Lady Montgomery I needed to speak to, but the world had moved on without us, and she might not even remember my name.

Zeph and I slowed our pace to let Becks run ahead, looking up at the peak of Arthur's Seat. As I'd seen yesterday, a huge chunk was missing from the hillside, which looked even worse in daylight.

"That wasn't there before." I tilted my head. The Ley Line passed through the hills, which I'd discovered the first time I'd crash-landed in the city. "Looks like something blew a chunk out of the hill."

"Wanna fly up and see?" Zeph's eyes gleamed invitingly.

A familiar rush of excitement rose within me, before a sure of guilt extinguished the flames. Ember should be here, and her absence twisted a knife in my chest. She'd *want* me to go on as if things were normal, and yet… "I don't know. I feel—"

"Like you're being watched?" whispered a voice.

My blood froze, my pulse roaring in my ears. I turned on my spirit sight, and sure enough, a ghost floated beside me, her eyes tinted with fire.

"Ignessa." My heart climbed into my throat. "What are you doing here?"

She should be in the other realm. *This is bad. Really bad.*

Zeph gripped my arm, tight. "Is it her? Ignessa?"

I dipped my head, unable to take my eyes off her. "What the hell are you playing at?"

"Ensuring you make good on your promise to help me." Fire licked at my arms and I backed away from her, stifling a gasp. She could still hurt me?

"I don't recall promising anything," I said. "You left me to die in jail and you captured my sister."

"I assumed you were capable of finding your own way out," she said. "And I didn't capture your sister. You let her die for you."

My fists clenched, and I made a mental note to ask Ilsa whether it was possible to learn how to punch a ghost the next time I saw her. "You left the other dragons behind."

"I had to go where the action is." Her ghostly breath whispered against my ear. "During your imprisonment, you found a ghost lost in the war, who informed you of an ancient spell which can repair the Moonbeam."

So she *had* been watching me from the spirit realm while I'd been in jail. Metallic rage coated the back of my throat and my hands shifted to claws.

"You cannot harm me, Coriander," she said. "But if you fail to perform the spell in a timely manner, more will suffer their fate."

"Who—"

The nearest house went up in a crackle of flames. I spun on the spot, cursing, but the flames devoured the bricks as though they were nothing more than cardboard. It wasn't regular fire, but the flames of the goddess. Nobody could have outrun it.

Flames licked the edges of the house and then

vanished into wherever they'd materialised from, leaving nothing but charred ashes all the way to the foundations.

There was nothing we could do for the people inside. She'd torched them in an instant, the same way she'd done to Lorne. To Lady Clare. Bile rose in my throat and I swallowed it down, clenching and unclenching my clawed hands.

Zeph took my arm in a comforting gesture. "We have to leave. If we're caught here, they'll blame us for the fire."

Humans wouldn't know the difference between dragonfire and the flames of a goddess. "Just… fuck her."

"I know." His eyes blazed with fury, but he knew as well as I did that two dragon shifters were more likely to be blamed for a fire than an invisible ghost. If we wound up jailed, Ignessa might take more innocent lives. The nearest humans were already calling the emergency services. There was nothing to be done here, except curse Ignessa for what she'd done.

We ran the rest of the way to Agnes's house, where I hammered on the door until she opened it.

Agnes's brows shot up when she saw my face. "What is it?"

"Her. Ignessa." I entered the hall with Zeph, then closed the door behind me. "She's here, and now she's setting people's houses on fire as an incentive to hurry up and set her free."

Agnes swore. "She's in this realm?"

"Maybe she slipped through the mirror when the mages weren't guarding it." My heart pounded in my chest.

Agnes muttered something unfavourable under her breath and walked into the living room, where a number of textbooks lay strewn all over the floor. Becks lay cat-napping on one of them.

"Hey." I snapped my fingers. "Wake up. We have a crisis."

Becks yawned and shifted to human form. "You were in there an hour. I nosed around the mages' place for a bit and decided to come back and help Agnes with her spellbooks."

"By sleeping on them?" I scanned the spread of ancient tomes, which looked even older than the ones Ilsa had been perusing in the mages' library. "Agnes, I don't suppose you have any spells which can repair—"

"That one." She pointed at a yellowed page spread covered in a language that wasn't English.

"What is this?" I frowned at the symbols on the page. "Wait—you *found* the spell? I thought you didn't want us to repair the Moonbeam at all."

"I suspected you might need the knowledge," Agnes said. "The translation's on the other page."

"Damn." I picked up the book. "I guess this is why Ignessa wanted us to hurry home."

Zeph leaned over my shoulder and read: "One lies where nothing dies.

The second grows where river flows.

The third hides where the hunt rides.

With breath divine, the three combine."

"Sounds like a faerie riddle," I said. "Three… what, are they the ingredients of the spell?"

"As far as I can work out," said Agnes. "I haven't had reason to study it in detail."

"They're way too vague." I read the description again. "Nothing dies? Where does nothing die? And which river?"

"Never mind that," said Zeph. "What is it we're even looking for? Does it say?"

"Three powerful ingredients," said Agnes. "I imagine they would be easy to identify when you reach the location. The spell also requires a catalyst."

"The breath divine," said Zeph. "Like a goddess?"

"The ghost in the jail said the goddess's fire was inside me," I murmured. "She implied that would be enough to ignite the spell and repair the Moonbeam."

Even if not, the goddess herself wanted in on our plan… which wasn't a good sign.

Agnes studied me. "Perhaps she's right."

I looked down. "Agnes, she's setting people on fire. If you help us thwart her, she might set you on blaze, too."

"She can't." A grim smile curled her mouth. "I carry a talisman that repels the goddess's flames. It doesn't work as effectively on anyone in the same house as me, but you should be safe here."

"You mean the pendant?" I asked. "You don't have a spare, do you?"

"No," she said. "The talisman is one of a kind. It used to belong to my sister."

Her sister Madison had died at Lorne's hands during his final massacre before the mages had hauled him in. I hadn't known the pendant was a talisman, but an item that blocked dragonfire *and* the goddess's fire was no ordinary magic artefact. Gratitude rushed through me, and I opened my mouth to thank her.

A sudden flash of light dazzled my eyes, and the smell of burning wafted in from the hall. Becks shifted into cat form with a yowl, while Agnes ran into the hall, her hands glowing with golden light. Burn marks covered the wall-paper, soot-coloured against the white background.

"Who is going to pay for that?" Agnes said.

"I can forward your bill to the fire goddess," I said. "Sorry, Agnes. I think she heard you saying she can't burn you and it ticked her off."

"I expected to draw her attention," she said. "Despite my promise to my sister, I can't seem to help getting involved in dragon shifter business. I believe she meant for you to read that."

"That's our clue?" asked Zeph. "What the bloody hell is that?"

I peered at the images on the wall. One was clearly a tree. The second was harder to figure out. A winding line. A river? Or a road? The third resembled a pointed hat. Or a rooftop. The fire goddess needed to take some art classes. Not that I'd be mentioning it aloud in case she burned *me* into the wallpaper next.

"There are three images," I said. "And three ingredients we need to find. Let's see the spell again—"

A resounding *boom* echoed through the house. My stomach lurched, and I yanked the door open, bracing myself for an attack. A dizzying scent wafted into the hall, making my eyes sting. Outside, I glimpsed smoke rising over the peaked rooftops.

"Get back in here," said Agnes. "Before you're blamed."

I made to close the front door, then spotted two familiar figures running towards the house, laden with bags. "Wait, that's Kit and Will."

Will reached the door and dropped the bags on the doorstep, breathless. "You've been back five minutes and you're already setting things on fire?"

"Not us." I backed into the hall to let him and Kit enter. "What did she set ablaze this time, a perfume shop?"

"No, a herb stall at the market," said Will. "And please tell me 'she' doesn't mean who I think it does."

"What's that?" Kit stared at the three images burned into the wall.

"Ignessa's idea of a clue." I rubbed my stinging eyes. "What did she take offence to at the witch market?"

"She's *here?*" Kit's bright green eyes rounded. "I thought she couldn't follow us."

"So did we," said Zeph, and Becks meowed from the sofa. "She's bloody persistent, for a ghost."

Will entered the living room, stepping around the pile of books on the floor. "What's all this?"

"We need three ingredients for the binding spell to fix the Moonbeam," I explained. "The recipe is a riddle and doesn't say what they are, so Ignessa decided to speed up the process by lighting things on fire and wrecking Agnes's wallpaper. And what in the world is that smell?"

"Bloodroot," said Kit. "It grows in Faerie, near the rivers."

My mouth parted. "One of the ingredients we need is on a river, according to the riddle."

"Let me see that." Will picked up the book. "Who the hell writes their spells in the form of poetry?"

"The witches' predecessors did, apparently," I said. "Maybe they were buddies with the Sidhe."

"They weren't," Agnes said, "but the paths between Faerie and Earth were very different in the days in which that spell was written. Bloodroot is a rare ingredient used in powerful binding spells. They say it can restore anything that touches it to its former state."

"I should have known the ingredients weren't the sort you find at the market," I said. "Nothing I've heard about Faerie has convinced me I want to set foot there. No offence, Kit."

"None taken," said the half-faerie. "I've never been to Faerie myself. I was born on Earth, though my faerie parent was a Summer noble. But she's right… pure faerie-grown Bloodroot is certainly rare and powerful."

"Knowing our luck, Ignessa set the city's entire supply on fire." I slumped into a seat. "Why'd she do that?"

Will moved his shopping bags into the room. "Bloodroot only blooms on one night per year, on the summer solstice. I reckon the supplies at the market were the dried sort, which doesn't have the same properties."

"We don't have time to wait for the solstice." Judging by Ignessa's trigger-happy use of her fire, delaying even a day might cost more lives. "Kit, does it grow in Faerie all year round?"

"In Summer territory, yes," said Kit, a thoughtful expression on his face. "It's rumoured that Bloodroot can bestow certain powers upon anyone who consumes it. The dried leaves they sell here on Earth possess almost none of that power."

"I'll take your word for it," said Zeph. "You mean we have to go to *Faerie* to find fresh Bloodroot?"

"They say the dryads guard the secrets of the Bloodroot's source," said Kit. "Perhaps there's a local we can ask."

"I wouldn't want to steal from a dryad," said Will. "People have died for less."

"We're not stealing, just getting information." *Yet.*

Kit dipped his head. "Don't worry, dryads are mild-mannered if you don't provoke them. They'd be more willing to trust me than the rest of you, I think."

"I bet," said Will. "Where's that bloody assassin? Does he know any of this?"

"Haven't seen him since last night," I said. "If he learns we're closer to getting Ember back, he'll want in on it."

"Can you picture him negotiating with faeries?" said Zeph.

I pulled a face. "No, you're right. The local half-faeries still live up in the hills near the Ley Line, right?"

"Last I saw," said Agnes. "For pity's sake, don't shift in front of them. They aren't fond of fire, especially dryads."

"Nobody seems keen on dragon shifters these days."

I walked out of the living room, followed by Zeph and Kit. "Coming, Will?"

"I'll get to work on these spells," Will said from the living room. "If we're going to Faerie, we'll need them."

"Becks, are you coming?" I called.

Becks let out a meow that I assumed meant no. We'd get on better with a smaller group, but I could just picture the look on Astor's face if we set off to Faerie without him. *Ah, well.*

"I don't think witch spells work in Faerie," Kit said, gliding ahead. Tall and slender with long dark hair, he was the only member of our group who looked remotely like he belonged among the graceful Sidhe with their glittering magic and shining tents pitched on the hillside.

Despite that, every one of them stopped and stared at us as we approached, even Kit. Maybe they could tell he lived among humans. As for Zeph and me, with our ashy eyes and auburn hair, we stood out like ogres among mermaids. Every half-Sidhe had pointed ears, slim features, and a regal air despite their ordinary T-shirts and jeans. They were also inhumanly beautiful, if a little ragged around the edges.

"I wonder if they remember the time I crashed their party?" Back then, I'd bet they assumed a dragon falling out of the sky would be the worst of their problems.

Zeph grinned. "Bet you're a legend now. The faeries tell their children about you."

"Yeah, that I'm the nasty monster lurking under the bed." I rolled my eyes. "Better to let Kit do the talking, at least until we convince them we're not going to breathe fire on their tents."

"I wouldn't use that word here." Kit lifted his head high and approached the nearest half-faerie. By the papery-looking armour he wore, he was either their leader or a designated knight. Not that I knew much about faerie hierarchies. His eyes were bright green like Kit's, a sign of his Summer Sidhe heritage, despite his fake armour and plastic-looking weaponry. "We'd like to speak to a dryad."

"Who are you?" asked the faerie.

"Uh…" Kit hesitated. "We're from out of town. We're on a quest, an urgent one."

"A quest?" His gaze sharpened. "The dryads uprooted and left. This isn't a safe place for us, not since the battle."

"Damn," I muttered. "Uh, we're looking for some Bloodroot. It grows where the river flows…" Now I was talking in rhymes, too. The ridiculous riddle was getting into my head.

"I know it grows there, human," said the half-Sidhe. "The Blood River is said to be the only true source, but you will not find yourselves welcome in the Court."

Kit's mouth fell open. "Of course! Thank you. You've been a great help."

"I'm lost." I hurried after him out of the camp, but Kit had kicked up his faerie speed like he sometimes did when he was overexcited. Panting, Zeph and I caught him up halfway to Agnes's house. "What's the Blood River?"

"It runs through the heart of the Summer Court," Kit said, beaming. "If we follow the river, it will lead us to the place where Bloodroot grows."

"You mean right through the Sidhe's home," I said. "Yeah, no thanks. Unless they want to volunteer to go to war with the fire goddess in our place. How do you even find this Blood River?"

"I don't know," said Kit. "Like I said, I've never been into the faerie realm. I was born in Cardiff, and I never met my dad. I just know he was Seelie. My human mother raised me. The Courts dislike half-faeries almost as much as they do humans, since we're mortal."

Zeph's brow furrowed. "They don't like mortals, yet they kidnap humans all the time anyway. How does that work?"

"They don't *hate* humans," said Kit. "They just view them as inferior. Same with us. No human steps into Faerie by choice."

"Then we're about to be the exceptions." I'd walk through hell for Ember without a second's thought, and she'd do the same for me. Faerie, on the other hand, was rumoured to make hell look like a tea party.

Bring it, then.

7

"Well, shit," said Will, when we'd updated the others on our meeting with the half-faeries. "I never thought I'd get to meet your faerie relatives, Kit."

"I don't even know who my father is," Kit said. "But the Court's still more dangerous for you than it is for me."

"You think I'm letting you go there without me?" Will said. "Not happening. Nor you, Cori. Don't even think about objecting. Ember would skin us alive if she found out you went into Faerie alone."

"She would," said Becks. "But if there's a way to do this without any of us going near Faerie, I'm all over that."

"Not sure we'll be that lucky." I looked around at our group. "Kit, you're the only one of us who can see through faerie glamour. That means you'll have to warn us if anything's sneaking up on us."

"Of course," he said. "We just follow the path of the river."

"I thought the first rule of Faerie was not to go near

the water," I said. "I mean, aside from not leaving the path, not eating or drinking anything, and not making a promise to anyone. We'll have to avoid merpeople, sirens, nereids, kelpies... anything else?"

"Each Uisge," said Kit. "They're shapeshifters who preys on mortal flesh."

"Is there anything in Faerie that *doesn't* prey on mortal flesh?" Will wanted to know.

"The Sidhe," said Agnes. "And they're capable of much worse. There's little I can do to help you. My type of magic doesn't work in the Courts."

Even Agnes's magic is nothing to the Sidhe?

I swallowed down my objections at the others coming with me. It was my quest, but there was strength in numbers, and everyone had their own skills to bring to the table. I just had to hope it would be enough. "We should let Ilsa know we don't need her help anymore."

"Ilsa Lynn?" said Agnes. "You're aware her family works for the Summer Court, right?"

They did? "It never came up."

I vaguely recalled Agnes mentioning that the Lynns' mother had been in Faerie when we'd met fifteen years earlier, but I hadn't pressed her for more details at the time.

"She does," said Agnes. "If anyone can get you into the Court, it's Ilsa."

———

When Zeph and I reached the mages' headquarters, fresh wards covered the gates, preventing us from entering.

"That's more like it," said Zeph. "I was beginning to think the mages' guild was about to collapse altogether."

"Don't speak too soon." I tensed as a cloaked figure walked out of the front door. "I think we've worn out our welcome."

The mage, a tall dark-haired man of around my age, looked us up and down. "Who are you?"

"I'm Cori," I said. "Um, we haven't met. I'm looking for Ilsa Lynn. She's expecting us."

Damn, I don't have the time to explain our situation to the entire mage guild. If he stalled me, Ignessa might set him on fire.

The mage didn't move. "I thought I saw you slinking around the place earlier. Do you think you can walk on the mages' property without permission?"

"Only because you left the door open," I pointed out. "If you hadn't wanted people to wander in, you might have left a sign saying *no outsiders.* Or just locked the gates."

His eyes narrowed. "Are you mocking me?"

"Nope, just making an observation," I said cheerily. "I do need to speak with Ilsa, though, and since I have no other way of contacting her, I guess we're all going to awkwardly stand here until she comes out."

The mage's jaw tightened. "You need to learn respect. What did you have to contribute to the war, pray tell? Did you make any sacrifices?"

"We missed it."

"You missed it," he repeated.

"Yep. Slept through the whole thing." I probably shouldn't push my luck, but being treated like a criminal was growing old.

Fortunately for both of us, Ilsa chose that moment to walk out of the mages' headquarters. "Oh, hey, Cori," she said. "Caleb—it's okay. They're with me."

"They aren't necromancers or mages," he said. "Witches, are you?"

Becks meowed. His gaze dropped to her, and his eyes narrowed.

"Shifters," I said. At the rate he was pissing me off, my claws would make an appearance soon enough. "We're from out of town, but we're friendly with Lady Montgomery of the necromancer guild."

The mage's suspicious expression didn't waver. "If you're lying, our dungeon has plenty of space for new occupants."

"They came to see me," Ilsa said. "Don't be a dick, Caleb. You don't have to challenge everyone you see. The wards would let us know if they were a threat."

He glared at her, but stepped aside. Not to let us in, but to let her out. "Make it quick."

Ilsa sighed. "All right, we'll go somewhere else."

"I'm getting the impression that dude doesn't like dragon shifters," said Zeph.

"I can't imagine what tipped us off," I added. "Maybe it was the part where he threatened to lock us in the dungeon."

Ilsa glanced over her shoulder. "Sorry. The mages are on edge at the moment. They did catch a trespasser earlier... a witch, I think."

Not Astor, then, I assumed. Though whatever mission he was on, he seemed to have no intention of involving the rest of us in it.

"I think you'd better come with us to Agnes's place," said Zeph. "You know her, right?"

"Yes, I do," said Ilsa. "Is she in on this, uh, scheme of yours, then?"

"You might say that," I said. "We think we know what we're looking for now, we just need a tour guide. I'm told your family works for the Summer Court."

Ilsa stopped walking. "You want a tour guide for *Faerie?* Do you have a death wish?"

"No, but we need to find something important, and Faerie is the only place it grows." I ran through our situation on the way to Agnes's house, and Ilsa's expression grew grimmer with every word. Then she pulled out her phone and tapped on the screen.

"I'm sorry, but I can't take you there myself," she said. "I don't work for Faerie, but my sister does, and she's busy at the moment."

"I thought the Sidhe hated humans," added Zeph. "Kit, our friend, said they don't even let half-faeries in."

"They do, but only if they have known family in the Court," said Ilsa. "It's not getting you in that's the problem, it's getting you out. Particularly if you steal from them."

"We'll worry about that later." I led the way to Agnes's doorstep and knocked.

Will opened the door. "That was fast."

"The mages wouldn't let us in," I explained. "This is Ilsa."

"Hey," said Will. "I'm Will. That's Kit, and he's explaining all the reasons going into Faerie is *not* a good idea."

"I never said it was a decision any rational person who

valued their life would make," said Ilsa, eyeing the marks burned into the wallpaper. "What's this?"

"The fire goddess's idea of a clue," I said. "We need three ingredients for the spell, so I guess each image corresponds to one ingredient. The actual text is in there. It's in the form of a riddle."

"It is?" Ilsa walked into the living room, leaning over the textbook Will had laid out on the floor. "So you think this tree is beside the river… which one?"

"The Blood River," said Kit. "It runs through the heart of Seelie territory."

"The name rings a bell," said Ilsa. "But the Seelie Court is a dangerous place for mortals, especially humans."

"We know," I said. "I wouldn't set foot near the Courts if there was any other way to save my sister's life."

"I understand," said Ilsa. "My boyfriend River is the son of a Sidhe lord. I messaged him to see if he'd be able to smuggle you into the Court, provided you don't do anything to draw unnecessary attention."

"Um… we'll try not to." Two dragon shifters drew unnecessary attention just by walking into a room. "Thanks, Ilsa. I appreciate it."

"Your boyfriend's called River?" Zeph eyed the drawing on the wall. "Does he have any Bloodroot?"

"No," said Ilsa. "He's a necromancer, not a faerie, but his dad owes him a favour. He should be on his way over… there he is."

A knock on the door sounded. Ilsa went to open it, and a blond half-faerie entered the hall. He wore the uniform of the necromancer guild and had short curly hair and pale, pointed features.

"I didn't know the necromancer guild was a career option for faeries," I said.

"I get that a lot," River said mildly. "My father is a Sidhe lord of Summer, but I can't say he'd be pleased if I told him I'm bringing a group of humans to visit. I do, however, have an open invitation to his house, which should allow you to accompany me into the Court."

"As long as nobody sees us." He looked familiar, and I recalled a blond kid I'd met when I'd visited Edinburgh fifteen years ago. "You're Lady Montgomery's son, aren't you?"

"Yes, he is." Morgan marched up behind him. "What do you mean by going off into Faerie without telling me?"

"We're not," said Ilsa. "That is—I'm not, and neither are you. We just need to get Cori and her friends in, and then…"

"And then we can find our own way out," I said. "Right?"

A short barking noise came from behind Morgan. A small dog ran up to us, yapping excitedly.

"You brought him into the other realm to rescue Ilsa," I recalled. "Did you call him a demon puppy?"

Small and covered in black fluff, the puppy looked about as much like a demon as a squirrel looked like a tarantula.

"Oh, that's a joke," said Morgan. "He's a faerie dog."

"He is," said Ilsa. "But Morgan, he's never even been to Faerie."

"He has an amazing sense of smell," said Morgan. "He's smart, too."

The puppy sniffed at me, then tried to climb my legs. I gave him a stroke, and he rolled over on the ground, tongue lolling. He didn't seem bothered that I smelled like a dragon. "Are you sure?"

Morgan looked at Ilsa. "You know what Faerie's like. He can see through glamour, *and* navigate the Ley Line. If I were them, I'd want him on my team."

The puppy lay down and drooled on my shoes. "He can navigate the Ley Line?"

"Well, I think so," said Morgan. "He's never tried, but it's in their blood, right?"

"I still don't think this is wise," said River. "I can take you into the Court on the pretext of paying my father a visit, but he's likely to react harshly if he realises you plan to steal from Summer. I have something of a reputation for helping humans escape the Sidhe's clutches."

"Don't scare them, River," Ilsa reprimanded. "Cori's sister is in trouble, and the only way to save her is to go into the Court."

And borrow something from a tree that might try to eat us alive. It was no more impossible than risking my neck in an arena match, right?

"Keep an eye on the time, too," said River. "Time in Faerie passes on a different scale to this realm."

"Not again." I pulled a face. "We already lost fifteen years in the other realm because we were locked in jail."

"Ouch." Ilsa winced. "I've met humans who got lost in Faerie for decades. Fair warning."

"That, or they show up dead," said Morgan helpfully. "Or mad."

Ilsa gave her brother a prod in the arm. "As far as magic goes, you should be able to shift, but no other magic works in Faerie aside from their own. Are you sure you want to do this?"

My heartbeat quickened. Talk was one thing, but setting foot in the faerie realms was another matter entirely.

"Give us an hour," said Zeph. "We'll be ready."

River inclined his head. "I'll meet you near the Ley Line."

"Thanks." Gratitude washed over me. "Believe me, if I can ever repay the favour—"

"You did," said Ilsa. "You saved my life back in the other realm. I was five minutes from being eaten by a fury."

"Fury?" said Zeph.

"You saw those winged monsters, right?" she said.

"So that's what they're called." Worse might await us in Faerie, but what choice did we have?

River turned to me. "It's appreciated. Thank you for helping Ilsa."

The faerie dog barked in agreement.

"He's called Pepper," said Morgan. "Make sure he doesn't get hurt over there, okay?"

So we had a guide. Now all we needed was to safely get in. Oh, and out. Funny how the stories never mentioned that part.

I surveyed my reflection in the mirror an hour later, tugging my jacket into place to cover my bright T-shirt. Like my jeans, it showed obvious signs of wear and tear but was still functional. I'd combed my hair but decided against covering it, since I doubted my red hair would be the brightest or most remarkable thing in the Summer

Court. Other than a single iron knife buried in my coat pocket, I'd have to rely on my claws. While carrying iron into the Seelie Court was considered a grave offence, going in unarmed would be riskier than the alternative. Besides, most beings in Faerie thought of us as somewhere between tasty snacks and harmless playthings. Levelling the playing field was only fair.

I met the others in the living room. Zeph wore jeans and a battered jacket, like me. Hardly high fashion, but if the Sidhe took offence, there was little we could do. Will's jeans had holes in the knees, while Becks's trench coat was ripped down the back. Since everyone in Faerie was covered in a thick layer of glamour to make humans see whatever the Sidhe wanted them to see, we'd at a disadvantage even if we dressed like royalty. If they objected, I could always try lumbering around in dragon form. I'd bet the Sidhe had never met a dragon shifter before.

Kit walked into the room in full faerie guise. He'd glamoured his hair to look longer and wore an armoured coat and trousers that moulded to his slim form.

"What in the world are you wearing, Kit?" I asked.

"I glamoured my clothes to look like Seelie Court high fashion," he said. "At least, it was high fashion the last time I heard. Which was about thirty years ago. So…"

"It'll work," said River, who wore a similar outfit. Despite his shorter hair, he looked as much the part of a Sidhe lord as Kit did, since they shared the same bright green eyes that marked someone as a Seelie faerie. "Can you glamour your friends, too?"

"I can try," said Kit. "I don't normally glamour that many people at once. But wouldn't it be better to turn ourselves invisible?"

"Most Sidhe can see through such enchantments," said River. "And please don't let them see the iron."

"No iron. Got it." Will paced in the hall, his blond hair standing on end where he'd been running his fingers through it. "Kit, are you sure—"

"Yes." Kit reached out a hand, and Will's ears turned pointed.

"Wow," said Becks. "You do look kinda like a faerie prince."

"Who, me?" Will leaned over to look in the hall mirror. "Huh."

"You'd need to grow your hair out, though," said Kit, smoothing Will's hair down. "And do something about your eyes."

At another gesture from Kit, Will's eyes turned green. His hair lengthened, while a snazzy Court outfit took the place of his scruffy T-shirt and jeans.

"With any luck, we won't have to get up close and personal with the Sidhe." Will gave a mock bow to his reflection. "What about you guys?"

"I'll go as a cat," said Becks. "Pretend to be a shapeshifter faerie."

"All right," said Kit. "Just don't shift into a human. Zeph and Cori… don't walk around in dragon form."

"Dammit," I said. "That's my master plan foiled. I was going to rampage through the Court until I'd scared off all potential threats."

"Believe me, there are beasts in Faerie that can rival a dragon shifter," said Ilsa. "So it's just the five of you?"

"Since the assassin hasn't shown his face," said Will. "Where is he, anyway? I thought he was dead set on rescuing Ember."

"It's probably better for all of us if he stays out of Faerie," I said. "What about the dragonling?"

"He went hunting," said Kit. "I'm sure he'll understand why he can't come with us."

At least he was taking a sensible approach this time, but then, he of all people knew Faerie and its dangers. "Are you glamouring Zeph and me?"

"Sure." Kit snapped his fingers. Green light flashed, and when it cleared, Zeph's ears had turned pointed. His newly green-tinted grey eyes widened in disbelief.

"Whoa," he said, touching my ear with his fingertip.

In the mirror, my ears looked pointed, but they felt no different. The green tint to my irises would look downright weird if I lost my temper and my eyes turned orange. "Reckon I could pass as a faerie princess?"

"Hmm." He ran his finger over the tip of my ear, leaving a trail of warmth. Then he seemed to realise what he was doing and dropped his hand. "Let's go."

"Time for a swift trip to Faerie," I said. "We'll just go in, get what we need, and get out again. Simple."

8

My bravado melted when our small group—minus Astor—halted at the foot of the hills leading to Arthur's Seat. The Ley Line was visible as a rippling current of energy slicing through the air.

"Is it true, then?" I asked. "The Ley Line leads into Faerie? We can just… walk through?"

"Only Sidhe and half-Sidhe with an invitation can enter," River said. "Ilsa, stay behind. I'll be back in a minute."

"Let's hope Faerie plays nice," said Ilsa, eyeing the Ley Line. "Don't make any promises to anyone, and don't accept any gifts. And Morgan, don't you even think about following."

"Like I want to go back to that place." He gave the puppy a stroke. "Take care of him, okay?"

"I will do." I gripped the reins, hoping having a faerie dog would make the Sidhe more likely to overlook my height and flaming red hair.

Will and Kit walked behind River, while Becks padded beside me. I hoped she wouldn't start a fight with the faerie puppy. She could never seem to help herself from swiping at any nearby canines as a cat.

River walked into the Ley Line, vanishing among its rippling currents. As we followed, the air shimmered around us, showing glimpses of paths snaking through woodland.

The dragonling leapt over our heads, and in the same instant, the world blurred into nothingness.

An instant later, a bright path appeared under our feet, winding between towering oaks. Beams of sunlight shone through the canopy, brighter than the average summer's day in England.

"This looks… normal," muttered Zeph. "I don't trust it."

"I'd advise you not to trust anything you see," said River. "I can take you as far as my father's orchard, then you'll have to make your own way from there. I'll wait for you for a while, but my father will grow suspicious if I stay too long. Take this."

I extended a hand and he pushed a cool green stone into my palm. "What's this for?"

"It's a token. It'll transport you to this path should you need to make an urgent exit, but it can only be used within a mile of the Court. If I'm not here, ask Pepper to lead you home. He can travel through the Ley Line. Just don't let go of his reins."

"Thanks." I pushed the token into my pocket. I didn't like the idea of depending on a faerie spell and a puppy to get us out, but it couldn't be helped.

"How do miles even work in Faerie?" asked Zeph.

"Wait—if the requirement to use the Ley Line is being half-Sidhe, wouldn't Kit be able to get us out?"

"He's not employed in the Court," said River. "I wouldn't risk it."

Kit himself was already halfway down the path. Will hurried after him. "Whoa. Don't go falling under their spell. I thought you were immune to it."

"Oh, even the Sidhe aren't," he said.

Well, that's not great news.

We were in Faerie. In *Faerie.* I was torn between trying to take in every detail and getting it over with before one of us fell into a trap. The dragonling was uncharacteristically quiet, his head down, tail dragging on the ground. "Why did you follow us?"

"He worries about us," said Kit, who'd brightened considerably at Thorn's appearance. "We need allies, right?"

"You need to focus on not drawing attention," said River, taking the lead down the winding path. He moved faster here, his movements more noticeably fae. He must have to hold back at least some of the time when he was playing human. With his graceful steps and Court attire, he looked like he belonged here. Then again, so did Kit. Will did his best to keep pace with him, but Kit moved like a river, fast and fluid. Becks walked behind them, her shifter speed disguising her non-fae nature.

And then… there was me. I was far too short to pass as anything other than human. Zeph looked the most out of place of all of us, with his bright auburn hair and his muscular frame. Considering the Sidhe had more magic in a fingernail than I did in my entire body, I had my doubts they'd be intimidated even if we shifted.

River took us on a winding route which led into deeper forest. "I'd prefer you not to be out in the open, in case anyone is watching," he explained. "It'll take longer, but it's safer."

"I thought it was unsafe to go into the woods." I ducked under a low-hanging branch, and undergrowth crunched beneath my feet. "Conspicuous, too."

"This is Sidhe territory. Nothing will harm us."

I did not share his confidence. It didn't help that I was a city dragon through and through, despite my love of open spaces. Paths wound between thick oaks and ashes, while every plant seemed to be carnivorous or poisonous, or both. The heat sent my dragon shifter senses blazing, while a thousand scents battled for dominance. Crushed grass, earth, odd plants incomparable to anything on earth, and sweet-scented flowers.

"How's a faerie dog supposed to sniff out anything in here?" I said.

"They have keener senses than even most fae," River responded. "I'll have to leave you here. Keep following this path until you reach the river, then go north."

The puppy strained against the reins, which snapped, and he plunged into the undergrowth. In a rustle of branches, River was gone.

"Did we just get ditched twice over?" said Will.

Becks gave an irritable meow, her fur prickling. Then the puppy's head emerged from the undergrowth.

"I think he wants us to follow him," said Kit.

"Bloody faeries," said Will. "Who wants to volunteer to go first, then?"

Thorn responded by diving into the undergrowth after the faerie dog. Kit followed, pushing a handful of undergrowth aside to reveal a tunnel beneath a wide spread of tree roots. Becks streaked through ahead of the dragonling, followed by Will and Kit.

"This is not my idea of a good time," Zeph said.

I had to admit I agreed. "Give me a simple problem to solve with my claws any day of the week."

I ducked down under the tree roots into the tunnel, which was tall enough for me to stand in. Zeph wasn't so lucky, being over six feet tall. I heard him swearing behind me as we trailed through in single file. I couldn't see anything except the dragonling's tail in front of me, which occasionally hit me in the face, so I had to trust the faerie dog was leading us in the right direction. Tree roots snaked above our heads, while the smell of leaves and fresh soil filled the air.

We emerged from the tunnel beside a fast-flowing river of glittering blue water as wide as a road.

"We made it." I scanned the water for any sign of potential threats. "Okay, where's that Bloodroot?"

"Not here," said Kit. "They say it grows beside a river of blood that runs through the heart of the Court. We'll know it when we see it."

"A river of blood?" I said. "Why is it always blood? Why can't it be a river of caramel? Or chocolate sauce?"

Now my mouth was watering. I should have packed more snacks.

"The deadly river of caramel doesn't have quite the same ring to it," said Zeph. "This *is* the faeries we're talking about."

The faerie dog padded alongside the river, keeping a sensible distance from the water. Considering one of the major rules in Faerie was to avoid going near running water, forests, or… well, anything, I was more than happy to keep my distance. Dragons didn't get along with water on a good day.

The path ended at a high cliff. On our right, a large stone bridge spanned the width of the river, leaving us to either turn back or walk over the water.

"Shit," I said. "We have to cross?"

"I think so," said Kit. "Walk in single file, directly down the centre, and keep an eye out for trouble."

In case anything tries to eat us. All my dragon shifter senses told me there was no way in hell I was getting on that bridge. Zeph met my eyes, orange fire simmering in his irises. "Want to shift and fly over?"

"It's a troll's bridge," Kit said. "If any of us cross the river without leaving a tribute, we won't be able to return to the Court."

"Don't piss off the trolls," said Will.

"I thought it was don't feed the trolls," I said. "What is this tribute supposed to be, then? Money?"

"A gift." Kit reached into his pocket and pulled out a handful of coins. "These will do. Follow closely behind me."

I dragged my gaze from the water. "You lead the way, Kit."

The half-faerie stepped onto the stone bridge. Will climbed up behind him, and one by one, we walked across the swift-flowing river. While the stone bridge was sturdier than a wooden one, no railings supported either side, so if anything tried to drag us into the water, we'd have nothing to grab onto. Each second dragged endlessly, while my instincts screamed at me to leave the river far behind. Midway across, Kit crouched down and dropped the handful coins over the side of the bridge.

Someone yelped. "Ow! Who's throwing coins at me?"

"Is there a person down there?" Kit peered over the edge, halting our procession. "Hey, there is."

Will caught Kit's fingers and tugged him back from the edge. "Please, Kit, don't fall into any traps. I want to get the hell off this bridge, now."

"Likewise." I waited for Kit to move, but before he could, a hand grabbed at his foot.

Becks leapt on the threat with a yowl, claws digging into the disembodied hand.

"Help!" yelled the voice the hand belonged to. "Please, you've gotta get me out. I'm stuck in here."

I glanced over the bridge and spotted a human-sized figure caught in a net in the alcove where Kit had tossed the coins. One of his hands was free, but the net ensnared his body, suspended above the water.

"Yeah, he's a trap," said Will, pulling Kit out of reach of the faerie's hands. "Nice try, mate, but we don't pick up hitchhikers in Faerie."

"I'm not a trap," said the faerie. "Please get me out, and I will grant you any favour you wish for."

Dammit. I wouldn't have wanted anyone to leave *me* lying in a net for a troll to eat, but rescuing him went against all the advice I'd ever heard about dealing with the faerie realm. Guilt twisted in my chest. Being owed a favour by a faerie wasn't as dangerous as owing one, but if any of us touched him, he might drag us with him into the deep. I met Will's eyes, seeing similar conflicting thoughts there, and everyone looked at Kit.

"Your call," said Will. "But don't touch him."

"He's not glamoured," Kit observed. "Or hiding anything."

His hands flashed green. At once, the net collapsed. The faerie scrambled for a grip on the bridge, pulling himself to safety. Other than his cat-like eyes and pointed ears, he looked human, his hair a mass of tangled black curls.

Becks hissed and swatted at him with a paw, positioning herself between him and us.

"You mistrust me." The faerie bared his teeth in a smile. "That will serve you well."

"Good for you," said Will. "If I were you, I'd run for it while you can."

"Now, I can't let a group of humans like you run around the faerie realms getting into trouble, can I?" He stepped into our line. "I owe you a favour. I will be your guide."

"We already have a faerie dog, thanks." Will made a shooing motion. "Consider your favour repaid if you leave us alone."

"Then I will see you again soon," he said, "Beware the Each Uisge."

The faerie hurried away, prompting me to look up at the end of the bridge. The dragonling and the puppy had almost reached the other side by now, so we resumed our trek to catch them up.

"Each Uisge," I said. "What're those again?"

"Water horses," said Kit. "Like kelpies, but they can change forms. And they aren't as friendly."

"Good job kelpies are lovely harmless creatures," I muttered. "What kind of fae was that guy, do you know?"

"He was half-blood, either a cait sidhe or a phouka,"

said Kit. "I'd guess a phouka. They can take on at least a dozen forms, including human."

Becks gave a hiss of disapproval and ran along the stone bridge, her swift cat paws reaching the bank first. She shook her head violently as though to say *never again.*

A bone-shaking roar came from behind us, making the while bridge tremble.

Will cursed. "What the hell was that?"

"I don't think the troll liked our tribute," said Kit, picking up speed. "Unless—it wasn't coins he wanted."

The image of the faerie we'd saved came to mind. "Oh, fuck. Don't tell me that guy was supposed to be the tribute."

The bridge gave another alarming tremble. Then it split in two, leaving Will and Kit on one side and Zeph and me on the other.

"Cori!" said Kit, his eyes widening.

I grabbed Zeph for balance, glancing over my shoulder. A massive misshapen head poked out of the water, and a pair of meaty hands gripped the bridge.

"We're gonna have to jump," I warned Zeph. "Or fly. To be honest, I don't care about pissing off that guy."

The water in the gap did *not* look inviting. I couldn't make the jump as a human, but if I shifted my feet, I'd be in with a shot. The bridge trembled under the troll's hands. I crouched, prepared to jump—

Ember's eyes met mine, her face shimmering below the water's surface.

"Help," she whispered.

"No," Zeph growled between his teeth. "It's a trick."

I know. I squeezed my eyes shut, my hands trembling. How could a faerie trick *sound* exactly like my sister?

I dragged my gaze back to Zeph. "Shift and fly."

Zeph didn't move. He was leaning right over the edge, his gaze fixed on the water, his face pale. "No."

"Don't look at it, whatever it is." I gripped his arm, my nails digging in. "It's not real."

"I could make it real," whispered a voice.

My claws slid out. I glimpsed movement under the surface, a horse-like shape. The Each Uisge. "Stop that, you bastard."

"Someone you love, was she?" whispered the voice. "You know… Faerie can give you anything you desire if you ask the right questions. I would be honoured to take you to the one you love if you promise me something in return…"

Zeph let out a roar, diving at the shape beneath the water.

"Zeph, no!" I caught the back of his shirt, but the momentum pulled me after him. The water gaped beneath us like the maw of a giant beast.

Then a vine grabbed me around the waist, binding me to Zeph and yanking us both out of the water. Kit's hands glowed bright green as he pulled the vines, depositing us on the other side of the bridge.

"Damn." I gasped. "Thanks, Kit. You just saved our necks."

A horse-like head emerged from the water, baring sharp teeth. "I will not be deprived of my prey."

"Go to hell." My claws shot out, and I lunged at the Each Uisge. The horse's head tilted back in a scream, blood trailing into the water.

"Cori." Zeph's hand caught mine, ice-cold. "His blood will draw more of them."

Ah, shit. Faerie predators were drawn to bloodshed. We wouldn't be able to return via the same route if we wanted to avoid being chased out of here by a swarm of angry water horses. Not that I regretted making him bleed.

"C'mon." Still holding Zeph's hand, I turned my back on the river. "You okay?"

"Fucker." His voice was low, pained. "I'm sorry, Cori. I nearly got both of us killed."

"It's not your fault. Whatever he showed you wasn't real. With me, he pretended to be Ember. You?"

A moment passed. "My parents."

I squeezed his hand. "I'm sorry."

We hurried away from the bridge down the path, relieved to be on dry land once more. The winding route continued all the way down the side of the river, bordering woodland on one side. My heart thundered from the near-miss. Living in the same house as a harmless half-faerie like Kit had somewhat lessened my impression of just how deadly most fae were to mortals. The closest I'd come was that banshee I'd brought down who was masquerading as a harmless little old lady, and she'd been weakened. Faeries who lived in their own realm were at full power, and I hated my human eyes for not being able to see the truth of this place.

But I wouldn't give up. Ember was counting on me.

The water darkened the further we walked, turning sheer and opaque. An odd greenish light drew my eyes to the surface, while an unpleasant coppery smell teased my nostrils.

My stomach lurched. The water was no longer clear

but wine-red under its shimmering green surface. "We're at the Blood River."

"Nobody fall in," said Kit.

"There goes my plan to take a swim." I swallowed down nausea, scanning the bank for any signs of the Bloodroot. The ground on either side of the river seemed bare, empty of life, an odd sight for Summer territory.

"This isn't a spot favoured by the Court," said Kit. "That's probably the only reason nobody's come after us. The Blood River is said to run red with the blood of those who wronged the Erlking. He's the ruler of the Seelie Court."

"Sounds like a real charmer." I gave a shudder. "The Bloodroot grows where the river flows, but it's not flowing, is it? It's just sitting there. Also, there aren't any trees."

"Who cares about semantics?" said Will.

"The Sidhe do," said Kit. "The tree grows where the river flows. So… we have to find a tree where the river is still flowing. Pepper can help."

The faerie dog took the lead, loping along the bank.

"Are the Sidhe really that literal?" Zeph said.

"Yes," I said. "I mean, I don't have a ton of experience with them, but Sidhe can't lie, and a lot of half-faeries don't like to. Their riddles have to be taken at their word, but that doesn't mean they can't get creative with the meanings."

Zeph grunted. "Why not just say what they mean?"

"That would defeat the purpose of screwing with us, apparently," I said. "With faeries, you either get people like Kit, who are incapable of being deceitful… or people like the Each Uisge, who *live* to fuck with humans and other prey."

Zeph's eyes simmered. "We're not prey. And to be honest, I don't like pretending to be."

"Feel free to breathe fire all you like once we find the tree," I said.

"I don't want to breathe fire," he said. "I want to fly the hell out of here. This place isn't good for dragon shifters. Can't you feel it?"

I could feel it, all right. Magic tingled in every particle of the air, in the earth beneath our feet, in the too-bright sky. My claws itched to come out and tear through the layers of illusion until I could see the world for what it really was.

Our group came to a halt on the bank. The dragonling let out a low growling noise, while Becks stiffened, her fur standing on end. Before us lay a tree, taller than any I'd seen before. Easily ten feet tall, its roots spanned a distance so wide they might have been snaking under-neath our feet for miles. It stood at a crooked angle on a slope, its roots extending into the water, its branches reaching upwards into the sky. The tree's trunk was the same red colour as the waters of the river.

"Are you sure that's a dryad?" I whispered.

"It's not a pony, I'll say that much," said Will. "I don't see any Bloodroot, though."

The tree's thick trunk and grasping branches were bare of leaves or moss, but something gleamed beside its roots.

I inched closer. Crimson leaves sprouted from the riverbank, and the tree's roots surrounded it like a cage.

"I'm gonna go out on a limb and say those roots will rip the hands off anyone who tries to steal it," said Zeph.

"Maybe we should ask nicely?" I peered at the trunk

for any sign of a humanoid face. Then I took one step closer.

A low-hanging branch swung around, and our group scattered as the tree came to life. Its branches whipped out in all directions, while the roots below the earth stirred, threatening to tip us into the bloody water.

"Whoa!" I held up my hands. "We're not here to harm you."

A branch whipped me full in the face, sending me sprawling into the mud. I tasted blood and lifted my head, only to find the roots had broken the surface of the earth. Around me, the others were trapped in the same manner, even the dragonling.

The roots closed in, locking around my body like a cage.

My claws slid out, and I pushed at the roots, looking up at the tree trunk. A face appeared in the bark, eyes as crimson as the water. The dryad. Somewhere behind her lay the Bloodroot, our one shot at saving Ember.

I put on my angelic little sister smile, which I hadn't used for so long it felt as odd as a glamour.

"Hey there," I said. "We wanted to ask you... a question."

I'd almost said *a favour,* but if I knew one thing about faeries, mentioning bonds, obligations or promises was a great way to end up ensnared forever.

"Mortals have come here to ask me a question?" She laughed, and the ground bubbled up with red water around her roots. Ugh. "What question is that, pray tell?"

"I'm told this is the only place in all the realms to find fresh Bloodroot," I said. "I wish to borrow some to use in a spell."

"You wish to take my Bloodroot? Did you know it bestows gifts upon those who touch it?"

"I heard." She couldn't lie, like most pure fae, but any of her words might contain a double meaning or trick. "If you require anything in exchange, please tell me now."

"Blood sustains me," she croaked. "That is what I require."

"Don't you already have enough blood?" Will said. "You could fill a swimming pool with it."

"Will," hissed Kit. "Whose blood?"

"Any of you will do." The dryad's bark-like teeth bared in a jagged grin. "One of you must bleed."

"For what?" said Zeph. "You never *said* you'd exchange the Bloodroot for blood. I want you to spell it out."

Good catch, Zeph.

"He's right," said Kit. "What do you wish for in exchange for the blood? You can't lie, can you?"

"I do not sully these waters with deceit, mortal," she said. "And you will give me what I want."

Roots stabbed out of the earth like knives. I shifted my hands to claws, catching them before they impaled me. Blood sprayed out where my claws severed the roots, and the dryad shrieked.

"That enough blood for you?" I clawed my way out of the cage, cutting down every root in my path. Green light bloomed around Kit, repelling the roots and forming a shield to push them back. The dragonling hissed and spat mouthfuls of fire at the grasping roots, allowing Will to escape and run over to join Kit.

I, however, had my eyes on the Bloodroot. *If I fly over and grab it in my claws, she won't be able to fight me.*

And I'd been trying *so* hard not to set everything on fire.

I shifted into dragon form. Roots grabbed at my scaled legs, but I flew higher, soaring over the river in an arc. I ducked and dodged branches, my gaze fixed on the roots sprouting at the riverside.

I released a breath, and the merest hint of fire singed the dryad's roots. At once, she withdrew them from the riverbank with an anguished howl.

I extended a claw, hooking it around the Bloodroot's leaves. They were stronger than they looked, and I had to tug with both claws before they came free, dangling blood-red roots. *Gotcha.*

The dryad screamed again. The waters of the river rose to the bank, surging under Kit's shielding spell and dragging my friends into the bubbling current of blood-red water.

Shit. Keeping my grip on the roots, I flew over the spot where the others had been standing. *Please, no. Please don't let them be dead.*

The dragonling exploded out of the blood-drenched soil, Will hanging onto his tail. Kit emerged a second later, and Zeph's head broke the surface. I exhaled in relief as they made for the safety of a patch of woodland some way off, out of reach of the waters.

I landed beside them, turning into my human form. "Got the Bloodroot. Where's Becks?"

"Get out, humans," said the phouka, appearing from the bushes. His face was streaked with bloody water, suggesting the flood had caught him in his escape.

"We don't abandon our friends." Damn. There were no

signs of her at all, and in cat form, the water might have swallowed her in an instant. "Becks!"

The phouka let out a growl. "I'll help your friend. You get out."

Becks's head broke the surface of the bloody water with a splutter, but the flood rose to swallow her again. Before any of us could move, the phouka leapt into the water. An instant later, he emerged, holding the scruff of Becks's neck and dragging her after him to the bank.

The phouka released her. Becks coughed, shifting to human, and vomited bloody water onto the ground. "Let go of me," she wheezed, pushing the phouka's hands away.

"You're welcome," said her rescuer. "If you fell into the river, you would be forever enslaved among Summer's armies. More than a few humans have ended up ensnared in this way."

"Aren't you a bundle of laughs?" Becks coughed again, struggling upright. Her hair was sopping wet and plastered to her cheeks, stained in the red of the bloody water. "Considering how much you hate mortals, you sure seem to love coming up with ways to get us trapped in your Court forever."

"I never said I hated mortals," he said. "I *am* one. I'm half-human. The name's Bracken."

"I don't want to chat," Becks said bluntly, striding away from him. "Where's the path?"

"Ah, shit," said Will.

The waters had flooded the entire area, making our surroundings unrecognisable. I dug in my pocket for the token, finding it empty. *Damn. "The token's gone. I bet those bloody roots pulled it out of my pocket."*

"We can't get out?" Becks's eyes widened, her hair standing on end like fur.

"Don't forget Pepper can travel through the Ley Line," Kit said. "River told us, remember?"

"I hope he's right." I scanned the flooded ground, but I had a nasty feeling the token had long since disappeared below the waters. *Damn that dryad.*

Rustling drew my eyes to the dragonling, who padded after the cu sidhe through the trees. I followed, seeing what I hoped might be a path, but it turned out to be a set of long, deep footprints gouged in the earth.

"I don't want to meet whoever they belong to, thanks," I said. "Though I might take them over the dryad."

A branch shot out from a tree and wrapped around Will's throat, lifting him off the ground. Kit exclaimed in alarm, firing a burst of energy from his palms at the tree. Will broke free of the branches and landed on his feet, massaging his throat. "Fuck. More murder trees?"

Bracken gave a low growl. "She's mobilised the forest against you."

"I take it we're not taking the shortcut?" I backed away from the trees, my stomach lurching. The only way out was to run was back to the river, but that would put us within reach of the dryad's roots again.

The trees rustled, and branches shot out in all directions. One lifted Becks off the ground, while another grabbed for my ankles and hoisted me upside-down. I kicked out, the blood rushing to my head.

The dragonling spat a mouthful of fire at my capturer, and the branches let go. I landed on my feet, claws sliding out. Bracken, meanwhile, transformed into a larger furry creature the size of a bear, reaching with a paw to pull Becks free of the branch and place her on the ground.

"Run," said Bracken, back in his human-like form again. "Run!"

We ran, feet pounding on the earth, roots and branches whipping at us from behind. Tendrils lashed my side, drawing blood, but I pressed on, veering away from the river.

A meadow came into view. It screamed, *trap, but* the alternative was going through the woods and getting speared to death by a tree, so I'd take my chances. I hurtled deep into the knee-high grass, and the sound of rustling branches slowly faded out.

"Damn close call there," wheezed Will.

Becks meowed in agreement. Kit's pale face was streaked with blood, while the glamour he'd put on Will, Zeph and me must have faded during the fight. Our ears were back to normal, no longer pointed, while the blood on our clothes would attract every bloodthirsty beast within a mile. Lucky the meadow smelled pleasant enough to mask the stench of blood. *I hope.*

I inhaled deeply. "No wonder faerie perfume is so popular."

Zeph slowed to keep pace with me. "You have twigs in your hair."

"I know, I know." I trekked ahead, cursing our rotten luck. I hadn't come here expecting an easy ride, but the token River had given me had been our only hope of making it out without inciting the wrath of the ruling Sidhe. "Lucky there are a few corners of Faerie without any trees."

"Hmm." His hand slid into mine—a surprise, but not an unpleasant one. "Nice place, this."

"If you forget the murdering faeries." The grass tickled my knees, a reminder that my jeans had torn. Wet mud clung to my shoes, while we'd left a bloody trail all the way through the field. "And we might as well be walking around with neon lights on our heads telling them we're here."

His hand squeezed mine. "Relax, Cori. None of this is your fault."

"I brought us here." His hand felt nice in mine and combined with my tiredness and the intoxicating smell of the meadow, I found myself swaying closer to him with every step. "For Ember. But I got the roots."

"You did." Zeph gave me a smile. "We did."

"Damn right." I punched the air with my free hand, a rush of dizziness piercing me. My ribs stung with sharp pain, but the smell was highly distracting, and so was the warm hand in mine.

Then Zeph wrapped his arms around me, kissing me firmly on the mouth. I stiffened in surprise, then kissed him back. His fingertips laced through my hair and stroked the back of my neck, and anticipation fizzled through my nerves.

"Now I've rendered you speechless." He grinned. "I'll take that as a compliment."

"Nah, I'm thinking in horror of what my sister's going to do to you." I grinned right back, feeling weirdly light-headed. "Sorry to deflate your ego."

"I think I'll survive it." He winked. "Besides, it would be worth it."

My face flamed crimson. "You might end up eating those words when she wakes up."

He brushed a strand of hair from my forehead. "We'll see."

Warmth pooled within me, chasing away the lingering fear from our near-miss. The pleasant smell soothed my nerves, and I wondered if the others would object if I just lay here with Zeph for a bit. There was a nice patch of grass over there which looked inviting.

Zeph kissed me again, lowering me to the grass as though he'd guessed the direction of my thoughts. His body was strong and hard and begged to be touched. "I think," he murmured. "We were supposed to be..."

"Crap." Faerie was at it again. I shook my head to clear the fuzziness from my thoughts. "Zeph, snap out of it. We're under a spell."

"Damn right." He tugged at the hem of my shirt, his fingertips brushing the skin underneath.

"Zeph, Faerie is in your head." It was in mine, too, the part of me couldn't ignore the ache between my legs and the tingle in my skin where his fingertips made contact. "We have to catch up to the others."

He blinked, his eyes glazed. "Jesus. My head feels stuffed with cotton wool."

"It's this meadow. It must be enchanted." My claws tore through the grass, ripping it out at the seams. "Hey. Guys. Will? Becks?"

I clawed another handful of grass out the way, then shifted to dragon form. My sharp senses returned as I kicked off the ground, above the grass and out of its intoxicating spell. Ahead, I spotted Kit dragging Will out of the meadow into the woodland. His faerie instincts would have seen the spell coming a mile off.

Zeph's dragon form rose behind me. Good. He'd escaped. I scanned the meadow for Becks and spotted her entangled with… was that the phouka?

I growled, but they ignored me. Uh-oh. Bracing myself to get scratched half to death, I grabbed the scruff of Becks's neck. She shifted into cat form and squirmed out of my hands, landing on Bracken's head. He crawled out of the grass onto the bank, dislodging her.

"This way!" shouted Kit, his eyes frantic. "Every dryad is out for blood, and they've drawn the Sidhe's attention!"

Becks shifted into human form and punched the phouka in the face. "You bastard. I don't even like you."

"Really." He smirked. "You seem conflicted when you tried to take my clothes off back then."

"It's a faerie spell," she snapped. "I'd have done the same if you'd been a troll."

"If I were a troll, I'd have eaten you." His grin widened. "Besides, you were the one who jumped on me."

I landed beside them and shifted into human form. "Not the time, guys. You can argue later. Where's the way out?"

The sound of beating hooves rang from somewhere nearby. Never mind the dryads—the Sidhe would do much worse than stab us with tree roots.

The faerie dog barked. He sat atop a hill which opened into a tunnel below the earth. *Thank you.*

Becks pelted in first, and we hurried along in single-file as hooves beat overhead and the sound of screaming dryads formed a ghastly orchestra in the background.

After several frantic minutes, we emerged onto a forest path.

"This way." Kit raised a hand, and a shield fell over our group. "Stay close to me—if the Sidhe catch us, they'll see through my glamour. Pepper will find the way out."

The faerie dog barked. He raised his paws, standing on his hind legs as though feeling for something invisible. Then the ground lurched away from under my feet.

I staggered, catching my balance on the damp grass. The slope of a hillside rose on my right-hand side, and the shimmering light of the Ley Line surrounded us once more.

We'd made it back to Edinburgh.

Heart hammering, I breathed out. "I bloody hope the other two ingredients aren't in Faerie. I don't think we'll be welcome there if we go back."

"No shit," said Zeph, as breathless as I was. "Everyone here?"

"Barely." Will picked a leaf out of Kit's hair. "Becks, you okay?"

Becks shuddered. "I'd never get attacked by a tree in London."

"You aren't wrong," said Bracken. He must have followed us home. I didn't blame him, considering the alternative was being a snack for a dryad, but Becks scoffed at the sight of him and walked on ahead of our group. The faerie dog ran past, diving into a puddle and splashing water everywhere.

"Hey—thanks for helping us get back." I followed after him. "We should return him to Ilsa and Morgan."

"He saved our necks back there," said Kit. "I'd never have got us all out otherwise."

"I'd have had to burn the whole forest." I triple-checked the Bloodroot was still in my pocket. After all the trouble we'd gone through to get it, I'd be keeping it close at hand. "Especially the meadow."

Zeph gave a grunt of agreement, not catching my eye. Did he regret what we'd done in the meadow? I had trouble telling my own instincts apart from the effects of the spell, but I'd been nursing a steadily growing attraction to him for a while. Maybe he was angry we'd nearly got ensnared in a faerie trap.

We'd look a real sight walking through the streets covered in mud, faerie blood, and heaven knew what else, but it was that or fly. Thorn took the lead, stopping to wash himself in a nearby river. I didn't blame him a bit. My clothes were torn to rags, while blood dripped from my sleeves and formed a gory trail where I walked.

"People will think we're serial killers at this rate." I spotted the phouka trailing along behind us. "Why are you following us?"

"You just made me an enemy of the dryads, too," he said. "I'm dead if I set foot in the Courts again."

"Someone already left you as troll bait," said Becks, who was limping. "Why do you keep staring at me? I told you, I don't like you. I was under a spell, nothing more."

"I didn't know you took on a human form," said Bracken. "I assumed you were fae."

"I'm a cat shifter, not a faerie," Becks responded. "Unlike some people, I don't make a sport out of toying with humans."

We reached Agnes's road, and I hesitated before knocking. "How much time did we lose in Faerie? We don't want to burst into her house and find someone else is living there."

Will groaned. "Please tell me it hasn't been another fifteen years."

"It won't have," said Kit, peering through the window. "She's in there, and she looks the same. Oh, she's seen us."

The door opened a moment later. "Good timing. I was just going to bed."

"How long has it been?" I asked.

"Less than a week," she said. "You'd better come in. Don't stand there dripping. And just who are you?" She addressed the phouka.

"A stray," said Becks.

"I don't mean to intrude," said Bracken. "I will stay outside. With your… friend."

The dragonling hissed at him. The faerie dog, meanwhile, had vanished. I hoped he could find his own way back to Ilsa, because the mages would never let me into their headquarters in this state. My ribs stung, reminding me of the wounds I'd suffered when the tree had taken a shot at me.

"Should we roll dice to see who gets to take a shower first?" I suggested.

"Kit," said Will. "Since he saved our necks back there."

"There's another shower downstairs," said Agnes. "That leg looks nasty."

Becks hissed in pain, rolling up the leg of her jeans to expose a jagged wound on her leg. No wonder she was so twitchy.

"You'd better clean that," I said. "The rest of us can wait, right?"

Zeph grunted in agreement, removing his jacket. I

pulled off my coat, wincing. Claw-like marks from the branches extended from my hip to my side.

"Ow," I said. "And I used to *like* trees."

"I have some healing salves over there," Will said. "I also have cleansing spells, if any of you can't bear to wait for a shower."

"I think I'll wait."

I'd never thought I'd find myself longing to jump in the water, but the stickiness of blood on my skin made me want more than a cleansing spell. The tree roots had left jagged slashes over my ribs I hadn't acknowledged in my panicked escape from the Court.

"I'll brew up more spells, then." Will made his way into the kitchen, while Kit headed for the upstairs shower and Becks went into the downstairs one. I, meanwhile, left the Bloodroot on the coffee table, then approached Will's collection of healing salves on the sideboard.

"Sit down," said Zeph. "I'll clean the wound."

"You're bleeding, too," I pointed out. Long scratches marked his chest, while blood soaked his torn shirt.

He waved a spell at me. "Don't make me pick you up and lay you down."

"Is that a threat?" I perched on the sofa, somewhat flattered by his obvious concern. I'd suffered much worse injuries than a few scratches, but I wasn't complaining about getting his attention. Not now I knew how nice his hands felt on my skin.

If I didn't know better, I'd swear he was deliberately drawing out the process, his fingers lingering on my ribs as he put the salve on the scratches, then skimming down to my waistband. I shivered, goosebumps rising to the surface where his fingers trailed. "You sure you're not still under the meadow's spell? I smell like blood and death."

"Actually, you smell like the meadow. It's distracting."

A meow sounded. Becks jerked her tail in the direction of the shower, wearing an expression which looked like it meant 'get a room'.

Zeph grinned. "You'd better go and shower first, Cori."

Agnes was in the living room when I came out of the bathroom, while both Kit and Will were absent. "Did you at least get what you went for?"

"We did." I indicated the Bloodroot sitting on the coffee table. "I don't think any dragon shifters will ever be welcome in Faerie again, though."

"I expected nothing less," said Agnes. "If you dragons have one consistent trait, it's your ability to leave a trail of chaos wherever you tread."

"Bit of an unfair generalisation." I caught her gaze, which focused on the symbols burned into the wallpaper. "Oh, come on, it was the fire goddess who put those there, not us."

"The mages stopped by while you were gone," she said. "They wanted to know all about my interesting new guests and took a particular interest in the wallpaper."

Oh, no. "Did you tell them where we were?"

"I did," she said. "After all, Faerie is one of the few places the mages can't get into without help."

"Even the mages would think twice before stealing from a dryad," said Zeph, walking into the room with his hair damp from the shower. "Tell you what, we should use that as our excuse no matter where we have to go to find the other two ingredients for the spell, if it keeps them from getting in our way. Tell them we're in Faerie. It's not like they can follow us and check."

"You might want to rethink that," Becks remarked. "There's someone outside."

Agnes swore. "Stay in the living room, and don't let them see you."

When she entered the hall, I pulled the living room door closed. Becks shifted into cat form and squeezed behind the sofa, while I remained standing against the wall, out of sight of the window. First a knock sounded, then low voices.

"Yes, I have guests," I heard Agnes say to the person at the door. "So do you. The entire necromancer guild, in fact, the last I saw. Mind your business and I'll mind mine."

"There are bloody footprints on your doorstep," said a male voice. "How did they get there?"

I didn't hear Agnes's response. A fiery hand locked around my neck from behind.

Ignessa.

10

I choked, Ignessa's phantom hand searing the skin of my neck.

Zeph whipped to face me, his eyes widening. "Cori..."

My teeth bared, my hands shifted to claws, and I grabbed for the fire goddess's invisible hands. A moment later, she let go.

The living room door opened, and Agnes stormed back in. "What is going on this time?"

I pressed my hand to my neck. "Ignessa just tried to strangle me. Well, she got halfway and gave up."

Zeph's hands curled into fists. "What was that for? We did what she wanted. We found the first ingredient for the spell. And, I might add, we still haven't figured out how to get rid of her when we remake the Moonbeam."

"I forgot to ask Ilsa." I pressed my fingertips to my neck and found the burned spot already cooling. "By the way, she probably heard you just then."

Zeph let the ashes drift through his fingers, his eyes

simmering. My neck stung where she'd grabbed me, and I knew from the furious expression on Zeph's face that she'd left a visible mark. His hands skimmed my neck, leaving a trail of goosebumps in their wake.

Becks emerged from underneath the sofa as Will and Kit hurried into the room.

"I heard someone yelling," said Will. "Did your goddess friend pay another visit?"

"She tried to strangle me," I said. "I think she might be upset we left her behind while we were in Faerie."

"Have you got another healing spell?" Zeph asked Will.

"I don't want to waste one on this," I protested. "It barely stings. Not sure what she was doing. Did she think we weren't moving fast enough?"

"Not sure there's much faster you can go than being pursued out of Faerie by angry dryads," said Will. "Did she say anything else?"

Agnes pursed her lips. "Your goddess friend left you another present."

On the carpet, below the spot where the goddess's ghostly hands had burned my neck, lay a pile of dust. Zeph crouched down. "It's just... ashes."

"That's no help." I peered into the hall, at the first three images burned into the wallpaper. "What about the other two images? We already faced the tree."

"One lies where nothing dies," murmured Kit. "Where does nothing die? Faerie?"

"Please no." I looked imploringly at Agnes.

Agnes's mouth pressed together. "I can think of a few places, but they're not anywhere you want to set foot unless you're sure of what you're looking for. There are certain areas of Unseelie territory... and the land of the outcasts is also said to be a place where death in the usual sense doesn't exist."

"We're spoilt for choice." I rolled my eyes. "Isn't the Unseelie Court meant to be *worse* than Seelie territory?"

"By reputation, yes," said Agnes. "However, most dryads live in Summer, so you won't encounter any of them if you do have to go to Winter."

"Maybe we'll piss off the redcaps this time," I said. "What else is Unseelie? Ogres, right?"

"Er, you're forgetting all the people we know with contacts in Faerie are linked to the Summer Court," said Will. "We have zero contacts in Winter."

"It might not be Faerie." I looked around at the others. "Where else does nothing die?"

"Death," said Zeph. "I mean, anything that goes into Death is already dead, right?"

A chill raced up my spine. "You can't go into Death. Not physically."

"A graveyard?" suggested Zeph. "I'm pretty sure everyone buried in a graveyard is already dead. Unless they're really unlucky."

I snorted. "Doesn't the riddle say where *nothing* dies? That implies more than just humans. Animals and plants, too. Also, the riddle is centuries old. It'll be somewhere older than humans."

"We'll make a faerie out of you yet, Cori," said Will. "Right, Kit?"

"It'll be a place of magic," Kit said, with certainty.

"Magic." My gaze drifted to the pile of ashes. "The dragons' realm qualifies as magical."

"No, thanks," said Becks. "It's almost as unappealing as Faerie."

"It's reasonably free from dryads," I said. "I did want to check in with Ember. I don't know how much time has passed for her while we've been gone, and I want to tell her we're working on the spell. She might have heard some gossip from the other ghosts, too." Like Ayla, for instance. Perhaps she knew what the other ingredients might be.

"I'd like to check if the eggs hatched," Kit put in. "The dragonlings have no idea how to fend for themselves without Thorn to teach them."

Will shook his head. "Are you forgetting the part where everyone in that realm wants us dead?"

"I know." I touched the tender skin on my neck. "Do the mages know the mirror belongs to the dragon shifters, or are they still claiming it's rightfully theirs?"

"From what we heard at the market, the latter," said Will. "They're also taking credit for winning the battle with the Ancients, even though they did almost none of the work. Of course they know the mirror isn't theirs. They just don't like giving up their acquisitions."

"Since when was this news?" said Becks. "I didn't expect that to change in the last fifteen years. The mages have been on top ever since the invasion."

"That might not be true for much longer," Agnes said. "Lord Addison faces a large number of threats to his power."

"Wouldn't that be a shame," said Will. "Never mind them. We have enough crap to deal with."

"We need their mirror," I reminded him. "Agnes, is there anyone who might believe the mirror is ours? Or should we just go with the stealth approach and hope their new wards can't keep out dragon shifters?"

"I have a better idea," she said. "Speak to Lady Montgomery. She holds some clout with the mages. I believe she's been arguing with them about the mirror since they took it into their possession."

"It's worth speaking to the necromancers," I allowed. "Who's coming?"

Only Zeph volunteered—and Becks, provided she remained in cat form. We bought sandwiches to eat on the way to the mages' place, keeping an eye out for any suspicious characters with red hair and grey eyes. Despite Ignessa's phantom assault on me, the fire goddess remained quiet. Becks walked ahead, sniffing at every corner. The phouka had vanished, as had the dragonling. I hoped Thorn hadn't eaten our rescuer.

I kept the Bloodroot zipped in my pocket. The mages wouldn't know what it was, but given their penchant for taking things that weren't theirs, I wouldn't let them have so much as a peek at it.

Becks reached the mages' gates first, slipping underneath the wards. A moment later, she emerged with Ilsa on her tail.

"Your friend sure is persistent," said Ilsa.

"We figured we weren't welcome here," I said. "Did Pepper find his way back to you okay?"

"He did," Ilsa said. "According to River, it sounds like half of Faerie was on your tail."

"Yeah, it didn't exactly go as planned," I admitted. "Is Lady Montgomery around? We need to speak to her."

"Yes." The door opened behind Ilsa and the woman herself came out. "Who are you?"

The words died on my tongue. Maybe she didn't

remember me after all. "I'm Cori. We met fifteen years ago."

Lady Montgomery's brown hair was now streaked with grey and her face more lined, but she remained as strong and sturdy as ever. Medals adorned her black necromancer cloak, highlighting her achievements as the leader of Edinburgh's necromancers. Her gaze travelled over us, including Becks, who hid behind my ankles in cat form. "You look the same as you did then. What manner of shifter are you?"

"Dragon, but we aren't immortal," I said. "We were stuck in another realm where time passes differently to this one. We need your help."

Her brow arched. "*My* help? With what?"

Good question. "Uh… have you heard of a place where nothing dies?"

"Is that a joke?"

"No," I said. "It's a faerie riddle."

Her eyes narrowed. "And you thought I was the person to ask?"

Oops. Too late, I remembered her son, River. For him to be half-faerie meant that she and a Sidhe had once been very close.

"I'm just asking everyone I run into," I said hastily. "I thought it might refer to the realm of Death."

Her mouth flattened. "Not even necromancers can survive a trip beyond the gates of Death. I wouldn't advise you to try."

"I really wouldn't," added Ilsa. "Where nothing dies? Sounds more like Faerie."

"Been there, done that," I said. "Lady Montgomery, we also wanted to ask the mages for a loan of the mirror. I heard you were trying to get it back from them."

"Without any success." Her nostrils flared. "Few of the mages remember how the mirror ended up in their hands, but they won't let anyone else claim it."

Then it's their own fault if they get burned. "You remember we brought it here from London, right? Is Lord Smyth still in charge over there?"

"Lady Montgomery!" a voice shouted from behind her. A cloaked novice approached, and the boss turned away with an irritable sniff.

"I have to deal with this," she said. "Ilsa, help Cori and her friends *unless* it involves skirting the law. Understand?"

"Of course," said Ilsa.

Zeph raised an eyebrow. "Do you often skirt the laws?"

"Still picking up invisibility amulets from Agnes's cabinets, are you?" I added, recalling the first time we'd met.

Ilsa grinned. "I forgot about that. The boss is more lenient than she pretends to be, and she's not the mages' biggest fan."

"Does that mean you'll help us sneak through the mirror?" I asked.

Her smile faded. "Is it that urgent?"

"My sister is trapped there," I said. "Also, I'm supposed to find a place where nothing dies, but I don't think it's in Faerie. That's the only other magical realm I know of. Did you hear anything when you were over there?"

"The only time I've spent in the other realm was when I was a prisoner," she said. "But now you mention it, I didn't see any ghosts."

I did. Ember. But she wasn't a typical ghost, right?

"I think my sister will know," I said.

"C'mon, we can let them in," said Morgan from behind her. "Couldn't help overhearing."

"Like hell," said Ilsa. "You were listening in the spirit realm again, weren't you?"

"I had to make sure nobody else was," he said. "Also, the mages are in a meeting, so if you want to sneak in, now's the time."

"No, it isn't," said Ilsa. "The mages still haven't let the last trespasser out of jail."

"Trespasser?" A suspicion hit me. "Do you know who it is? Because if it's a dragon shifter, they're all Ignessa's pawns, and she can set this whole place on fire with zero effort."

Ilsa's eyes widened. "I'll go into the spirit realm and check."

She closed her eyes, her body going still, as though she was in a trance or a deep sleep. Was that what I looked like when I left my body behind to go into the spirit realm? She *looked* alive, but unnaturally still, as though frozen in time.

Then her eyes opened. "It's a male human. I don't think he's a shifter. Someone you know?"

"I thought you said they caught a witch." Unless they couldn't tell the difference between a witch and someone who wore magical marks formerly used by the Orion League.

"Nobody has seen Astor in ages, have they?" said Zeph.

Oh, no. The mages had Astor. He must have sneaked back through the mirror and straight into their trap.

11

"You've got to be kidding," I said. "Astor got himself arrested?"

"Is it really a surprise, though?" said Zeph. "He walked through the middle of a battlefield, for crying out loud. He has no concern for his own safety."

"He's not the careless sort." Not in any ordinary circumstances, anyway. Considering how badly he must have wanted to see Ember, though, he might have let his guard down.

"If he got caught, he can get himself out," said Zeph. "We don't have time to stage a rescue mission."

I shook my head. "We can't leave him in there. Ember would kill us."

"She wants us to set her free, though, right?" said Zeph. "And she's in a worse situation than he is."

"I know." Damn Astor. If he'd just cooperated with us from the outset, this wouldn't have happened. "He can't have said a word about any of us, or they'd have come after Agnes next. He must have led them to believe he was acting alone."

"At least he didn't betray us," said Becks, who'd shifted to human form. "That doesn't make me feel sorry for him. What did he expect to happen?"

"We're about to do the same," I pointed out. "If one of us were in the same position, he'd get us out. Not without complaining, mind, but he'd do it."

The one thing we had going for us was that the mages seemed to have foregone their usual protective measures, and their basic wards were no match for Will's unlocking charms. Maybe all the witches they'd employed had died in the battle.

"If you're certain you want to do this, we can stage a diversion for you," said Ilsa. "Right, Morgan? That puppy has broken into places he's not supposed to be in at least three times a day since we got here."

Morgan smirked. "Sure, causing trouble for the mages is not gonna be an issue."

"Is anyone guarding the jail, do you know?" I wished my spirit sight was as accurate as Ilsa's seemed to be, but I hadn't had nearly enough time to train it. "They're who we need to get out of the way."

"On it." Ilsa's expression zoned out again.

"I'll get the puppy." Morgan ducked back through the oak doors into the mages' place.

"Why not fly to the village and use the other mirror instead?" asked Zeph. "Better than risking arrest."

"Because we need to get Astor out of jail, otherwise he'll put us on his hit list." I was mostly joking. Astor meant no harm to any of us, and if the mages were no longer a safe element, I didn't like the idea of leaving him in their custody. Especially if they figured out he'd once been an Orion League hunter.

"I can help with the diversion," Becks said. "Wish I'd known, I'd have asked Will to make some of those rat illusion spells."

"Or itching spells," I added. "We can take Astor to the mirror… wherever that is."

The mirror hadn't been in the library, so they must have stored it elsewhere. I turned on my own spirit sight, and grey blurred out the world. It'd been so long since I'd used it on Earth that it took me a few seconds to spot Ilsa hovering in front of me. She glowed brighter than the other ghosts, while the symbol on her forehead was visible in the spirit realm but not in the real world. Strange.

Her eyes widened. "What the bloody hell are you doing in here, Cori? You're not a necromancer."

"I have the spirit sight." I looked past her at the crowds of mages swarming the east wing of the building. "I was looking for the mirror."

"It's in the dungeon." She floated closer, looking me up and down. "How did I not notice you're a necromancer?"

"I didn't come by my talent in a typical way." To say the least. "Lady Montgomery knows. Did you say the mirror's in the dungeon?"

With Astor? Maybe that's how they'd caught him.

"That way." Ilsa pointed through the doors to the mages' guild. "Keep going towards the back, left of the stairs. The dungeon door's reinforced, but not warded."

I turned off my spirit sight to find Zeph watching me, a furrow in his brow. "Were you two… *talking* in there?"

"Yep." I hitched on a smile. "Coast's clear, for now. Becks, do you want to keep watch?"

She shifted to cat form and mewed an affirmative. Ilsa beckoned Zeph and me into the carpeted lobby. "I'll watch out for trouble."

Crashing noises came from the east wing, along with disgruntled shouts from the mages. It sounded like the puppy was having a blast. At least someone was getting some entertainment from our dilemma.

Becks halted at the foot of a grand staircase, her sleek cat form blending into the shadows. Following Ilsa's instructions, I found the door to the dungeons, which opened at a simple unlocking spell.

"It's a wonder nobody's murdered them in their beds." I led the way down the short staircase into the dungeon. "We never should have left the other mirror in the village."

"If we hadn't, Agnes would have had to hide it in her house while we were in Faerie," said Zeph. "And then if the mages had searched her house, they'd have brought it here."

"True." *Bloody mages.*

The smell of iron drifted out of the dungeon, cold and sharp. Rows of cells greeted us, some reinforced in iron but otherwise free of wards, while others were larger, covered in thick layers of protective spells.

"Those ones will be for dangerous criminals," said Zeph. "Would they trial Astor as human or otherwise?"

"Depends if they saw his tattoos or not."

"They didn't," said a voice from behind a door. "Let me guess, you were foolish enough to get caught, too."

"You're supposed to say, 'so nice of you to join us'," I said to Astor. "I have to say, I expected something a little nicer than the dragons' prison. Did the mages blow their budget on chandeliers?"

Astor didn't answer. Didn't find me amusing, I guessed. Oh, well. You couldn't have it all.

"Also, we didn't get caught," added Zeph. "I thought you were a master of stealth."

"*You* certainly aren't," said Astor testily. "If they catch you—"

"There's a demon puppy wreaking havoc upstairs." I considered the door of his cell, trying to see if it had any alarms built into it. None that I could see. My claws slid out, and easily sliced through the lock on the door.

Astor stepped out. "I think you just blew your chance at being the mages' ambassador."

I shrugged. "They pretty much think we're trouble-making arsonists anyway."

"That is an accurate description of a dragon shifter if I ever heard one," Astor said.

"Even Ember?" Zeph raised an eyebrow. "You'll have to go through the mirror and stay on the other side, since the mages will lock you up if you ever come back."

"That's where I was trying to get to begin with." His eyes narrowed. "Why are *you* risking your necks?"

"We think the second part of the spell might be in the other realm." Not that Ignessa had given us much of a clue. "Where's the mirror?"

Astor strode to the right, leading the way into an alcove. The mirror stood against the wall, for all the world as though someone had tossed it in there and forgotten. Considering the city of dragons on the other side, it was lucky the others *hadn't* come through, given the worrying lack of defences.

Footsteps came from upstairs. "Better go."

And we'd better hope the Moonbeam is where we left it.

The three of us stepped through the mirror. The world faded out, then the shape of a giant golden dragon appeared in front of us. We'd landed in the square in the centre of the dragons' city, and three dragon shifters advanced on us, their ashy eyes glowing with embers.

Oh, bugger.

"I thought you abandoned us for the human realm," Azalea said. Despite the hostile glint in her eyes, she looked much less downtrodden than she had before Ignessa had corrupted her mind, the weight of responsibility vanishing under the fire goddess's influence.

"We're looking for a way to fix the Moonbeam." Might as well go with the honest approach. "We're here to help you."

How long had passed in this realm? Not as long as we'd spent on Earth. A few hours at most. They must have flown some of the Moonbeam's shattered remains over to their city immediately after we'd left.

"You think we will forgive you for the damage you did?" Her eyes flamed. "You doomed us."

"Do you not remember how my sister and I helped free you from Lorne and destroyed the Orion League? How we cured the sickness?" Desperation saturated my words, yet I knew it was no use arguing. Ignessa's influence had seeped into the heart of the dragons' city, into their minds and bodies alike.

My gaze snagged on the glowing shards of stone, and I swore I saw *her* eyes flickering inside, watching me. *I knew it.* She was in the Moonbeam's broken shards, and through them, she had the others in her thrall.

Repairing the Moonbeam wouldn't fix the damage... but short of destroying every shard and giving up on my sister, we had no other options.

The air flickered, then Ignessa appeared above the shards of broken stone as a ghostly human-sized figure.

"You assume I don't know you mean to betray me the instant you remake the Moonbeam?" she said.

"I've been open about how much I don't like you, so it's not a surprise you cottoned on." My fists clenched. "And I'm in this for my sister. Not you."

"Oh, I know." Flames burst from the Moonbeam's shards, warm enough to sting my bare arms. "Who should I burn next, I wonder?"

"If you hurt them," I said, my voice a low rumble, "I will make you suffer for the rest of your existence. And I'm told that for immortals like you, it's a *long* time."

A deafening growl echoed overhead. Ember descended in a sweep of wings, positioning herself over the flaming Moonbeam shards, and preventing the goddess's fire from reaching the other dragon shifters.

The goddess's ghostly form vanished from sight, and the flames winked out.

Holy crap.

As the other dragons began to stir, Ember swooped down and picked up Astor, placing him on her back. Getting the message, I shifted into a dragon and took to the sky, Zeph on my heels. My body trembled even in dragon form, and I knew without a doubt that if not for the bond between Ember and Ignessa, the fire goddess wouldn't have hesitated to torch her on the spot.

We flew beneath the colossal volcano that shadowed the dragons' city. Clouds masked the peak, while its jagged outline brought a rush of recognition. Ayla's words stole into my mind: *Nobody believed me when I warned them of the Moonbeam's history of corruption. It lay in the mountains for hundreds of years before it was found.*

The Moonbeam had been lost in the mountains, along with its owner, before both had resurfaced. The second image burned into Agnes's wall entered my mind's eye, the one that resembled a mountain. Might the second ingredient be somewhere in the mountains?

Ember's flight angled away from the city, and I adjusted my path to catch up with her. We flew with swift wingbeats, landing on the hillside near where I'd rescued Ilsa. Astor climbed off Ember's back, while I shifted to human form to speak to her.

"Thanks, Ember. We got the first ingredient for the spell to fix the Moonbeam." I fumbled in my pocket for the Bloodroot and held it out.

"I'll take it," Astor said.

"You're staying here?" said Zeph. "Everyone in this realm wants to kill you."

He gave a shrug. "It's not an unfamiliar scenario for me."

I handed him the Bloodroot. "Be my guest. But for god's sake, don't lose that. We nearly died in Faerie getting hold of it."

"You did *what?*" Ember's ghost appeared, her eyes wide with alarm. "Cori."

"That's a slight exaggeration," I added. "We had to steal from a dryad—"

Zeph tensed, his hands shifting to claws. Then two monsters exploded from the fog, jagged wings beating, talons slashing. *Furies,* Ilsa had called them. An appropriate name. I brought out my claws, more than happy to spill their blood on the hillside.

"Where the hell are they coming from?" I tossed a fury's headless body over the hilltop, watching it bounce out of sight.

"Who cares?" Astor hurled his knife into another fury's eye. "You found one of three ingredients. How are you going to kill Ignessa when she's free?"

"Haven't got that far." I ducked sharp talons, my claws sinking into a fury's spine, and waved at the dark peaks shadowing the dragons' city. "Zeph, doesn't that volcano over there look like the illustration Ignessa drew on the wall?"

"The illustration looked like a toddler drew it," Zeph pointed out.

I cringed. "Word of advice, don't insult the mad goddess of fire's drawing ability."

"What the hell are you two talking about?" Astor tossed his knife into the air and caught it by the handle, as though debating whether to stab one of us next.

"Our esteemed goddess was kind enough to leave us a few clues," I said. "Which you'd know about if you hadn't taken off alone and got yourself arrested."

"Astor," said Ember's ghost reproachfully. "What were you thinking?"

"He's not," I said. "Thinking, I mean."

"Are you talking to Ember?" Astor lowered the knife. "What's she saying?"

"That you're a liability." I regretted those words the instant his eyes narrowed. "Chill, Astor. I'm joking. She asked what you were thinking, getting arrested. I think we'd like to know the same, to be honest. How'd they catch you?"

Astor's jaw locked and he didn't say anything.

"Cori, why would you think the volcano might be our place?" asked Zeph. "The ashes she left us?"

"That, and the ghost I met in jail here mentioned the Moonbeam was lost in the mountains before Lorne 'accidentally' stumbled across it." I turned to Ember's ghost. "The spell was a riddle. *One lies where nothing dies, one grows where river flows, one hides where the hunt rides.* We found the Bloodroot near a river in Faerie."

Her eyes rounded with understanding. "Where nothing dies? You think it might be here?"

"It's as good a guess as any," I said. "Not sure even a dragon shifter can fly into an active volcano without getting burned, though."

"I'll take a look," said Ember. "I can get there within a few seconds. This disembodied state comes in handy sometimes."

"What did she say?" Astor asked.

"She's going to the volcano," I said. "Oh, don't look at me like that. Even if it erupts, nothing can hurt a ghost. Ignessa didn't give us any more clues."

Astor made a disparaging noise and sat down on the grassy slope. He looked more ragged than before, after a week in jail, but I doubted he'd accept any comforting words from me. He had eyes only for Ember's dragon form in the sky.

The minutes stretched out. I paced in circles, but Ember didn't return.

"She can't be in trouble, can she?" said Zeph.

Astor rose to his feet. "Have you sent her into danger?"

"She volunteered," I said. "And I reiterate, she's a ghost. Nothing can harm her."

At least, I didn't *think* so. I turned on my spirit sight, scanning the grey for any signs of Ember. Not even the fire goddess showed her face, though no doubt she was watching me.

"Ignessa," I said, loudly. "Where is my sister?"

No answer.

"Ignessa!"

The fire goddess answered in a burst of flame which nearly knocked Astor off his feet. He leapt away from the grass, cursing. "What the fuck?"

"Sorry!" I glared at the burning grass, but the goddess herself didn't appear. "Stop burning my friends and tell me where the hell my sister is."

Astor's knife appeared in his hand. "What did she do to her? Let me talk to that fire goddess and I'll convince her to give Ember back."

"Astor, she'll burn you to cinders," I said. "If she can hurt a dragon shifter, she can do much worse to you."

"I'd like to see her try."

Astor was usually the epitome of cool and collected and excelled at making sensible decisions rather more than the average dragon shifter. Ember's plight had burned away his cool exterior and left him burning with the need for vengeance. If he'd been a dragon, his eyes would have been blazing with fire.

"Astor, Ember will follow you into the afterlife to yell at you if you get yourself killed now," I told him. "Hell, she's already *in* the afterlife."

"I'm going after her," he said, turning around as though to march up to the volcano on foot.

"You can't teleport there," I said. "You'll have to fly with one of us."

"Not quite." He dug in his pocket and pulled out a few pieces of broken stone. He must have stolen them from the city while we were confronting the dragon shifters. Sneaky assassin. "They're supposed to be a shortcut, right? It'll be easier to fly if you're not carrying me. Take one with you and I'll leave another here, so you have a way back."

"You can hop between one piece and another?" said Zeph. "We could scatter them everywhere we want to go."

"That might come back to bite us when we want to forge them into one again," I reminded him. "What if we need all the pieces?"

"They've already scattered," said Zeph. "All right, we'll take a couple each. Can't hurt."

I picked up one of the shards and slipped it into my pocket. "This is the quickest way out."

"I'll wait here for you," said Astor.

"Sure you aren't running away?" Zeph said. "Or are you scared I'll drop you?"

"No, I'm giving *you* a way out if you run into trouble up there, which you will." His gaze travelled to Ember's dragon form. "I'll wait here with her."

"I didn't really want to give you a lift anyway," said Zeph, rolling his eyes. "C'mon, Cori."

"Last chance to back out, Astor."

He didn't answer. His eyes were fixed on Ember's dragon-shaped shadow within the foggy sky.

I shifted to dragon form and bounded up to join her. Then with Zeph at my side, I flew on, toward the volcano shadowing the dragons' city.

12

I half expected an ambush from the other dragon shifters, but nobody accosted us as we flew around the edge of the city. The volcano appeared larger than every up close, the clouds peeling back to reveal a huge expanse of rocky cliffs that looked hard for even a dragon shifter's sturdy claws to grip.

I found a bare ledge and landed, staggering a little. I shifted to human form to give Zeph space to land alongside me, then turned on my spirit sight to look for my sister.

Grey fogged my vision, but no ghosts. In the spirit realm, souls appeared as glowing lights, and Zeph's was easy to pick up on—but not Ember.

Where was she?

Zeph turned to face the stone cliff. "Do you see anything at all?"

"No. I'll have a closer look."

I turned on my spirit sight, floated towards the mountain and crashed into a brick wall. Not a physical one, but an invisible force that sent me reeling back into my body.

Like… a spirit barrier.

Where nothing dies.

I turned on my spirit sight again, extending my consciousness outward. A solid barrier met me, somewhere behind the cliff face, and pushed me back into my body again.

I gripped the cliff with my fingers. "I think there's something inside the volcano which keeps the dead imprisoned."

"How? With candles?" Zeph's tone was sceptical. "They don't even have necromancers in this realm, do they?"

I shook my head. "I can't *see* the barrier. I just know it's there. And I think Ember is on the other side."

Zeph swore. "Can you get her out?"

"I sure hope so." I scanned the cliff face. "We're gonna have to find a way in."

The cliff gave a tremble, and several pebbles fell down. Then a head appeared over the edge, covered in ridged scales and twin horns on either side of a pair of milky white eyes.

"*What* is that?" said Zeph.

"I don't know, but it sure as hell isn't a dragon shifter."

The creature resembled a wingless dragon with long legs and pinkish scales. The beast let out a cry, and lumbered down the cliff face, its tail swinging.

I shifted into dragon form, launching myself into the air. Zeph did likewise, catching the worm-like creature by the tail and throwing it against the cliff. The worm's head moved, and a jet of a foul-smelling substance shot out of its mouth. I ducked, and the substance hit the cliff side, leaving a sizzling puddle of liquid behind.

Lovely. It can spew venom as well as thwacking us to death with its tail.

Fire rumbled in my chest. The beast dodged the flames, its head disappearing under the cliff. My flames evaporated, revealing a tunnel entrance. There didn't seem to be any other path inside, but my instincts rebelled against crawling into a dark tunnel after a monster.

"There is no other way, Cori," whispered Ignessa. "Can you survive the lindworm?

That's what it's called, huh?

I landed on the cliff above the spot where the worm had vanished and turned human again. "I really appreciate how you keep saving everything till the last minute, Ignessa. Keeps things interesting, know what I mean?"

"You're not crawling after that monster, are you?" Zeph climbed up behind me, peering into the tunnel.

"You and I could eat that monster for breakfast," I said. "You know we could."

"Tempting, but I bet that thing tastes foul."

"Yeah, I wouldn't advise it. I'll buy you dinner when we get out."

He grinned. "Aren't I the one who's supposed to buy *you* dinner?"

"Hey, it's the twenty-first century. I can pay for our date."

His amused grin widened. "I'm glad you clarified it's a date. And I would take you up on the offer, but I thought you had no money."

Oops. I'd forgotten that part. "I can almost afford a

packet of crisps and some chewing gum. You're not exactly rolling in cash either, are you?"

He leaned closer, his hand brushing against mine. "I can afford a date. I've been saving for one, actually."

The volcano rumbled beneath us, jerking us apart. I tensed, ducking down to peer into the tunnel, but no signs of the worm appeared. Within, the passage branched in two directions.

"Left or right?" I extended a hand and poked the tunnel wall, which felt sturdy enough. "I could try breathing fire to get rid of that monster, but it might collapse the tunnel."

"Left, and I'll go first." Zeph ducked into the tunnel entrance. It was a tight fit, especially for his broad shoulders, but the tunnel widened as it split in two directions. I crawled after Zeph down the left tunnel, hoping we weren't about to come nose to nose with the lindworm. There was no room to shift in here.

The tunnel sloped uphill, rounding a corner, then another. Just when I was about to lose patience and punch through the ceiling, the tunnel widened and gave way to an open cave.

I followed Zeph out, straightening to a standing position. Light filtered down from a gap somewhere higher up, onto the circular path surrounding a deep pit. I approached the edge, looking down into a bubbling pool of lava. I'd have been more freaked out at the lack of any safety railings if I hadn't been ninety percent sure lava had as little effect on dragon shifters as flames did.

"That looks more appealing than a river of blood. Fancy a swim?" I quipped. "Nah, I don't want to have to comb lava out of my hair."

"Can you sense Ember here?" Zeph's shoulders were tensed, his ashy eyes wary.

I turned on my spirit sight. The grey fog remained as empty as ever, but the invisible barrier must be closer than before. I inched forward—

Zeph roared, and I jerked back into my body in time for him to haul me out of the way of the giant worm's tail. Inch by inch, it dragged itself out of the lava, rows of pointed teeth gleaming like shards of rock.

"Thanks," I gasped to Zeph. I ducked a spray of venom, which splattered on the path where I'd been standing. The lindworm's scaly hide looked as tough as a dragon shifter's, too hard for my claws to penetrate. Not good.

The worm's tail whipped out, forcing me to jump perilously close to the lava. Zeph's claws cut into the beast's tail, drawing blood. I summoned my own claws, slicing at its scaled hide. My claws jarred against scales as tough as rocks, but I dug deeper, rewarded when several scales broke free. Its tail swung again, forcing Zeph right to the edge of the path. The worm loomed over his head, its teeth poised to bite.

"Hey, fuckface! Get over here." I grabbed the Moonbeam piece from my pocket and waved it in the air.

The bright light caught the beast's attention, drawing it away from Zeph. I held the gleaming light high, then leapt, feet shifting to claws, and landed on its back.

The beast shook itself, trying to dislodge me. I held on tight, clawing my way to the tip of its head. Then I dug my claws into the pits of its eyes.

The lindworm screamed, its head tipping over the cliff's edge. Zeph grabbed its tail and yanked it back before we both plummeted into the lava. I leapt clear of the beast's shuddering body, landing on the edge of the pit.

"Nice one, Cori," said Zeph.

I shook my bloodstained claws and picked up the Moonbeam shard where I'd dropped it. "Thanks for not letting me fall in."

"Likewise." He gave me an approving look. "You've really got the hang of what we practised."

"I had an incentive to learn." I shifted my claws back to hands again, scanning the lava pit for signs of any more giant worms. None, but no other way in or out either. The lava pit lay at the heart of the volcano.

So where was Ember?

I tapped into the spirit realm, extending my consciousness in the direction of the lava pit. While my surroundings were a uniform grey in colour, I hadn't been imagining the invisible barrier. It surrounded the lava pool itself, and as the spirit realm grew clearer, less blurry, distinct shapes began to form above the pit.

I recoiled. Those were *people* on the other side of the barrier. Ghosts. The world came to a halt right there in the lava, a gaping hole full of spirits. A sense of wrongness pierced me to the very soul. This was the place where nothing died, a void in the heart of the volcano.

Ember… she must have ended up trapped on the other side, too.

"Damn," I whispered. "This is a literal dead end. They're trapped."

And I'd have to leave my body behind and join them if I wanted to get Ember out.

"Cori?" Zeph squeezed my hand, a questioning look on his face. "What is it?"

He couldn't see the void, nor the ghosts. If I didn't have the spirit sight, I wouldn't be able to, either. Dead eyes watched me, and among them, I spotted a flicker of life.

Ember.

"Zeph," I said. "Can you do me a favour and hang onto me?"

"Cori, what are you planning?" His brow furrowed in confusion, his gaze darting to the lava pool and back again. "You're not diving in?"

"There's a spirit barrier around the edges of the pit, and Ember's stuck behind it. I have to go in as a ghost to bring her out, unless I dive into the lava and risk drowning while I'm on the other side."

He shook his head. "You'll die."

"I've done it before."

Okay, I'd never floated through an invisible spirit barrier into a void which trapped the dead, but by the look of those ghosts, I was in no danger of passing through Death's gates. The veil didn't even exist here. Something was rotten at the heart of the dragons' realm, beyond Ignessa's influence and the eerie fog that never went away. Necromancers didn't even exist in this realm, but someone, or something, had trapped all these ghosts in a place they couldn't move on.

"Cori." Zeph's hand brushed my cheek. "This is risky."

"My sister is in there. She came here for my sake, and…"

And the volcano also held the second piece of the puzzle. *Where,* I didn't know, but I could figure that out when Ember was back where she belonged. With me.

"I know." Zeph's arms came around me. "I'll keep you safe. Don't take too long."

"I won't." I turned on my spirit sight. Then I floated out of my body, over the edge of the pit and through the invisible barrier.

At once, a dazzling white light pierced my vision. I squeezed my eyes shut, fighting the urge to flee back into my body. While the light was the same colour as the Moonbeam, no answering fire burned inside my chest. The light dimmed, replaced by grey nothingness when I opened my eyes.

One lies where nothing dies...

I floated around, whispering spirits drifting past on either side. The ghosts wore the vacant expressions of those who'd long forgotten their names and lost all sense of identity.

"One lies where nothing dies..." A voice echoed back at me, from the abyss, and I recoiled. I hadn't known I was speaking aloud, but the lost spirits caught my words and threw them around like a series of ghostly echoes.

"Where nothing dies... she lies, she lies..."

Then I saw her. Her body was transparent, her gaze vacant, but I'd know my sister even as a ghost. She hovered among the lost spirits, her eyes blank and staring.

"Ember." I grabbed her hand, but my grip passed right through her. I tried again, but it was like trying to catch mist in my hand. Her eyes didn't recognise me.

"Leave her," whispered a voice.

"Stay here with us."

"You're warm. So warm..."

"Get away from me." My voice came out stronger than I felt, a living person's voice among the dead.

I was more than a ghost, and I *would* get her out. My hand closed around Ember's wrist. The stronger the will to live, the stronger the ghost. "Stay strong, Ember."

She didn't return my grip, but her hand solidified, allowing me to tug her with me towards freedom.

One slight issue… I'd lost sight of the barrier. The grey all looked the same, uniform, drab, the ghosts within as pale as the fog. Ghosts of humans. No, dragon shifters. Insubstantial though they might be, they shared the same ashy grey eyes.

Had all the spirits of those who'd died in the war somehow ended up trapped behind the barrier? Were my *parents* in here?

I faltered, my grip on Ember's hand slipping. Another ghostly hand took her place. Whispers surrounded me, the moans of the lost and forgotten dead. Hands grabbed at me all over, eager to feed on my life, to drag me into the abyss along with them.

Fear choked me, filled my mind with images of a cage without bars, a prison with no end. A chill that went deeper than any fire could penetrate.

Ember's hand grasped mine, her grip stronger.

She knew me.

A jolt of renewed hope burned in my chest, and we struggled together, out of the endless abyss and into a world so bright it burned my eyes.

Lava closed over my head, choking my breath. I lost sight of my sister, and alarm flickered through me as the crushing weight of the lava bore me down into its depths.

———

Images exploded before my eyes. Dragons, flying above the volcano. A plume of fire reaching into the clouds. The sky splitting open, revealing dark shapes beyond description, and the fire goddess emerging from the flames, borne on a tide of lava. Her eyes blazed with fury as she clashed with the oncoming tide of monsters until they swallowed her up.

I jolted back into my body with a gasp, struggling for breath. A pair of ashy grey eyes looked down at me—not a ghost's, but alive, so alive.

Zeph's voice was raw. "I thought I lost you."

His embrace cradled me, surprisingly gentle considering the scales still on his arms, the claws replacing his hands.

"I found her," I whispered. "Ember."

"Good." His lips brushed my forehead. My heart began to beat faster. "I'm sorry. It was like some invisible force dragged you over the edge and into the lava. I had to shift into dragon form to pull you out."

"You saved my life," I said. "I don't know what created that barrier, but it didn't want to let me go."

A confusing mess of images filled my mind, remnants of the visions I'd seen. Visions of the universe cracking open, and horrific beasts pouring from a split in the sky. The Ancients.

And Ignessa, emerging from the void with vengeance in her eyes.

Did I see her memories? Maybe I had. The images had been far too vivid to be a simple hallucination. Ignessa *had* been there, I was sure, trapped in the void along with the other gods.

When she'd been imprisoned... *this* had been her cell.

Perhaps the Moonbeam had been trapped in here, too, before she'd pushed it into the outside world. Then it had fallen into Lorne's hands, and his actions had split the world open and brought Ignessa and her fellow monsters raging back into this realm.

And then...

From what I'd seen in the vision, she and her fellow gods had not emerged to conquer the world but to fight with one another. When Lorne had taken the Moonbeam to Earth and traded it to the Orion League for power, she'd remained stuck here. Until Ember had used it to bring me back to life, giving the final catalyst for her to rise.

Zeph brushed a strand of hair from my forehead. "Are you okay, Cori? I forgot to look for the second ingredient, but I'm not sure it's here."

"Ah, shit." I lifted my head. "I couldn't get any sense out of the ghosts. I was lucky to get Ember out, and if I hadn't been alive, I probably wouldn't have managed it."

She wouldn't have gone in there if not for me. My chest tightened with guilt.

"But you did," he said. "Does she have any idea about the second ingredient?"

"Good question." I turned on my spirit sight. "Ember? You there?"

"Cori." Her voice was faint. "I don't think it's a good idea for me to stay close to that barrier. Something in there is trying to pull me in."

Zeph moved, jostling me. "Look, Cori."

I looked down at my clothes... or what was left of them. Lava coated my chest, already hardening. Its sheer white surface glowed with iridescent light. "That's… the same colour as the Moonbeam."

Zeph gently scraped a handful from my arm. "It's magical, whatever it is."

"That's got to be it." The lava must contain magical properties. It was tied to the spirit barrier at the heart of the volcano, keeping those ghosts imprisoned. Perhaps the barrier was all that remained of the spell imprisoning the gods in the void, and it had instead swept up all the victims of the dragon clans' war.

"Ashes." He held out a hand, and I sifted some of the stone into his palm. "Do you want to fly out or use the Moonbeam pieces? Because the lava did a number on your clothes."

"You mean I'm naked, don't you?"

Sure enough, when I stood up, all that remained of my clothes were a few rags that did little to make me look decent. Zeph's shirt was a wreck, but he'd half shifted to get me out, so his jeans remained intact.

"That's unfair," I said. "At least you get to keep some dignity."

"I'm just glad you're in one piece." Amusement sparkled in his eyes despite his serious tone. "I'd loan you my shirt, but most of it's in the lava."

"Hey… it burned you." Lines of lava ran down his chest, leaving reddish marks behind.

"I know." His fingertips traced a line over my collarbone. Where my shirt had melted away, reddish marks covered my chest. His touch feathered over my skin, bringing a blush to my chest. The sensation distracted me from the pain, and I ran a hand over his bare shoulder. A faint growl escaped, his eyes simmering with heat. I wanted to lose myself in his fire, to chase away the coldness of that dark pit, but the images I'd seen in the vision kept intruding.

Did Ignessa know? Was she the reason I'd seen those images of the gods breaking free? Unlikely. She couldn't control my dreams. Even when I'd thought she'd been visiting me in my sleep, she'd actually been communicating with me through the spirit realm. What I'd seen hadn't been in her control any more than it had been in mine, I was sure.

I released Zeph, my gaze darting to the lava pit. "Zeph, I think this place formed when the gods broke free. When Lorne freed them during the war."

"Damn," said Zeph. "This is… Death, right? In this realm?"

"Maybe it used to be." I swallowed hard. "All the ghosts I saw in there were dragon shifters. Maybe… maybe even my parents. But none of them remembered their names. They don't know who they are, or who they were."

Zeph drew me closer to him, his warmth chasing away the lingering chill of the dead. "Let's get you some clothes."

He placed the Moonbeam shard on the ground, and we stepped into the light, leaving the volcano behind.

13

Zeph and I appeared on the hillside where we'd left Astor. "We should leave the stones here along with the Bloodroot so we can easily get back here if need be," I said.

"Wise idea," he said. "I'm not all that keen on going back into the dungeon, to tell you the truth."

"How do you think I feel?" I indicated my obvious lack of clothing.

"Oh, there's the assassin," said Zeph.

Astor approached, his expression impassive. "I didn't know you had to be naked to find a ghost."

"I jumped into a volcano. Don't tell my sister."

His brows shot up. "You found her?"

"After a fashion, yes," I said. "We also found what we were looking for. I'm really glad I gave that Bloodroot to you. I'd be pissed if I went to all that trouble to get hold of it and then dropped it in a lava pit."

"So you're going to walk into the mages' jail, naked

and covered in burns, and hope they let you walk free?" Astor said.

I glanced at Zeph. "Got a better idea?"

"Or," said Astor, "you could go to Agnes's place. Becks smuggled some of the Moonbeam shards out of here while you were gone."

"You might have mentioned that first." I looked past him, spotting a crate tucked away beneath a jutting slab of stone partway down the hillside. "The dragonlings haven't hatched yet?"

"Is that why you wanted to stay here?" Zeph asked Astor. "You want to start a colony of dragonlings with Ember?"

"Nope," Ember herself said, making me jump. "Take him with you, Cori. That's an order."

I relayed her words to Astor, who shrugged and stepped through the Moonbeam shard at his feet without looking back.

Zeph and I followed, emerging in the middle of Agnes's living room. Becks jumped to her feet. "*There* you are."

I looked around in bemusement. Agnes stood in front of a chalk circle, while Will and Kit sat on the floor, surrounded by piles of spells and cardboard boxes.

"I thought you were locked in jail again," said Becks. "Why are you naked? Did you and Zeph get it on in the dragons' city?"

"No, I jumped into a volcano," I said. "I need a shower."

"A cold shower?" Will said.

I didn't dignify that with a response. Instead, I turned to Astor. "You lot can catch up. I'm going to find some clothes."

I heard the others bombarding Astor with questions as I hurried upstairs, ducking into the bathroom. Shower on, I set about scrubbing every trace of the volcano off my skin.

I returned to my room wrapped in a towel and damn near dropped it when I found Zeph sitting on my bed, his hair shower-damp and tousled, his shirt off and his feet bare.

"Knock, why don't you?" I was fairly sure every inch of my exposed skin had flushed crimson at the sight of him —and not from the volcano's aftereffects.

"You left the door open." He held a bottle in his hands. "You need to put some salve on those burns."

"So do you." My heartbeat quickened as he watched me walk to the bed and sit down. "Or is this just an excuse to see me naked?"

"Everyone saw you naked, Cori." He unscrewed the bottle's lid, then brushed my curls from my shoulder with his free hand. "Lie down."

I sprawled on my front, feeling oddly self-conscious with only a towel between me and Zeph.

Zeph tipped some of the healing potion into his palm, applying it to my back. His hands massaged my shoulders and the coolness chased away the burning sensation on my skin. Then his hands moved down my back, and the towel dipped further. *Oh.*

I bit my tongue to stifle a moan as his strong hands massaged the tension from my muscles. "Damn, you should try out a career as a massage therapist."

He chuckled. "Turn over."

"Er..." I gripped the towel around me as I rolled onto my back to avoid flashing him. The combination of his closeness and the lack of clothing sent anticipation fizzing in my veins. I found myself reaching for his bare chest, running my fingertips over the faint claw-like scarring at his hips.

"Run into another dragon shifter?"

"Yeah." His voice was husky. "I can't reach my back. Can you...?"

I obligingly sat up, and he turned around. A livid mark stood out across the back of his neck.

"Ow. Did the giant worm do that?" I picked up the bottle and squeezed some onto my palm, massaging it into his shoulders. He wasn't heavily scarred—a few scrapes and bruises, but he'd shifted at a young enough age that his scales had probably kept off the worst of the damage.

My hands lingered a little longer than necessary, and his body stilled. "Damn, Cori, you're making it difficult to think clearly."

So he felt it, too. I climbed over him, hooked my fingers into the waistband of his jeans and pulled him onto me. "Maybe I don't want to think."

He lowered his mouth to mine, his hands cupping my face.

"You scared the shit out of me, Cori," he murmured. "That volcanic dust... it's dangerous, whatever it is."

"Get down here, Cori!" Will called upstairs. "Astor's refusing to tell us anything. We need you."

Honestly.

Zeph grumbled under his breath. "We're never going to get a moment's peace, are we?"

"I did just tell them I took a bath in a lava pit," I reminded him. "Go on, get dressed. We'll finish this later."

"Yes," he said. "We will." His heated gaze lingered on my bare skin, then he pushed to his feet and walked out of the room.

I pulled my clothes on, mourning the loss of yet another other outfit.

"I liked those jeans," I muttered. "Dickheads."

Dressed and ready, I went back downstairs to find Will waiting expectantly in the living room. "Astor said you jumped into a volcano. Is it true?"

"More fell than jumped," I admitted. "Ember was stuck behind a barrier. The whole inside of the volcano is like a death trap for ghosts."

"But you got the second ingredient, Astor said," Kit said.

"The lava from the volcano is the same shiny colour as the Moonbeam." I watched Agnes's face carefully, and sure enough, a shadow fell over her expression. "Not only that, it traps spirits. It's like a natural spirit barrier."

"A spirit stone," Agnes murmured. "I've heard the name, but I didn't realise there was any left in that realm."

Huh. It made sense that the necromancers must have used something else before spirit candles became mainstream, but everything about that place creeped me the hell out.

"Spirit stone?" said Zeph, entering the room behind me. He wore a clean shirt, the slight flush to his skin the only sign of our upstairs escapade.

"Stones that can trap ghosts and roots that feed on blood," said Will. "What's the third ingredient, a man-eating turnip?"

"Whatever it is, it can be found where the hunt rides,"

said Agnes. "I'm afraid I still don't know where that is, but it won't be in the dragon shifters' realm."

"Good," I said. "How long did we miss this time?"

"Three weeks," said Becks. "Astor came out of the mirror after you left and told me to bring some of the Moonbeam shards here to use as portals."

"Won't that make it harder to fix?" Zeph said.

"I hope not," I said. "The dragon shifters have pieces scattered all over their city, and we left a shard inside the volcano, too. You couldn't pay me to go back in there."

"Likewise." Zeph sank into an armchair. "What've you all been doing for the last few weeks, then?"

"Kit and I are delivery boys for the witch market." Will waved a hand at the piles of cardboard boxes on the floor. "Not the best pay, but it beats stabbing monsters for profit. Becks signed up, too, but she quit when she got into a fight with a local."

"Really, Becks," I said. "I'm glad you're all okay."

"Thanks to Agnes," added Becks. "She kept the mages off our tail."

"Since they arrested you." I turned to Astor. "Why'd they lock you up with no trial?"

Astor shrugged. "I wouldn't tell them anything, so they had no reason to let me go."

"I thought the Orion League started here in Scotland," said Zeph. "Didn't they realise you were an ex-hunter?"

Astor shot him a frown. "No. I've never lived here in Edinburgh, and I don't exist on official records, even in London. We're fifteen years out of our time. None of us would even be listed among the dead, like in the invasion."

We don't exist. Perhaps that was why the idea of going

back to London filled me with an inexplicable sense of dread.

London had always felt more like home than anywhere else. When I'd first laid eyes on the dragon city, I'd imagined it might feel more familiar to me with time, but that wasn't the case. Not just because my experiences in the prison cell and volcano had somewhat soured me on the place, but because what I'd seen in that volcano cemented my certainty that something was fundamentally wrong in the dragons' realm, invisible to anyone without the spirit sight.

"Did you find anything else while we were gone?" I asked the others. "About how to get rid of Ignessa?"

"Oh, sure, we just strode into the mages' guild and asked." Will rolled his eyes. "Look, the *mages* couldn't kill the Ancients. One of them even murdered their last leader, a guy who was in power for over twenty years. All I'm hearing at the witch markets is that the public no longer trusts the mages to do their jobs."

My jaw dropped. "Whoa. Is this just because of the war?"

The Mage Lords had been the centre of magical power since the faerie invasion, and I couldn't imagine things being any other way. The magical world's trust in the mages had always seemed immutable, if just because they had the money and resources to fix any problem if they chose to.

"That Lord Addison is the most incompetent excuse for a Mage Lord I ever met," said Agnes.

"Didn't he only recently get voted in?" I said.

She grunted. "He made a bunch of false promises to

clean up the city after Lord Sutherland died. He won't last out the year."

"I'd rather he didn't jail us again before then," I said. "Agnes, I think we're going to have to leave. Once we work out where the third ingredient is, anyway."

And learn how to kill an Ancient. I refused to believe it was impossible.

"You haven't had any more clues from Ignessa?" asked Agnes.

"She's been quiet since we went into the volcano."

Zeph frowned. "Do you think she was scared of falling into the lava along with the other ghosts?"

"She *was* in there, once," I said. "Actually, I'm sure that's where she escaped when she woke up fifteen years ago."

"Excuse me?" Will dropped the handful of spell ingredients he was holding, while the others gaped openly at me. Even Astor's gaze was more intent than usual.

"The goddess was trapped behind the barrier?" said Zeph. "Didn't you leave a Moonbeam shard in there, right by the ledge?"

"Yes..." My mouth parted. "Yes, we did."

Well, damn. We might be in with a shot of getting rid of Ignessa after all.

14

Despite my exhausted state, sleep eluded me that night. I couldn't get the sight of those miserable ghosts trapped in the void out of my head, and despite knowing the volcano might be the only way to be rid of Ignessa, the thought of leaving the other ghosts at her mercy made my insides churn with guilt.

What trapped them there? Was it the other Ancients?

Just as I fell into a light doze, the smell of burning reached my nostrils, and a fresh wave of pain seared my neck. I sat bolt upright. "Ignessa, I'm not going to be in any fit state to find the last ingredient if you won't let me sleep."

"You don't have time to rest," her voice whispered. "They are hunting for you."

"What the hell are you talking about?" I listened for an answer but heard nothing. Swearing under my breath, I slid out of bed and grabbed my clothes. Mad or not, I wasn't about to ignore a warning from an Ancient.

I trod downstairs, my nerves jangling, and tripped headlong over a body.

"Ow!" I climbed to my feet, steadying myself against the wall. "What kind of place to sleep is this, Astor?"

A former assassin could probably fall asleep anywhere. He sat up, scowling. "I'm listening for intruders. You had a visitor, didn't you?"

"How did you—" I broke off. He pulled up his sleeve, exposing the lines of the Orion League's symbols visible beneath his tattoos. They glowed with silvery light, as though lit from underneath. "Whoa. When did that happen?"

"They've been doing that for a while. Since we first came back from the other realm."

"You mean when we lost fifteen years?" Wait. "That's when something went wrong with the spirit lines and the gods woke up, right? Did it have a knock-on effect? I mean, those marks are linked to the gods' magic."

"I have no idea," he said irritably. "They were glowing when I was in jail, too. I'm lucky the mages didn't see."

No kidding. "Can't you cover them up with a spell?"

"Show me a spell that can hide the gods' magic."

"Okay, no need to be rude. Ignessa seemed to think someone was looking for us—"

The door slammed open, and two cloaked mages marched into the hall. One of them was Caleb, the dark-haired mage who'd hassled us at the mages' place.

"You." Caleb turned on Astor. "I knew Agnes was harbouring an escaped criminal."

"You're breaking and entering." Dammit. We were more than a match for them, but striking the mages would put *all* of us on their hit lists. "Get out before I call the police—"

Heat seared my hands, and the two mages burst into white flames. A second later, nothing was left of them but ashes.

I stood stock-still. "Dammit, Ignessa."

A light snapped on, and footsteps descended the stairs, punctuated by Agnes swearing. "Thought they'd break into my house in the middle of the night, did they?"

I dragged my gaze away from the twin piles of ashes. "I'm sorry. I'd tell the mages the truth, but—"

"If they lock you up behind bars, you'll never remake the Moonbeam and defeat Ignessa." Her expression was grave. "I'll handle this, Cori, but you need to leave."

Slight problem... we still don't know where the final ingredient is.

More footsteps heralded Zeph's arrival. His gaze went from me to the piles of ashes. "She's back?"

"The mages broke in here to arrest us and she decided to take matters into her own hands." I swallowed. "We need to go—"

A shadowy figure appeared behind the open door. I turned on my spirit sight—and saw Lady Montgomery looking back at me.

Bugger.

The door nudged open and the leader of the necromancers walked in. Her gaze travelled from me, to the marks on the wall, and finally to the piles of ashes on the carpet.

"I think you'd better come with me," she said. "All of you. If you don't want to be in a jail cell by the day's end, that is. I have some information I think you'll need if you want to continue with your quest."

"Go with her," said Agnes. "She's an ally. I should warn Everett about that blasted goddess."

"Is she here?" Lady Montgomery looked directly at me. "You *know—?*"

"Explain later," Agnes said. "I give it ten minutes before the mages send someone else."

"All right, we're coming," said Will's voice from upstairs. "Just let me gather our supplies."

Astor scowled. "Enough of this. I'm getting out."

Before any of us could object, he'd picked up one of Becks's Moonbeam shards and vanished into it.

Within five minutes, we were all armed and ready to head out into the night with the head of the necromancer guild. Bands of grey light shone over the castle on the hill and the peaked roofs, illuminating the cobbled streets. The further we walked, the more piles of rubble we found, along with trench-like gouges in the roads that we had to hop over or walk around.

"Where are we going?" Zeph asked Lady Montgomery. "I mean, we're not welcome at the mages' headquarters. At all."

"We finished rebuilding the necromancer guild's old headquarters," said Lady Montgomery. "It rests on top of a spirit line, so it required some reconstruction, but nothing unfixable."

I looked where she pointed. A shimmering line cut through the road's centre, passing through an old stone building which stood out among its neighbours. Despite its age, the bricks looked sturdy and grey light shone from the walls, suggesting anti-faerie wards had been built right into the very foundations. A deep trench split the road in front of the building, creating splintering cracks beneath the rippling spirit line. The line itself was semi-transparent and as bright as the Ley Line. Had it always been like that?

"Is that where—?" I broke off, recalling the spirit line writhing with shadowy magic I'd seen on my flight to Edinburgh. No shadows darkened it now, but it shone brighter than any other spirit line I'd seen.

"What did that?" said Zeph.

"Dark magic," said Lady Montgomery. "A god's magic."

"Not Ignessa."

The leader of the necromancers glanced over her shoulder. "I assume it's safe to use that name, but I'd advise you to exercise caution when naming the gods."

"What do you mean?" I followed her through the glass doors into a wide lobby, more modern than I'd expected, considering most other necromancers made their homes in run-down buildings next to graveyards or morgues. Few people were around, but I imagined most necromancers would be asleep by now, after spending their night hunting down ghosts.

Lady Montgomery led us up a stone staircase to a corridor. Then she unlocked a wooden door embossed with her own name and invited us into her office. The plain wooden furniture and sparse decor matched the woman herself. Several framed photographs of River, her son, sat on the bookshelves, the sole personal touch to her office.

Lady Montgomery spoke. "This will have to be quick. It's not safe for you to stay in the city for much longer."

"It's not safe for us to be anywhere," said Will. "On

account of how everything we touch seems to catch on fire."

"Safe or not, we have a job to do," I said. "We'll worry about being on wanted lists when we're rid of Ignessa and we have Ember back. My sister," I added, for Lady Montgomery's benefit. "We need to fix the Moonbeam to get her back. We have two of three ingredients for the spell."

"Agnes told me about your situation," she said. "I've been looking into records of Ancients who've interacted with this realm. Dragon shifters have had a history of navigating the spirit lines, which makes sense, considering your origins."

"What does that mean?" Becks asked.

"Ignessa is our ancestor." I glanced at Zeph, who looked unsurprised. He'd guessed, too.

"Not just her," said Lady Montgomery. "Recent research suggests that the shapeshifter gods preceded all shifters in their modern form, though many do not believe the stories."

"*All* of us?" Will looked stunned, as did the others. "All shifters?"

"That's the current theory among experts," she said. "However, this fire goddess is something of an oddity. Little information exists within this realm, but Agnes has some theories based on the time she spent in the dragons' city herself. She believes Ignessa lay in a dormant state for years, perhaps centuries."

"We know she did," I said. "She used the Moonbeam to get out. Firstly, she made sure Lorne found it, then she escaped imprisonment during the war between the dragon shifter clans."

She nodded, as though I'd confirmed a theory of hers.

"Travelling into the other realm was rare even in the days before the war, and I imagine those mirrors were created for that reason. In any case, the war closed off the spirit lines, cutting off all contact."

I turned this information over in my mind. "One thing I wondered... we never saw much of the other realm beyond the dragons' city. Is there nobody else living there at all?"

Her mouth pressed together. "I can't claim to be an expert. I'm going by what Agnes told me, and also the records she unearthed from her sister Madison's will. But both of them believed the realm of the dragons was in fact a liminal space, a small pocket of reality hidden between two spirit lines. The dragons hid there to escape persecution and built the city from the ground up."

"Wait, the entire realm is a liminal space?" *Of course. That explained the lack of native dragon shifters, and the fact that everyone I'd met in that realm, with the exception of Ignessa, had originally come from Earth.*

And that must be why Death didn't exist there. There was nowhere for the dead to go except back into our realm.

"Damn, that's weird," Will said.

"Not really," said Kit. "Parts of Faerie are like that. Even in this realm, whole Courts exist in the liminal spaces, if you can find them. Usually, they don't want to be found."

"Exactly," Lady Montgomery said. "It was believed until recently that no humans had the ability to traverse the spirit lines, even necromancers..." She trailed off. "Morgan, do stop eavesdropping and come in. You too, Ilsa."

The two Lynns walked into the room, both looking slightly sheepish.

"Sorry," said Ilsa. "I was—"

"Trying to stop your brother from listening in," Lady Montgomery finished. "Oh, and bring the other one in, too."

The phouka walked into the office, his head held high and a wolfish smile on his face.

"What are you doing here?" I asked.

"The mages chased me out of my shelter and tried to arrest me." He bowed to Lady Montgomery. "I mean no offence."

Ilsa gave him a sideways look. "Ally, is he?"

"He helped us in Faerie," I relented. "And ended up getting chased out. We did warn you about getting involved with us."

"Considering I was about to get devoured by a troll when you found me, I rather think I got the better deal." He looked up at Ilsa with interest. "You are the Gatekeeper of Summer?"

"My sister is," she said. Turning to the rest of us, she added, "Is the third ingredient you need for that spell in this realm or somewhere else?"

"The riddle says it lies where the hunt rides," I said. "Does that sound familiar?"

"The hunt," she said. "It can't refer to the Wild Hunt of Faerie, can it?"

I groaned. "Not Faerie again."

The phouka cleared his throat. "They say the Wild Hunt rides when the veil is thin, between the fae realm and this one, following the paths of the dead."

"The what?" said Zeph.

"It's another name for the spirit lines," said Lady Montgomery.

"Spirit lines?" I echoed, looking up at the ceiling. "Like the line right here?"

"Maybe." Ilsa gave Bracken an appraising look. "It might be on any line, or in a liminal space. There are a lot of them…"

A chill gripped me. "I bet I know which it is."

Where had Ignessa chosen to make her escape and force my hand? It would be her idea of a spectacular joke to send me back to the place where both of us had been reborn, our lives entwined.

The phouka looked at me. "Yes, I see it. You have traversed the path of the dead more than once already, have you not?"

What was it with faeries and saying creepy shit about how I'd died? "I know where it is. We have to go back to London."

15

"London?" said Lady Montgomery. "If that's the case, I will let Lord Glover know you're coming."

"Wait, he's still alive? I mean, dead?" Necromancers had no need for a retirement plan, considering how many of them seemed to continue doing their jobs after they'd kicked the bucket. "If we warn people we're coming, Ignessa might target them, too."

"He's a ghost," Zeph reminded me. "I doubt Ignessa would bother with him. We need allies."

"You also need to leave before the mages shut down my guild." Lady Montgomery turned to Ilsa. "If you want to make yourselves useful, please escort Cori and her friends through the spirit line."

"Come again?" I said. "Through the spirit line? I thought you just told me it's impossible to travel through them."

"This one is an exception," said Ilsa. "Not that it's technically open for public use… Morgan, you can keep an eye out to make sure nobody sees us."

"Sure," said Morgan. "So this Ancient lives in the spirit realm?"

"Don't even think about it," Ilsa said to him. "Ignessa can burn even a dragon shifter, and it's a safe bet she's immune to necromancy."

"I don't blame you for staying out of this one." I followed her outside into the corridor.

"I'm glad you're not in jail," said Ilsa. "I'm guessing you lost time in the other realm again?"

"Yep." I walked at her side down the narrow corridor, my footsteps echoing from the stone walls, and descended the stairs into the necromancers' lobby. "Then Ignessa decided to set two mages on fire for breaking into Agnes's house and trying to arrest us, so you probably don't want to mention you helped us."

Ilsa swore. "Agnes could claim self-defence. She'd be justified in reacting to a break-in. Everyone knows she's fielded enough assassination attempts that trying to ambush her is a bad idea."

"She implied the mages are losing power." I quickened my pace as we crossed the lobby to the doors. "She thinks they won't be leaders of the supernatural community for much longer."

"Oh, that won't happen for a while." Ilsa pushed open the front door. "Things are fractious at the moment, though, and to be honest, a goddess wandering around setting people on fire is the last thing they need."

"With any luck, they won't have to know about her." I walked outside the guild onto the street. "Wait, are we about to walk into the same place as whatever did that?" I indicated the deep cavern in the road.

Ilsa stepped aside to let the others exit the guild. "Definitely not. This spirit line is a god-free zone."

Let's hope it stays that way.

Kit halted outside the guild. "I need to find Thorn. He won't know we're leaving the city."

"Be quick about it," said Becks. "We don't even have a home to go back to, do we?"

Will watched Kit leave. "You never know. The rest of Magic Avenue might have turned our house into a shrine in our honour."

"Yeah, right," said Becks. "Either they burned it down, or someone else bought the place."

"Or we owe fifteen years of rent," I added. "What about the shelter?"

"I got that off our hands before we left," said Will. "As for the house, unless someone else swooped in, it's still mine. Is anyone going to tell the assassin where we're going?"

"I have the Moonbeam pieces," Becks said. "He's welcome to join us, but I'm not responsible for what happens if he materialises on top of me."

The dragonling bounded over to us. In the last few weeks, he'd grown another foot in height, making him the same height as the average dragon shifter. How he'd fit into the house if it was still standing was anyone's guess, but we'd deal with that later. Kit walked behind him, his green eyes glimmering in the dawn light.

I turned to Ilsa. "I don't know how much you heard of what we said to your boss, but have you ever heard of a place where Death just… stops? A place where ghosts don't have anywhere to go?"

Her brow wrinkled. "What, a spirit barrier?"

"A natural one," I said. "In the dragon shifters' realm, everyone who dies ends up trapped behind an invisible barrier. I nearly got trapped there, too, when I followed my sister. I guess there's no gates of Death in a liminal space."

Ilsa drew to a halt. "You floated outside of your body? Cori, you know most necromancers can't do that, don't you?"

"I got that ability from Ignessa, too," I said. "But I wonder if you knew… if someone died in a liminal space, would they remain trapped there?"

"If they were behind a spirit barrier? Yes, they would," said Ilsa. "Why?"

"You're Gatekeeper of Death." I wished there was a way to be certain of our success before risking everyone's lives. If my plan failed, Ignessa would unleash her wrath on the other dragons *and* on earth.

"Doesn't make me an expert on liminal spaces, believe me." Ilsa paced outside the guild, halting at a spot midway through the spirit line. The currents rippled outwards like the roots of a giant tree. "You can enter the line here."

I stopped at her side. "I'm still lost on how we're supposed to get to London through a spirit line."

She pointed. "Walk that way and look for the right key point. I'm not really supposed to let anyone else in, but most people can't see the spirit lines and Lady Montgomery seems to think you won't abuse that knowledge. Also, are you coming with us?" she added to the phouka, who walked behind us.

"I have no home to go back to." His gaze travelled around our group, lingering on Becks. "If you need a guide to help you find the place where the hunt rides, I owe you a favour."

Ilsa's eyes narrowed. "Don't try anything. You're half-blood, right? You can lie."

"I mean no harm. They saved my life."

Becks made a sceptical noise. I wasn't all that keen on Bracken tagging along either, even if he had ended up facing the wrath of the dryads *and* the mages because he'd had the misfortune to run into us. Then again, being eaten by a troll wouldn't have been much fun either. And I hadn't the faintest idea how to find the place where the hunt rode, so it would be useful to have someone to help us figure it out.

I stepped to the edge of a crack in the road. At once, the spirit line became solid and a path appeared beneath my feet, but a winding earthen path laced with tree roots. That explained why the line appeared so tree-like from the outside.

"This is the spirit line?" I turned on the spot, marvelling at how the line cut through the middle of the city, inches away yet never quite touching it. "How'd it end up like this?"

"The line was damaged in the war," Ilsa said. "Repairing the damage had a few interesting side effects."

"So anyone can use the spirit line to travel through key points?" I stared down the path, which extended as far as the eye could see. "Damn, that's handy. If you don't have wings, that is."

Ilsa smiled. "I'll check nobody's following you. I've never been to London before, but your spirit sight should help you track your location. Keep an eye on the path and you won't get lost."

She stepped back to allow the others to pass, disappearing into the mist that bordered the path on either side. It reminded me of the dragon's realm, and the thought brought a chill to my skin. I began to wish I'd opted to fly instead.

"Is this supposed to be like *walking* to London?" Will wanted to know. "Because we haven't the time to walk four hundred-odd miles on foot."

"Lady Montgomery wouldn't have sent us here if it was a trick." I took a step onto the earth, which felt pretty damned solid for a transparent path between worlds.

"I'll take your word for it," said Zeph. "I hope you can see where you're going, Cori, because I can't see shit. And if he's never been here before, how can he show us the way?" He jerked his head at the phouka.

"Because many of us fey know the liminal paths by instinct," Bracken said, a glimmer of teeth showing as he smiled. "The hunt rides along the paths of the dead, and we know them well."

He took the lead, shifting into a furred shape the size of a dog. The dragonling followed, hissing at the tree roots as though they offended him.

"Of course the dragon's realm is a liminal space," I whispered to Zeph. "No wonder the ghosts are trapped over there. Everyone Lorne killed, everyone who died in the war…"

"Cori, I know you want to help the other dragons, but the living ones need you," he said. "Ember does."

"I know she does." I glanced down and instantly regretted it. The line was transparent, showing the earth below—suddenly *really* far below, as though we walked on a glass bridge in the sky. A wave of dizziness hit me. I wouldn't make much of a dragon if I feared heights, but it wasn't the height that bothered me. Rather, the weird paradox of looking at two places at once.

Zeph squeezed my arm. "C'mon, Cori. You're the only one who can get us out of here."

He looked as pale and nauseous as I felt. After his reaction to riding in a car, it shouldn't surprise me that walking on the magical equivalent of a sky-high bridge wouldn't be his favourite mode of transportation.

I gritted my teeth and took one step and then another, my gaze on the phouka's furred shape in the distance. He was the only one of us who didn't look freaked out. The dragonling flew, refusing to let his feet touch the ground, while Becks retreated into her cat form and walked as lightly as possible.

I glanced down to get my bearings, and my stomach lurched. The line seemed even higher than before, each step carrying us for miles. Each glittering spark below represented a key point, dotting the country in glowing patterns. One step and we were in England. Another step took us through the Midlands. *We must be getting close.*

I scanned the rolling mass of green and spotted a tangle of spirit lines intersecting at key points spread so close together it was impossible to see which one we needed.

"There it is." There was only one place with *that* many spirit lines overlapping—Hyde Park. "Uh… how do we get down?"

As though in response to my thoughts, the ground beneath our feet buckled, seeming less sure, less solid. I reached out and gripped Zeph's arm. He looked as though he might throw up.

"Get me out of here, please," he said, through clenched teeth.

"Where's that phouka?" said Will from behind me.

I peered into the fog. Our little friend had vanished. "I don't know, but one of these paths must lead into the key point we need. Where the hunt rides."

Hyde Park was a huge spirit hotspot, and in the last two decades, it had turned from a tourist attraction into a home for wild fae and anything with strong enough magic to withstand the fluctuating energy of the spirit lines. The image of those lost souls filled my mind, and I shivered, taking careful steps over the tangle of key points. I'd fought Lorne close by, and the spirit lines had torn open, sending us into the dragons' realm for the first time.

A hoarse cry sounded from further down the path.

I jerked my gaze up. "I think something got Bracken."

"Whatever it is, I'd rather it didn't get us, too." Will said.

Kit stiffened, his hands glowing green and forming a shield in front of our group. Then a furred shape hurtled around the corner, fleeing a giant beast which resembled a cross between a dog and a wild boar. The smaller beast transformed into the phouka, hiding behind Kit's shield.

The giant furred monster faced us, drool dripping from its mouth.

"Hellhound," said Zeph. "Bastards."

"Hellhounds are part of the Hunt," said Bracken. "This is their natural habitat."

I raised my claws. "He doesn't look like he's about to give us directions."

The beast leapt. I dodged to the side, swiping at its flank. Blood sprayed across the path, and the beast veered away, straight into the path of my claws.

"Better move," said Bracken. "Hellhounds are drawn to death, and the body will attract more of them."

"Ugh, they would be." I stepped around the monster. "Please tell me the third ingredient isn't a hellhound tongue."

Kit shook his head. "One hides where the hunt rides. This beast is not hiding, so it cannot be part of the spell."

Zeph growled and kicked the hellhound's body aside. "Are the faeries really that pedantic?"

"Yes." Kit glided past the fallen beast. "We need to get out of here."

I stepped forward and emerged from the spirit line onto a patch of burned ground. The scorched earth brought an ache to my chest. Here, in the centre of Hyde Park, Ember had breathed fire to destroy the Faulkner brothers' spell. I looked across the park, breathing in the smell of traffic and a thousand supernaturals rubbing shoulders.

Home.

The others halted, taking in the sight of London coming to life around us. We'd been through so much together since we'd left, and our lives were intertwined as deeply as the tangle of spirit lines. My fond gaze travelled along our group. Becks, who'd had our back since the first days of the invasion. Will, who'd taken us under his wing and given us the closest we'd had to a permanent home in years. Kit, who'd escaped captivity at the Orion League's hands and helped us get through Faerie unscathed. Zeph, who'd come to mean as much to me as any of my other friends. Astor, though absent at the moment, who'd turned from enemy to ally and risked his life for us.

And yet… there was one person whose absence gnawed at me like a gaping hole in my chest. Being in London without Ember made me feel like something fundamental was missing, the same emptiness I'd felt in that awful void in the heart of the volcano.

The place I needed to shove Ignessa if I wanted rid the worlds of her for good.

Home wasn't truly home without Ember.

16

W e searched the whole area for signs of anything that might be an ingredient in a rare spell, finding little more than scorched grass.

"Didn't Ember breathe fire here?" said Zeph. "What if the ingredient was destroyed?"

"Fifteen years ago," I reminded him. "Doesn't seem to have hurt the trees much."

At the edge of the scorched patch of earth, nature had reclaimed the park.

A rustling noise came from the trees nearby, the sound of crackling branches and shifting roots. Then a feminine face appeared in the nearest trunk.

"Murderer!" she screamed. "Evil murderer!"

Bloody hell. Even the dryads in London had heard about our exploits in Faerie?

"The faerie rumour mill is really something," Will remarked. "I vote we get the hell out of here."

"Agreed," said Kit.

Thorn yowled, flying out of range of the dryads' grasping branches. Roots burst from the ground like knives, surrounding us in a circle. At least these ones didn't come equipped with a river of blood.

"Get out!" shrieked the dryads.

"Believe me, we're trying to!" I jumped over the protruding roots and skidded to a halt against a wall of trees. *Okay. Shifting it is, then.*

The phouka gestured to a hidden passage beneath a raised tree root. "Come quickly!"

Not like we have a choice.

Becks squeezed through first and meowed, letting us know it was safe. I let the others go first, using my claws to stave off the grasping branches until the path was clear.

The tunnel snaked beneath a web of writhing roots, opening into a wider earthen passage beneath the park itself. We emerged at the roadside, London's noise crashing overhead like a waterfall. Taxis took corners at a breakneck pace, cloaked mages walked in tight-knit groups, and despite the chaos we'd left behind, London hardly appeared different to the day we'd left.

"Damn, nice going," I said to Bracken, who straightened upright. "Thanks for helping us out there."

"You're welcome," said the phouka.

The others murmured thanks, except Becks, who was too busy washing the mud off her fur in a puddle. Shifting to human, she shook out her trench coat.

"Say, he is kinda useful to have around," I said to her in an undertone. "I mean, he knows how to get through faerie traps. Comes in handy."

Becks made a disgruntled noise. "We can't keep

picking up strays. We might not even have a house to go back to. Where are we going now?"

"Home," said Will. "Or what's left of it. You're welcome to go ahead to the necromancer guild, though, Cori, if you want to get it over with. Just in case Her Fiery Highness starts nagging you again."

I glanced at Zeph. "Good point. You guys go ahead. Be careful, and if you see any signs of Ignessa, let me know."

I didn't want to split up, but it made sense for me to speak to the necromancers' leader alone. If he even remembered me. Ghosts weren't known for their skills at recollection, but Owen had been nice enough, for a necromancer's assistant.

"You sure about this, Cori?" Zeph asked. "Don't get me wrong, Lady Montgomery saved our necks, but I'm not sure the necromancers will have the faintest clue about Ignessa, the binding spell, or any of that."

"I don't get the impression Lady Montgomery sends people on the mages' most wanted list to speak to her colleagues unless she thinks it's worth the risk," I said. "Maybe he has friends on the other side of the veil who know what the third ingredient might be."

"What, their drinking buddies? Or whatever it is ghosts do in their spare time?" He shook his head. "I guess rehiring the same people after death is one way to be certain nobody new has come into power in the last decade and a half."

"Can you even fire a dead person?" The mental image amused me, but the word 'fire' reminded me too much of a certain goddess. Still, Owen and Lord Glover must know the local spirit lines, even if they didn't know about the ingredients. If nothing else, it would be nice to see someone who *hadn't* changed in the last fifteen years. At least, I assumed Lord Glover hadn't, being a ghost and all.

Zeph walked side by side with me. He slid his hand into mine, and I smiled. If I was a rocking ship, he was the anchor preventing me from sinking. We reached the necromancer guild, which was the same dull, squat building it had always been.

"It hasn't changed at all," I said. "Why is Edinburgh's guild so much better put together?"

"You think I know?" he said. "Their leader isn't a ghost, for a start. Maybe the ones in Edinburgh didn't lose so many in the invasion."

"Yeah, because their headquarters is the only one I've seen that doesn't look like a tool shed," I said. "Actually, that's kind of an insult to sheds everywhere. I can't believe they sleep in here. The ones who aren't ghosts, I mean."

Shed-like or not, the place looked sturdy enough. Maybe not immune to the goddess's fire, but I was reasonably confident even she couldn't make a ghost burst into flames.

"Maybe there's a reason he's the one she sent me to talk to," I said. "If Ignessa throws a temper and sets the place on fire, it won't touch him."

"I think you're onto something," Zeph murmured. "Some of us might not be so lucky, though. I'll keep watch outside for wayward zombies."

"Cheers." I scanned the guild's porch, but saw no sign of Owen, the spindly man who'd been there before. I knocked, and the door blew open as though in a sudden breeze. Behind the door floated a transparent figure, trying in vain to grab the door handle. Owen was a ghost, too?

"Oh," I said. "Sorry you're dead."

He'd been old the last time I'd been here, but had they really not managed to hire anyone new in the last decade and a half?

Owen stared through me. "You're alive."

"Everyone seems shocked to see that, but yeah, I am," I said. "Long story short, I wound up in a place like Faerie and lost fifteen years."

"I see," he said. "Then you'd better come in."

I caught Zeph's eye to let him know I had the situation in hand and entered Lord Glover's office. The man himself wasn't there, but the office looked utterly unchanged. "This place looks like it's been frozen in time since I left."

"No, well, the dead aren't known for innovation," Owen said. "I assume you're here because of the magical outbreak. We've had record numbers of people checking into the guild with the spirit sight, including those much older than the usual age."

"What—humans?" I blinked at him. "Humans are developing the spirit sight?"

"The local witch covens are experiencing the same," he said. "I can't say I know the cause, but it seems a shift has awakened the magical potential in large numbers of humans."

My mouth fell open. For witches and necromancers, magic wasn't hereditary—anyone

could develop it. The last time there'd been a mass outbreak had been during the invasion, when the levels of magic in the world had suddenly spiked.

Had the recent war caused a knock-on effect? It had been weeks after my 'death' that I'd started to see ghosts, and months before it happened often enough that I couldn't brush it off as an accident. Most of the humans would likely have done the same, hoping the weirdness would go away—but if there were dozens of people with untrained talent out there, they'd be prime targets for unscrupulous rogues to take under their wing.

"That's not what you came to ask me," said Owen. "Is it?"

"It's news to me," I admitted. "I'm here because Lady Montgomery from Edinburgh's necromancer guild referred me to you. She said you could help me with something… something related to the Ancients."

Lord Glover strode through the wall into his office, making me jump. "We heard the rumours, and we want no part in this. The gods have ears everywhere, and from the reports, we're lucky they didn't wipe us out."

"They're not as all-powerful as they claim to be," I told him.

Even Ignessa. I refused to believe she couldn't be beaten.

"That's a dangerous statement to make," he said. "You weren't involved in the war up in Scotland, were you?"

"Not exactly," I hedged. "I missed most of the action. But I *am* dealing with an issue involving one of the Ancients, and I was told you might be able to help me. She's called Ignessa, the fire goddess, and she's the one who killed Lady Clare fifteen years ago. She's also a ghost, hence my need to hire a necromancer."

Lord Glover's mouth parted. "I heard the rumours that all anyone found of Lady Clare was a pile of ashes, but there were no witnesses who recalled how she died."

"Ignessa can turn anyone to ash in a heartbeat," I said. "Don't worry, I'm pretty sure ghosts are immune."

"That's why you came to us?" Lord Glover said in incredulous tones. "You brought her to our doorstep on purpose?"

"She's already here, I'm your best shot at being rid of her," I said to him. "If there's anything you can tell me—"

"No," he said. "Our job is to banish the dead, and the Ancients transcend both life and death."

"She's still a ghost," I said. "Her body has gone. Also, she might not be mortal, but I am. And I have the spirit sight because her magic brought me back to life."

The two ghosts stared at me. "Brought you back to life? You're a product of necromancy? A soul binding, or a shade?"

"I don't know, but that isn't important," I said. "I'm telling you the truth. There's a talisman called the Moonbeam which contains the essence of the goddess's magic, and its fire links to the dragon shifters because we're her descendants. I was ripped out of my body five... er, twenty years ago, and my sister used the Moonbeam's magic to bring me back to life."

Neither of them spoke. Oh, yay. I'd freaked out the ghosts.

"I can't set anyone on fire like her, don't worry," I added. "I think the only magic she gave me via our connection is the ability to use the spirit sight. I can probably use regular necromancy, too, but Ignessa is using our link to blackmail me into helping her."

Owen said, "If you have the spirit sight, you must have seen the appalling state of the damage the gods did to the spirit lines. If the Moonbeam contains this goddess's power, no wonder the mages kept it locked away."

Ah. Maybe I should have asked for help locating the third ingredient for the spell *before* bringing up the fact that it contained Ignessa's magic.

"The Moonbeam is broken," I said. "Don't worry, the spirit lines aren't in any danger."

"I beg to differ." Owen indicated a metal device on the desk, encased in shimmering blue light.

I recoiled. "Lorne's spirit devices are still around? I thought they were destroyed."

"There are always those willing to sacrifice others to further their own goals," said Lord Glover. "Our team confiscated this from a local vampire."

"They're still around?" I picked it up, and the two ghosts backed off. Oops. I'd forgotten the spirit devices could absorb spirits of the dead as well as the living. "Can I use *this* on Ignessa?"

"Highly unlikely," said Owen. "The power of a goddess is far beyond a regular spirit. Most likely, the device would explode and damage the spirit lines."

Worth a shot. I turned the metal device over in my hands. It looked a little like a remote control, flat and smooth and unremarkable. My claws dug into the surface, and I peeled off the cover to expose the mechanisms inside. Brightness shone from within—a *familiar* brightness.

A shard of stone lay encased in metal. Not the Moonbeam, but a piece of something that resembled the lava from the heart of the volcano. "*Who* had this?"

"Does it matter?" said Lord Glover. "They've been on

and off the streets for over a decade. Edinburgh's guild had to deal with them, too."

Lady Montgomery didn't mention that. Lorne's first attempt to break open the spirit lines had involved those soul-stealing devices, which were built along the same lines as the Moonbeam and fed by stones that absorbed spiritual energy. When they got overheated, they blew sky-high. Who the hell had been tinkering with them this time?

"What are you looking for in there?" said Lord Glover. "Put that device down."

"All right, chill." I dropped it on the desk. "I'm looking for an ingredient used in a rare binding spell. We're not sure what it is, exactly, but it was located in the liminal space between the spirit lines over Hyde Park at some point."

"A binding spell?" said Lord Glover. "You'll have to ask a witch. Spell ingredients aren't our area of expertise."

I shook my head. "I'm not sure even a witch would know. It's an ancient spell, and the instructions told us the ingredient is located on an intersection of the spirit lines. Whatever it is, it looks like someone stole it before I could get to it."

The two necromancers exchanged glances. "You were involved in an incident there a few years ago, weren't you?" said Owen.

"Ah, kind of," I said. "The Faulkner brothers used a spell to send all the shifters in the area into a frenzied state, and the only way to destroy it was to breathe... fire..." I trailed off.

What was the Moonbeam's most insidious quality? Controlling shifters against their will... or to be more accurate, suppressing the human side until nothing remained but the animal.

We'd never found out how the Faulkner brothers had sent every shifter in the arena into a frenzy with a simple witch spell. Nothing aside from the Moonbeam was supposed to have that effect, but since the Moonbeam itself had been stolen not long later, it'd slipped my mind until now.

"Yes?" said Owen. "What is it?"

"Is there a magical item that can turn a shifter's instincts up to max against their will?" I asked. "Not like a spell, but just... anything that might be used as an ingredient?"

"What, Moonbeam leaves?" he said.

Moonbeam leaves.

I pressed a hand to my mouth. Of course—of *course*. Moonbeam leaves were like shifter catnip, as my sister put it, and had been in the Orion League's hands since long before they'd kidnapped me.

"The mages banned trade in the substance over a decade ago," added Owen. "Don't look so alarmed."

At least the mages had done one thing right. I'd known they were rare, restricted, but not that they might be used in a spell.

"Guess I'm heading to the black market."

Owen recoiled. "Not the arena?"

My heart gave a sickening dive. "Please tell me the arena isn't back."

"I wasn't aware that it ever shut down," he said. "Though I admit my memory isn't what it used to be."

"You have *got* to be kidding me. We blew it up. You

mean people are still hypnotising shifters and forcing them to fight?"

Hypnotising. Moonbeam leaves. *Of course.* Would the Faulkner brothers' schemes ever die?

"I'm afraid I couldn't say," said Owen. "I wish we could be of more help… and if you need training in necromancy, there's a spare novice textbook or two in that cupboard, I believe. Have a look."

I doubted any novice textbook would tell me how to banish the ghost of a goddess who could burn someone to cinders at a touch, but it couldn't hurt to have more resources. I found the book, said goodbye, and went outside to join Zeph.

He listened to me in silence as we walked down familiar roads, in the direction of Magic Avenue.

"Damn," he said quietly. "Moonbeam leaves… you know, I've heard of them, of course, but I didn't realise they were rare because they only come from one location."

"Might not just be there," I said. "The hunt rides along every spirit line, Bracken said. The riddle can be interpreted in more than one way. So… we know what the third ingredient is. Now all we need is to find it."

Slight problem: without a way to destroy Ignessa, rebuilding the Moonbeam wouldn't rid us of her wrath. If pushing her into the volcano didn't work, we'd be out of options.

"Do we have time to search all the spirit lines?" he asked.

"There's one place they'll be," I said. "The arena's back. It never left."

17

A s we turned the corner near Magic Avenue, a tremendous scraping noise like metal dragging on tarmac drowned out all other noise. "What the hell is that?"

Zeph grabbed my arm. "Tell me that's not what I think it is."

A large metal shape appeared at the end of the road, the source of the scraping noise, and a familiar current of fear jolted through my nerves. *An automaton.*

No freaking way. The Orion League's automatons had perished when they had, over two decades ago now. So what the bloody hell was one doing rampaging around London?

Claws sliding out, I advanced forward, my heart thundering. I'd once feared the automatons as much as the League who owned them, but up close, they looked as though they'd been designed by a child with a fascination with homemade robots. Their box-shaped bodies were clothed in metal armour made for practicality, not aesthetics. They were built, in short, to look like they meant business. And to shifters, they'd once meant death.

I lunged forwards, my claws slicing through the automaton's exterior like paper. I wrenched off one of the metal plates, exposing a glowing framework of wires within.

"I always wondered what powered these things." I reached inside, and magic sparked against my hands like an electric surge. I glimpsed a box inked with glowing symbols. Like the ones on Astor's skin. *I knew it.*

"I don't think it's the League's," said Zeph.

"Human tech sure as hell isn't this advanced, though." Not post-invasion, anyway. Yanking the box out, I turned it over. "I assume Will has already seen it…"

Zeph punched the automaton's head off with his clawed hand. "Bastards. These monstrosities destroyed my village. Who would bring them back?"

"If there are new enemies in town, they'll have to get in line behind the mad fire goddess." I marched around the corner to Magic Avenue.

A decade and a half without dragons crash-landing in the streets and brawling with gargoyles had done Magic Avenue a world of good. Wards protected the winding street, shimmering on the brick walls of the houses. It wasn't long before I saw someone I knew well. A black woman with braided hair exited a house on the left carrying a bag of herbs. Fifteen years older, but as healthy as ever.

"Keira!" I said. "It's nice to see a friendly face."

Her eyes widened. "What in the world happened to you, Cori?"

"Long story," I said. "Really long. Are Will and the others here?"

She beamed. "Yes, they are. We hoped you'd survived, but even if not, nobody wanted to claim your house."

"Let me guess… zombies moved in. Or fae." I couldn't complain, though—our house was intact. More than I'd ever hoped for.

"They tried. I chased them off. I'm afraid looters took your weapons after you left, but my pets are good at chasing off intruders."

My eyes widened at the sight of a huge cat behind her in the hall. "That can't be the kitten we saved from the London Eye."

Keira stepped back and stroked him behind the ears. "Remarkable creature, isn't he? He's getting old now, but he can give a gargoyle a run for their money."

"Thank you so much. For looking out for us."

"You're very welcome." She gave me a cheery wave, and I all but skipped down the road to Will's house.

If anything, the small brick house looked better than it had the last time we'd been here. No missing roof tiles or shattered windows. Someone had moved into the shelter next door, as expected, but when I pushed on the door to the shop, it opened at my touch.

"There you are," Becks said from the living room. "Check it out. Almost everything is where we left it."

"Except the mirror." I hurried into the empty shop and through into the back room, elated to find some part of our lives had remained intact. After the invasion, I'd learned not to settle on one place to call home, but the idea of the neighbours keeping our house safe warmed me inside.

Thorn was too big to fit on the sofa, but that didn't stop him from trying. His huge scaly body lay sprawled over the cushions, while Kit sat on the floor, his long legs stretching across the carpet.

"We have a substitute." Will indicated a heap of Moonbeam shards on the kitchen table. "Astor left these here."

"You know the mages from Edinburgh could follow us through there, don't you?" said Becks.

"They're not even using the mirror, are they? They left it in the dungeon." Also, if they picked up the wrong piece, they'd walk into the middle of the volcano, which might at least make them think twice about stealing other people's magical artefacts.

"My wards are still up," Will said. "Didn't stop people from stealing all our leftover weapons, mind, but I guess the zombies put them off moving in. Don't go in the basement."

"I guess this road isn't on your typical looter's route." I flopped into an armchair.

Will, meanwhile, moved around the kitchen checking the cupboards. "Nobody open the fridge until I decontaminate it. It smells like a zombie's armpit in there."

"You can deal with that," I said. "Where's Astor? And Bracken?"

"Astor went to see if any of his old contacts are still alive," said Becks. "As for our new friend, he went to scope out the tunnels. And speaking of contacts, we're gonna have a hell of a time getting work when we're supposed to be dead several times over. If we walk into the mercenaries' place, they'll tip salt on our heads and hire a necromancer to exorcise us."

"Who even runs the place now Darcy's dead?" Some of

my elation faded. "Guys, I know what the third ingredient is. It's moonbeam leaves. You know, shifter catnip. And it's a banned substance now."

All eyes turned in Will's direction.

"Don't look at me," said Will. "Half my contacts are either dead, think *I'm* dead, or they packed up and left. Besides, I don't work with people who trade in illegal goods."

"There's always the underworld," I said. "Guys… I have some bad news about the arena."

Becks jumped to her feet. "It can't be back, can it? What the hell have the mages been doing for the last fifteen years?"

"I don't know for sure the arena still exists," I added. "But I think the underworld is our best bet. We don't have much time before Ignessa sets her sights on London again."

And then? She might well finish what Lorne had started.

Becks bared her teeth. "I'll go and sniff around. I'm sure there's some back-alley shifters I can shake answers out of."

Were all our old enemies coming back? First the automatons, now the arena. Speaking of the former. I dug in my pocket for the box I'd yanked out of the automaton and put it down on the kitchen table.

"What the bloody hell is that?" Will asked.

"Did none of you see the automaton?" I said to the others. "You know, big clanking human-shaped thing covered in metal plates, not much of a talker?"

"Oh. That." Will picked up the box. "So that's what they use to power them. I did wonder."

"They're the hallmarks of the Orion League," said Zeph. "You're not saying you're cool with it rampaging around?"

"It's not the League's," said Will, opening the box. "The witches say it isn't, anyway. I *knew* this was magical."

Light poured out of the box, and I backed away in case it exploded. "I cut it to ribbons. You're welcome."

Will put down the box. "Chill, Cori. The League is dead, and someone left that automaton as a lookout. I reckon it belongs to a witch. They reclaimed it, like the blood magic symbols."

Kit looked up. "Will, if you build a giant robot—"

"I'll never come up with anything as batshit as adopting a baby dragon," he said. "And no, it was *not* me who built the bloody thing. I have no idea who did it."

Zeph and I exchanged blank looks. A giant robot was the least of our problems, and I doubted *that* was Ignessa's. She'd been strangely quiet since we'd arrived in London, for that matter.

The door opened and Becks streaked in, her cat form scooting across the floor. She turned human again, leaning on the sofa to catch her breath. "The arena's back, all right, but they say it's voluntary now. A likely story."

"Who told you that?"

"A local." She scowled. "I noticed *someone* following me, so I came back here before he gave us away."

"Hmm." The arena had left a gaping hole behind in the supernatural underworld which had paved the way for the sickness to take root. That someone had revived it came as no surprise, but it was kind of depressing to find our actions against the Faulkner brothers might have made no difference at all. "Did you see Astor?"

"No." Becks flopped into an armchair, since the dragonling had taken the sofa, and tossed a leaflet to the carpeted floor. "I *did* pick that up."

I examined the leaflet, which proclaimed that an 'exclusive supernatural extravaganza' was scheduled for tonight at one of the local theatres.

"A supernatural extravaganza," Zeph read over my shoulder. "Fights, contests… fire-breathing?"

"What, dragon shifters?" I frowned. "This looks way too snazzy to be a dirty underground fighting ring."

"Let me see that," said Will, walking over. "Yeah, no. What's the betting Ignessa set the whole thing up as a trap?"

"If so, and we don't take her bait, she might imitate the Faulkner brothers and suck out the souls of everyone there," I said. "Or something equally heinous. Besides, if the only place to get the moonbeam leaves is the supernatural underworld, then she won't stop us."

"Yeah, about that," said Becks. "Once we have that third ingredient, there'll be nothing stopping Ignessa from forcing you to remake the Moonbeam there and then without figuring out how to kill her first. If this is what she looks like with her magic weakened, I don't want to know what she can do when she's back at full power."

"I know." I lowered the leaflet. "I have a plan. You'll have to trust me on it."

"Don't you want to ask the mages for help?" said Will. "I mean, maybe not if they heard Ignessa turned those two guys into ash back in Edinburgh…"

"They don't even know she killed Lady Clare," I said. "They thought we were dead for fifteen years, though, so I can see them giving us no end of grief if we show up at their headquarters again. Also, if the mages in Edinburgh are anything to go by, even *they* don't know how to deal with the Ancients. Certainly not one who's a ghost. The necromancers don't either. I think we're on our own."

Bracken cleared his throat from the doorway. Becks sprang to her feet, her eyes narrowing. "Watch you don't go wagging your tongue, or you might find yourself without one."

"I won't tell anyone your secrets," he said. "I escaped the wrath of the Sidhe, and I have no desire to fall victim to the Ancients."

Becks scowled. "You know, the only reason we're letting you stick around is so we'll have someone extra to hide behind if she tries to torch us, too."

"I'm honoured," he said dryly. "There are zombies in your basement, by the way. That's what I came to tell you."

"Yay." Will grabbed a salt shaker from the kitchen table. "It's like the good old days."

All that was missing was my sister. Her absence cut me like a blade in the chest, and wandering around our former haunts had only cemented my certainty that I was running out of time to save her.

Despite my plan, I couldn't help wondering if Ignessa was manipulating me even now. She'd made it quite clear that she and Ember were bound in a manner that wasn't easily undone. If I'd calculated wrong, we might all pay the price. But I wasn't one to give up without a fight, especially not on my sister.

18

"I think Ignessa's sulking," I told the others as we walked to Leicester Square. "She's been outright ignoring me since we got here."

"You didn't expect to find her squatting in the basement?" Zeph scanned the road for any signs of interlopers—including automatons—but the evening was quiet, the sky tinged pink with sunset.

After we'd evicted the zombies from the basement, we'd eaten, changed into clean clothes, and otherwise prepared for the arena's big event. I'd been on tenterhooks waiting for a message from Ignessa in the form of something else catching on fire, yet aside from Thorn setting an armchair ablaze and eating the barbecued remains, the house remained flame-free. Even the tunnels, though after a few thankless hours dealing with the zombies, I wouldn't have minded torching them.

"Glad they picked a new location." Becks turned human, her trench coat brushing the floor. "Hopefully one that *isn't* on top of a key point."

"Me too," I said. "Then again, nobody seems to have learned from their mistakes in the last decade and a half."

"Don't speak too soon," said Becks. "Damn, he's *still* following us."

I glanced behind us at the phouka, who walked far enough behind us that I was reasonably sure he couldn't hear her.

"If you don't want him to stay with us, tell him to fuck off," I said. "Or I can do the honours."

"Eh." She shrugged one shoulder. "I wasn't kidding when I said he might be a handy shield if Ignessa breathes fire on us again."

"Uh-huh." Despite her words, there was no heat in her tone. "He's helped us more than once, remember? He saved your arse back in Faerie. And he got us out of Hyde Park. Obviously, he thinks some of us are good company."

"Gah." She made a disgruntled noise. "Why would anyone throw their lot in with us, anyway?"

"You're asking a dragon shifter who hangs out with a gargoyle-witch, a cat who's afraid of mice, a half-faerie, a dragonling who eats furniture, and an ex-assassin."

"You left out Zeph. Or is he more than a friend?"

I watched the back of his head, but he showed no signs that he'd heard her. "Assuming we don't die? Yes, he is."

"I always thought you two were made for one another," she said. "As for Astor and Ember… *where* he's wandered off to this time, I have no idea. He'd better not have been arrested again."

Kit and Will had stayed behind with the dragonling, keeping one of the Moonbeam pieces at the ready in case we needed to make a quick getaway. That left Becks, Zeph, Bracken and me to storm the castle. Or theatre.

Advertising billboards for the supernatural extravaganza were plastered on half the buildings.

"We should have applied as a novelty act," I said. "Might have covered the ticket costs." Becks would sneak in as a cat, but Zeph and I would have to pay on the doors if we wanted to get into the new arena, and the pricey tickets had eaten through most of the cash Will had found in a safe box under the floorboards.

Becks made a disgruntled noise. "They're still using shifters for entertainment. It's like nothing we did made any difference at all."

"Give it time," I said. "We haven't been here a day yet."

I knew what she meant, but what had Ember once said? We had to get up and fight again and again, because if we didn't, the enemy—whichever form they took—would win.

Zeph turned the corner into a bustling street. The arena's new location was on a corner in the still-thriving area of the theatre district where the mages paid a fortune to watch West End shows in heavily warded arenas free from any danger of supernatural assaults. Given the location, it must be legit, but the security guards looked suspiciously like the gargoyles who'd worked for the Faulkner brothers. Their huge bodies were crammed into smart suits, their features a cross between gargoyle and human. If it was the same guys, they'd gone up in the world in the last fifteen years.

An objection rose to my tongue, but Zeph had already reached the theatre, tossing a handful of notes at the rat shifter guarding the doors. The rat shifter took the money, frowning at me as though trying to puzzle out where he might have seen me before. I kept my head high, as though I belonged here, and nobody accosted me. If anyone had seen me come to the arena fifteen years ago to save a dragon egg and end up rescuing Zeph instead, they'd never know I was the same person.

"You're not volunteering?" I whispered to Zeph.

He gave a grin. "Nah, I think I'll enjoy a spectator's position this time around. Unless that shifter dude wants a rematch."

"You still think you would have won?" I snorted.

"You're supposed to feed my ego and tell me I'd have wiped the floor with him."

"I'm pretty sure your ego is fine." I stepped onto the red-carpeted stairs. "Damn, this is fancy. I guess this is the closest we'll get to a date, the way things are going."

"It can be a date if you like." He led me upstairs and into the theatre itself. The stage, bathed in spotlights, was the polar opposite of the dirty, bloodstained basement which had held the old arena. The mages seated in the premier seats at the front and back cemented my certainty that they'd taken the idea of the arena and monetised it for their own benefits. At my feet, Becks slipped past in cat form, ready to spy on the patrons. Zeph and I carried a single Moonbeam shard each, both as an escape route and a way to implement our plan against Ignessa if she showed her face tonight.

"This isn't an arena," Zeph murmured. "It's a theatre. The mages must have given the go-ahead for a legal version of the arena to replace the illegal fighting rings. That way they get the profit."

"Just as long as nobody's wagering dragon eggs." I took a seat next to him, scanning the row in front. "Nobody looks like they're trading you-know-what, either."

The other patrons seemed to be shifters, for the most part, but a few witches sat in groups among the crowd. None of them looked like they might be traders for illegal substances, though with the mages occupying the rows at the very front and at the back, nobody would dare try anything within public view. We'd have had better luck slinking around back alleys if we wanted to find some moonbeam leaves.

The row filled on either side of Zeph and me, and I scowled when the muscular gargoyle shifter next to me accidentally elbowed me in the face. *Yeah, this was a mistake.*

I fidgeted. "You know, I'm not really a theatre person."

"Nor me." Zeph's body tensed. "It's starting."

The audience hushed as the spotlights came on. Then, two people walked onstage. They wore red masks covered in scales with twin horns on either side of their heads, but their beaks beneath marked them as gargoyles.

"Introducing Coriander and Ember!" a voice roared through the speakers.

The crowd erupted into applause, while I sat in stunned silence. *We* were the star act? I wouldn't lie, it was kind of flattering, in a bizarre way.

"Nice," said Zeph. "Which is you?"

"That's me," I said, pointing to the one on the left.

"No, it's Ember. She's bigger than you are."

I gave a mock pout. "Nobody said they had to be accurate."

Zeph chuckled. "Way to go, Cori. See, you did change the course of history. Everyone in London remembers your name."

"Very funny." I gave him a light smack in the arm. "For all we know, we're notorious."

And where the hell was Ignessa? For all I knew, she was lurking backstage, ready to torch the whole place. Even the display of magical flamethrowers as the 'dragon shifters' entertained the crowd didn't put me at ease.

The person who was supposed to be Ember said, "Introducing our first match—"

Becks nudged me in the hand. I ducked my head, wincing when she dug in her claws to indicate she wanted to talk to me. I nodded to Zeph to let him know I had it handled and attempted to duck out of the row. The huge shifter on my right grumbled when I squeezed past him into the aisle, but I ignored him, heading over to join Becks.

Becks jabbed a paw at a half-open trapdoor in the aisle, one I wouldn't have spotted if she hadn't pointed it out. I peered through it, and hot air whispered on my neck, like a blast from a warm fan.

Ignessa.

"Don't even think about asking your friend for help," she whispered in my ear.

Fear coated my throat, my heart jackhammering. All eyes in the room focused on the stage, and nobody saw me push the trapdoor up to reveal a hidden staircase.

Becks slipped inside first, mewing at me to follow her. I didn't want to leave Zeph, but Ignessa would burn the whole place down if the mood took her.

The dark staircase led into a darker corridor which set my wings itching to break out. I felt my way forward to a pair of twin doors which opened into a smaller theatre.

I stifled a gasp. The second theatre was much smaller

than its upstairs neighbour, with no barriers between the seats and the stage. Judging by the spotlights and the utter silence, the show had yet to begin. No wonder I hadn't known the place was here—not a sound nor any movement came from the audience at all. Too quiet to be natural. *Ignessa. What did she do?*

"I thought you'd never arrive, Cori," said Ignessa's voice, projected through the room as though spoken through the loudspeakers.

"Show yourself," I said. My voice rang out, louder than I'd intended. The audience didn't move. *They're under her spell.* She wasn't content to just let me buy the moonbeam leaves, she wanted to make our lives into a performance her own amusement. I should have figured she had a theatrical streak.

"Come to the stage, Cori, or they die."

The spotlight fell on a number of cages at the back of the stage, containing cat shifters, wolf shifters, countless others. *Damn her.*

Becks nudged my ankle. I gave her a nod to let her know I was okay. Then I walked down to the stage, holding my head high. The spotlights dazzled my eyes, and when I blinked the glare away, someone else walked into view from the opposite side of the stage.

Astor.

Ignessa spoke again. "Would you kill your sister's lover to save her life?"

I tried to catch Astor's eyes. His shirt was torn to rags, revealing the dragon tattooed onto his back and chest, which seemed faded beneath the glowing marks the Orion League had painted onto him. *What did she do to him?*

My hands clenched. "What is the point in this?"

"Does there have to be a point?" she said.

"For someone like you?" My voice grew louder. "Yes, there does. You always have your reasons, even if they're petty and self-serving."

"You dare to insult me at a time like this?" she said.

"I think we're past the pleasantries, Ignessa." If she spotted the Moonbeam piece in my pocket before I figured out how to shove her through it into the volcano, then I'd need to come up with a new plan. Assuming she didn't just torch everyone in the room. "What's this in aid of? You want to punish me by forcing me to fight my friends?"

"Your sister defiled the name of my people when she lay with this man," she spat. "This assassin, whose fellow hunters slaughtered my brethren."

So that's what it was. She saw Ember's relationship with Astor as a personal betrayal.

"You don't need to take it personally," I said. "I mean, I'm in a relationship with another dragon shifter and we both still think you're a piece of shit."

I didn't hear her reply, because Astor *moved*. I jumped out of range, shaken by his speed and the knife blade gleaming in his right hand. With the goddess calling the shots, rules were meaningless. I could fight as dirty as I liked, but hurting Astor would play into Ignessa's hands.

Astor moved like a human whirlwind, his knife slicing open the back of my jacket. I deflected another strike with the side of my claw, but the knife blurred out of sight before I could grab it. Faster than a shifter, he spun the knife and drove it towards my neck.

I threw myself flat, tangling my legs with his in an

attempt to trip him. His torn shirt revealed fresh tattoo marks for speed and stamina. The Orion League's marks contained the magic of the Ancients, and Ignessa must have hijacked them and used them to control him.

If I shifted, I could end the match in seconds, but then, Ignessa would be the only victor. How could I take him down without hurting him? *Damn, think, Cori.*

The Moonbeam shard in my pocket dug into my hip, reminding me of my escape route. I wouldn't abandon Astor, not if I wanted to get Ember back safe and whole. The audience, too, were victims in Ignessa's deranged schemes. At a single word, she might slaughter them all. I needed to play along, and then find a way to break her hold over Astor.

I feinted a strike then dove low, tackling him onto his back. Astor rolled to the side and was back on his feet in a blink, hitting out with a strike to the sternum that sent me flying off my feet. My back crashed to the ground, and the stage lights spun above my head. *Ow.*

Astor stood over me, the knife in his hand. He'd moved quicker than a breath, the light of the fire goddess shining from the marks on him. After everything I'd been through, it seemed I'd meet my end at the knife of an Orion League assassin after all.

I rolled onto my front, my eyes watering with pain, and grabbed the Moonbeam shard from my pocket. The stone caught the stage lights and Astor's next strike missed, the dazzling light throwing off his aim.

Then he whipped a second knife from his pocket and hurled it at me. The knife struck the Moonbeam shard hilt-first, knocking it flying from my hands. Astor lunged, catching the shard in his extended hand.

Dammit.

"Any last words, Cori?" said Ignessa, her voice echoing through the loudspeakers. "Or would you like to shift into your true form, unleash your fire, and end this? Would your sister forgive you?"

"My sister would forgive me for anything."

"Then we'll see if you can resist my fire."

Astor raised the shard, and fire exploded in my chest, roaring through my veins. The Moonbeam's magic drew out the beast within me, and I shifted, my dragon form filling the arena. My breath rumbled, the fire longing to break out. The Moonbeam shard gleamed, white-hot, enticing.

No. Stop that.

Ignessa laughed. "You're no match for my influence, Cori... I told you."

Fire burst from my lungs, engulfing Astor and the stage along with him.

No!

The human inside me screamed, stopping the flames in their tracks—but Astor was still there, holding the Moonbeam shard, as though the fire hadn't touched him.

I swayed on my feet, shocked back into human form. My gaze fell on the cages behind the stage—cages which were now empty—and the audience, who'd thrown themselves to the floor out of range of the fire.

What the hell? Had the Moonbeam shard absorbed the fire? Perhaps, but Astor hadn't been in control of his actions at all. He'd stood right in my path, and now remained still, his gaze distant and zoned out.

I reached for the Moonbeam shard in his hands,

expecting resistance, but instead, he pressed the shard into my hand.

He's not under her control. Instead of burning him, my flames had extinguished the glowing marks on his arms, freeing him from Ignessa's influence. Didn't explain the empty cages—but when my gaze drifted to the side of the stage, I glimpsed a line of furred shapes vanishing out of the entrance. Becks and Bracken must have sneakily unlocked the cages while Ignessa was occupied watching our fight.

In a flash of light, Ignessa appeared, hovering above the arena with flaming eyes. Her expression echoed my own disbelief and shock. "You dare to defy me?"

Yes. I gripped the Moonbeam shard, holding it high. "You bet we do, Ignessa. Come and get us."

She turned on the audience, who'd frozen in the middle of returning to their seats. "Kill them both."

The crowd moved, on their feet, surging towards the stage. If they reached us, they'd tear us both to shreds before I could open the portal.

The Moonbeam piece glowed in my hands. Dammit, I'd been so close.

Wait a second. If she could use the shard to awaken my fire, then its other powers must be active, not just the portal.

Facing the audience, I raised the Moonbeam shard above my head and intoned, "Stop!"

The shifters stopped mid-charge, their gazes fixed on the shard. Nobody moved an inch.

I'd brought her army to a standstill.

"Stop that," she growled.

Certainty hit me. "You can't control it, can you? Not all

the time. I have just as much influence over the Moon-beam's fire as you do. Any shifter can use it."

"And *you* just gave me the means of getting to your friends." She flew at the Moonbeam shard, her ghostly form vanishing through the portal.

Shit.

"Nice try, but too late." Zeph's voice rang out.

He climbed onto the stage, holding up his own Moon-beam piece. Ignessa's ghost shot out of the shard in his hands, pivoting on the spot. With a snarl, she flew at me again.

This time, I was ready. I focused on the volcano's fire with everything I had, picturing the void in my mind's eye. The Moonbeam shard I'd left on the edge of the abyss, inches away from the trap that held a thousand captive spirits.

The goddess disappeared into the glass, vanishing in a flash of light.

"NO!" Her scream reverberated through the arena, but the light dimmed, and she was gone. Sucked into the fire.

Zeph lowered his own shard. "She's gone."

"Holy shit." I swayed again, seeking out Astor. "What the hell did you do? Steal Agnes's pendant?"

"No," said Astor.

"Sorry, *borrow* her pendant. Or liberate. Take your pick."

"This mark—" He pointed to his tattooed arm—"pro-tects me against fire. We walked on burning hot coals in initiation training as League members, that's how I know."

"And you decided not to mention it until now?" Zeph

strode to my side, placed a hand on my shoulder to steady me. "Did you come here on purpose?"

"Of course not." Astor spoke in calm tones, as though he hadn't narrowly escaped being burned to a crisp. "The marks the goddess used to control me burned off when Cori breathed fire on me."

"You can be the one to tell Ember you *let* me burn you," I said, with an eye-roll.

"It worked, didn't it?" He scanned the arena floor. "By the way, I think the audience is still under your spell."

"Oops." I lowered the Moonbeam shard and willed its light to dim down. The other shifters came to life, and I caught Becks's gaze watching me from the shadows. "I'm glad she got the other shifters out."

"Me, too." Zeph stroked my forehead, planted a kiss on my brow. "You're okay, Cori. You did it."

"I did."

I just hope I can save Ember, too.

19

"This isn't a permanent victory," I told the others, when we gathered back in the living room at Will's house.

"Usually when you push someone into a volcano, they're not getting up anytime soon," Will responded.

"This is an Ancient we're talking about," said Zeph. "Also, she's fireproof."

"And she got out of there once already," I added.

"Wait, she did?" said Will.

"She used to be imprisoned in there," I explained. "I… sort of saw into her memories when I fell into the lava. She was stuck in the volcano for years, but when Lorne woke the gods…"

"It brought her out of the volcano, too," Zeph finished. "So you think she might try to escape again?"

"I hope not, but I also hoped to remake the Moonbeam *before* banishing her," I said. "That way, Ember would escape, and she wouldn't."

When I remade the Moonbeam, it might well

reverse what I'd done to Ignessa. I'd need to be ready to toss it into the volcano the instant my sister was at my side.

"Also, I got these." Becks threw a bag onto the table. "Moonbeam leaves. Found a trader in a back alley."

"Wait, you did?" I peered into the bag, then withdrew before the sharp smell infiltrated my senses. "Nice job."

"Wait, you sneaked around in back alleys and saved those shifters at the same time?" Zeph asked.

"No," she said. "I sent Bracken to buy the leaves. They only affect shifters, so I figured he'd be in with a better shot at getting hold of them without spending the whole night fighting locals."

I frowned. "So you *are* working with him? Where is he?"

"I don't know." She looked decidedly shifty. "What? I don't see you interrogating Astor about the stunt *he* pulled back there."

I looked around for Astor and spotted him hovering near the door.

"Astor…"

"I appreciate you sparing my life," he said. "Thank you."

From Astor, that was like a hug and a declaration of friendship for life. "You know I breathed fire on you, don't you? You'd be dead if not for those marks."

"I planned for it," he said. "I suspected the marks would make me susceptible to Ignessa's control."

"You knew my flames wouldn't burn you to a crisp?" I arched a brow. "Or were you willing to risk me having to live with the knowledge that I killed my sister's boyfriend?"

"I already tested the fire," he said. "How do you think I sneaked past the dragons so many times?"

"Are you sure you're not actually a dragon shifter?" Zeph said. "You take enough risks to be an honorary dragon, at any rate."

"Or Ember's rubbing off on him," I put in. "How'd Ignessa get you, then?"

"I told you, the marks have been gaining strength the longer she's been in this realm," Astor said. "I realised she might use them against me, so I decided to let her. After all, I knew her only possible aim was to set us against one another, and that I was immune to your fire."

"Ember is going to skin you alive," I said. "I hope you know that."

"I'm sure you'll tell her all about how you breathed fire at me." His eyes were glittering with amusement. Astor was teasing me now? "And how horrified you were when you thought you killed me."

"Too soon, Astor. Too soon." I turned to Zeph. "One impossible task down. One more to go."

I didn't want to delay using the spell to remake the Moonbeam, but if it *did* bring Ignessa back, I was in no shape for another fight to the death. Astor hit bloody hard for a human.

Zeph's hand squeezed mine. "You've done enough for today. You need to rest, or else you might end up sleeping for days."

"Hey, I'm past that stage by now," I said. "But I'll let you tend to my wounds."

He grinned, hearing the double meaning in my words, and pulled me after him upstairs. "It's your room, so you'll have to invite me in."

"Aren't you the gentleman." I made a big show of opening the door. "Poor Becks will have to sleep outside. Not that she minds, being a cat."

"Hmm." He closed the door behind us and gave me an appraising look. "Are you hurt anywhere?"

"I think I skinned my knees."

"I'll kiss them better." He reached down behind my knees and tipped me backwards onto the bed. I sprawled out, and he leaned over and stole my breath with a kiss. "Better?"

I wrapped my legs around his waist. "Better."

He snatched another kiss, pulling off my shirt. I scrambled to do the same for him, and the next few seconds were a frenzy of shedding clothes and bare skin. I'd never been with another dragon shifter—for obvious reasons—but when his touch sparked heat inside me, I saw that same heat reflected at me in his eyes. His fire stoked mine, kindling my desire.

Zeph slid his hands over my bare skin, to the slick wetness between my legs. I gasped in time with his fingers' movements, writhing beneath him, almost embarrassed by how quickly I peaked.

"Hmm. Make that noise again." He removed his fingers, his eyes gleaming. "You do have protection, don't you?"

"You bet." I yanked open a drawer and pulled out a box of condoms. "I'm taking a witch-made contraceptive, too. Thought I might get lucky."

"I like a dragon who's prepared." He took out a condom and I helped slide into onto his hardened length.

He entered me with a thrust which tugged a gasp from

my lungs. We moved together, heat and fire against fire and heat, my desire far from quenched.

It turned out the rumours about male dragon shifters' stamina were not exaggerated.

———

I woke early, refreshed, happy, and more than ready to see my sister again. Leaving Zeph to sleep in, I took a quick shower and went downstairs to grab breakfast.

"Hey guys." I sat down at the kitchen table. "Ready to kick some arse?"

"Why are you in such a good mood?" Kit asked.

"She got laid," Will supplied.

"I get to see my *sister* today." Zeph was just the icing on the cake. I was positively buzzing. "Is Becks around?"

"She went off with the phouka."

"I thought she didn't like him." I poured cereal into a bowl. For once, the lack of milk didn't bother me. Just being back at home, with the people I loved, was enough. Once Ember was back, life would be perfect.

"Becks does what Becks does."

"Cat logic there," I shovelled cereal into my mouth. "Oh, there she is."

Becks padded in, shifting to human form, and walked to the table to help herself to breakfast.

"Seen Astor?" I decided not to comment on her dishevelled hair and muddy coat.

"No," said Becks. "I assume he's still sore about you kicking the crap out of him last night."

"More like the other way around." I rolled my eyes. "Those tattoos of his are something else. I should have seen it coming, really. Those marks the League gave him have been acting up since the spirit lines opened."

"Damn," said Will. "Is that why he's being so moody lately? I mean, aside from his girlfriend being stuck as a ghost. I heard him skulking around outside last night. Unless that was you, Becks."

"You didn't come back last night," I added to Becks.

"You think I wanted to walk in on you and Zeph boning? No, I slept in the gutter."

I grinned. "So you didn't hook up with Bracken? Without faerie magic this time?"

She scowled. "No."

Will mouthed, *she totally did.*

Zeph entered the kitchen, distracting everyone. "Hey," he said. "What're we doing today?"

"Saving Ember." I walked to the living room area and fetched the Moonbeam shard and the bag of moonbeam leaves. Inside the bag were the Bloodroot and the spirit stone. "Guess Astor brought them here ready to do the spell."

A knock came from the front door. I dropped the bag on the kitchen table. "Who knows we're living here?"

"The whole street," said Will, getting to his feet. "Also, you made a spectacle of yourself in front of the entire arena last night, in case you've forgotten."

A second knock, louder. On his feet, Kit disappeared into the shop.

"It's them," he hissed. "The mages."

Damn. Even if it was merely a friendly social call, and I had my doubts, the last thing we needed was to be caught hiding an illicit substance less than a day after our return to London. I picked up the bag with the moonbeam leaves and the other ingredients and stashed it down the back of the sofa cushions, then I ran after Will to answer the door.

A cloaked man with dark hair stood on the doorstep. He must be a newer addition to London's mage guild because I'd never seen him before.

"Hello," Will said from beside me. "Can I help you?"

"So it's true," said the mage. "The dragon shifters have returned to the city."

I met his gaze, unintimidated. "Yes, they have."

"Or some of them have," he added. "Where's your sister?"

I was about to visit her when you interrupted. "She's gone away for a bit," I said. "If you don't mind my asking, who are you? What happened to Lord Smyth?"

"The Mage Lord retired two years ago."

Oh. He hadn't been that old, but the job of the leading mage was demanding, especially in a major city. I didn't blame him for wanting to get some peace.

"So are you the new Mage Lord?" I asked.

"No, I'm the Mage Lord's assistant," he said. "I'm here to speak to Coriander."

"That's me." Suspicion rose. "How did you know we were back in the city?"

"You were seen at the West End last night," he replied. "You put on quite a show, they say."

So the mages do *know about the underground fighting ring?* Unless they'd seen us in the audience in the upstairs theatre, but I had my doubts.

"We were going to visit you later," I said. "I don't know if you've heard from Lord Glover yet, but—"

"You paid him a visit," he said, "to ask about the Ancients."

"Yes..." *So he knows, then?*

"I also spoke to the mages from Edinburgh," he added.

"They didn't get the best impression of us. Look, we just have one thing we need to do here—"

"Rescue your sister? Or kill Ignessa?"

Shit on toast. His eyes carried a familiar glint.

Ignessa had the mage under her spell. And I bet he wasn't alone.

"Excuse me." I slammed the door in his face, whirling to face the others. "She has him."

Question was—when? Had she escaped the volcano the instant I pushed her in?

A current of air slammed into me, forcing me to grab the door frame. He must be an air mage. We had a few spare Moonbeam pieces, but if we used them to escape, the mages would be able to follow us.

There was a crash, then the mage toppled over on the doorstep. Astor stood behind him, a baseball bat in his hands. "He's not the only one. I spied on the mages. They took down their wards. They're following the voice of the goddess without knowing she's manipulating them."

"That figures." Like with the other dragon shifters, she'd let them believe they were acting of their own accord. It was easier for her that way.

I hurried back into the living room to grab the bag of ingredients, shoving it deep in my pocket. Then I pulled out a Moonbeam piece, peering through into the heart of the volcano. Ghostly shapes hovered on the other side of the barrier, but not her. *Where is she, then? In this realm, or back in the dragon shifters' city?*

"What are you doing?" said Astor. "The mages will be back to pick up their little friend soon."

I cursed, lowering the Moonbeam shard. "Astor, do you know where Ignessa is?"

"I don't, but I do have these." He threw a handful of tattoo pens on the floor. "Mark everyone with a fireproof spell. It'll be temporary, but if she sends the other dragon shifters after you, you'll have some measure of protection."

"Whoa." Will picked up one of the pens. "Where'd you get these?"

"Does it matter?" Astor pushed up his sleeve, revealing a new mark on his arm. "Copy this mark."

"Okay, okay." Will inked a rune on his arm. "It won't work on you, Kit, but your shielding magic can deflect fire."

Not the goddess's fire—but no magic was a match for her, not even dragonfire. And like the healing symbols that we'd used to combat the virus, the marks would need to be reapplied frequently even to deflect dragonfire.

I put down a Moonbeam shard. "I'm going to the dragons' city to remake the Moonbeam. When I do, all her attention will fixate on me. That'll give you the chance to send out a warning throughout the city. I'm not going to order you to flee, but the spare mirror is in the dragon's village where I left it, and as far as I know, it's safe there." Whatever happened, I would not let my friends sacrifice their lives.

"You can't go alone," Zeph protested. "Cori…"

"This is my last shot, Zeph." I blinked tears from my eyes and hugged him. "If I get Ember back, we'll have one more dragon shifter on our team."

With Ignessa in control of London, I had nothing to lose by remaking the Moonbeam and freeing Ember from her prison. Then we'd be together, even if we had to face the end side by side.

Zeph released me. "Please be careful, Cori."

I stepped into the light, emerging in the dragons' city. Silence surrounded me, still and absolute. I pulled out the bag of ingredients, turning to the pile of shards on the ground. "With breath divine, the three combine…"

"Until the fire becomes your pyre," whispered the goddess in my ear.

I jerked upright. She hovered above the shards, twin flames simmering in her grey eyes.

"I did what you wanted." I tipped the bag of ingredients onto the ground. "You have no reason to complain."

"When I escaped my prison, I was weak," said the fire goddess. "I'd forgotten my history, let alone how to work magic."

"Uh-huh." I let her speak. The longer I gave my friends to warn everyone in London, the better. "Very interesting."

"Over time, I have regained some of my strength," said Ignessa. "Yet you sought to trap me within the fires, as though I were a simple mortal spirit?"

"I really struck a nerve there, didn't I?" I said. "Look, you killed people. Forgive me if I don't break out the welcome banner. Just tell me what you want."

"London," said Ignessa. "It should have been mine, but Lorne failed at every task I gave him. Even the mages have failed me, over and over. Humans are unreliable and weak."

"No, they just have this pesky thing called free will," I said. "And so do I."

"This realm is dying," said the fire goddess. "I need a

new domain to rule over, and London will more than suffice."

"Yeah. World domination. Hmm." I moved the ingredients into place, and a wave of light pulsed from the Moonbeam shards. *Whoa.*

"It's starting," said Ignessa, her voice brimming with excitement.

That's... not the reaction I hoped for.

Before I could speak a word, Ember flew overhead, her flames engulfing the shards of glass-like stone along with the three ingredients. A torrent of white light surged to the heavens, blotting out my vision.

It's working. Ember's bond with Ignessa fulfilled the requirements of the spell—but why had the fire goddess sounded so triumphant back then? Had I got this all wrong?

Ignessa vanished beneath the Moonbeam's light, which spread over our surroundings until whiteness encompassed the world.

The light dimmed, and the first thing I saw was Ember. But it wasn't my sister's eyes who looked back at me.

"Now we are truly one," said the goddess's voice, speaking through Ember's mouth.

The cheating Ancient had stolen my sister's body for her own.

"You can't," I whispered. "You can't possess a human. Even a dragon shifter."

"Except for the one whose soul is bound to mine," she said. 'Thank you for your assistance."

The glow dimmed, revealing a solid white stone lying on the ground, the mirror image of the original Moonbeam. Splintered pieces of the old one lay scattered around it, but the stone in the centre was whole. And so was Ember… except it wasn't her.

Ignessa. She tricked all of us, even Agnes.

Did Ember's spirit even still exist anymore? Or had she moved on—or worse, been cast into the void in the volcano, like so many others? Even if it was too late to save her from Ignessa, the idea of never seeing her again… no. *I won't lose her. I can't lose her.*

"Don't look so sad," said Ignessa. "You were far from my only pawns. The rest of your kind are the same—designed to be used, tossed aside, and broken."

The Moonbeam glowed, reflecting the burning void in the centre of the volcano. Its heat seared me even from the other side of the portal.

"Don't do this," I warned. "Destroy me and you'll destroy yourself."

"You're nothing to me, Cori."

The portal swallowed me up, casting me into the heart of the volcano.

20

The void of souls caught me, tugging me into its depths until greyness surrounded me on all sides, encompassing hundreds of ghosts, countless lost spirits severed from the world they'd left behind.

I threw myself against the barrier, pushing as hard as I could. *I have to get out or I'm dead. How long would it take before my body drowned in the lava? Not long at all.* I hurled myself into the barrier again, agony splintering through me even though I shouldn't be able to feel pain. Then a ghostly hand caught mine.

"Don't, Cori," said a voice. "You can't."

I pulled my hand free, wheeling to face the stranger who'd grabbed me. A woman with long curly hair—a dragon shifter, judging by the ashy cast to her otherwise transparent eyes.

"Who are you?" I asked. "How do you know my name?"

Her hand dropped to her side. Something in her features was... familiar...

"No." My throat closed up, a knot twisting in my chest. "No, you can't be…"

A man floated to her side, a man with curly hair which would have been auburn had he not been as transparent as the woman at his side, the woman with her face shaped exactly like my sister's…

My *parents.*

I was right. Everyone who'd died in the war had been trapped behind the barrier, unable to shift, unable to move on.

"I'm sorry," I whispered. "I'm sorry you're trapped in here."

My parents' arms felt almost solid as they pulled me into a hug between them. None of us spoke for a long moment. Tears stung my eyes, unable to fall. I'd never believed I'd ever see my parents again in any form, yet for this, I'd paid with everything else I had left in the world.

"Is Ember here?" I choked out. "God… she *possessed* her and stole her body. Ignessa did."

"Oh, Cori," Mum said softly. "Ember isn't here. I saw her, though, the first time you came in here. She told me how she returned you to life…"

"And woke Ignessa." Bitter pain seared me from the inside. "It's not her fault. If anything it's mine. Ignessa tricked us, and I thought the volcano could hold her. And now she—Ember—"

"Cori, your sister isn't dead," said Dad. "She cannot move on as long as she exists in this realm. There's no afterlife here."

She's still a ghost. But hope bloomed in my chest, extinguished in an instant. Ember and I were both trapped in different ways, on opposite sides of the barrier. Close, yet never so far apart. And my friends would be waiting in London for Ember to return, with no idea the person controlling her body wasn't my sister at all. My body trembled with sobs, and my parents embraced me, offering comfort in the only way they could.

"Has it always been this way?" I whispered. "I saw visions… I saw the gods breaking free from the void. Were you here when it happened?"

"Yes," said my mother. "We were among the last to leave the city. Most of the other dragons had relocated to Scotland by that point. We left your sister and yourself in the hands of Madison and Agnes and stayed here to fight against Lorne, but…"

But they'd died at Ignessa's hands. *She'd* killed my parents—not Lorne, and not the Orion League. Not only that, she'd condemned them to an eternity of suffering.

"Ignessa was here, too," I murmured. "She used to be trapped in the void."

Mum inclined her head. "She woke when the war started, but we later found out she'd been speaking to Lorne for some time, through the Moonbeam. Note that his clan mostly survived the war, but the others died. The others, who were descended from Ancients other than Ignessa herself, perished in the fight."

Ignessa's influence explained so many things about Lorne's reckless destruction of the dragon clans. He hadn't killed at random, but he'd targeted the descendants of the other Ancients, so only Ignessa's people were left. Any who challenged her rule joined her in death.

"Our family is directly descended from Ignessa's

bloodline," said Dad. "I imagine it gave her much displeasure to have to kill us when we refused to concede to her rule."

"I should have known you guys gave her hell," I said, with a shaky smile.

"We did," said Mum. "She tried to use the Moonbeam to escape this realm, but Lorne thwarted her plans by taking it with him back to Earth."

"I thought so," I said. "If she used the Moonbeam to control her armies, she didn't have to kill you. You shouldn't have died."

"Don't mourn for us," he said. "We have had a long time to think about our decision to fight her, and we have no regrets."

"Not even that you didn't get to see me grow up?" I blinked tears from my eyes. "I understand why you had to oppose her. Madison died for the same cause, thanks to Lorne and the Orion League. Sometimes it feels like as soon as we beat one enemy, another one appears, and it's worse."

"There are always people like her," said Dad. "She found it easy to find supporters. Mages desperate to hold onto their power. Humans, steeped in hate and looking for a target."

Despair choked me. "Is there nobody else who might stand a chance of overpowering her? It seems wrong that one goddess should be able to do so much damage."

"The Ancients who opposed her have long since disappeared into the void," said Mum.

"Wish I could send her to join them," I muttered. "I should have known she'd get *something* out of me remaking the Moonbeam. Since her body is gone, she wanted another one."

"Don't blame yourself, Cori," said Dad softly. "Not ever."

"That Moonbeam is the reason I never got to know you," I said. "It took Ember from me, and yet I still thought it might save us anyway. And now I'm *dead.*"

"You aren't dead, Cori," Mum said. "Your soul is trapped on this side, but Cori… your body is alive."

I'm alive? I sure didn't feel it. I'd assumed I'd fallen into the lava and drowned. Right?

"When this realm collapses into the void, we will fall along with it," said Dad. "You can see it already."

I followed his gaze. The wall of grey faded at the edges, and beyond, a crack lay in the wall. Ghosts floated out, their quiet moans disappearing into the ether.

"But—the other dragons." I looked back at my parents in horror. "You mean the city is going to collapse, too?"

"Yes," said Ember's voice. "Cori, we have to leave."

I spun on the spot. My sister floated towards me, her eyes fixed on our parents' ghosts.

"It's you," I whispered. "What are you doing here?"

She dragged her gaze away from Mum and Dad. "It's my turn to save you, Cori."

"You're not…"

Her hand reached out to me, a fierce fire burning in her eyes. Her hand locked around mine. The void answered, threatening to pull her in along with me.

And then my parents blocked the void, hand in hand, pushing Ember and me towards the barrier. I gripped her hand, hard, pulling her along with me. My parents' voices faded into the background.

"You knew," I whispered to Ember. "You knew they were trapped, didn't you?"

Ember glanced at me, her eyes shining. "Yes, but I didn't want to distract you, Cori. I'm sorry. You have to live. One of us has to."

Tears blurred my eyes. "Ember, please don't be gone. I can't deal with it if you are."

"Cori…" And then we were out of the void, and she was embracing me as solidly as a real person. "I'm okay."

"No, you're not," I sobbed, holding tightly to her. "She played all of us for fools, and you paid the price."

"I knew, Cori," she said. "I knew there'd be a catch, and I didn't want to return to my body if it meant giving her a second shot at life. I'm not worth that."

"You are," I mumbled." It should have been me who made the sacrifice, not you. It's my turn. The little sibling is supposed to get a shot at playing the hero someday, right?"

She let out a half-laugh, half-sob. Tears were pouring down her own face, unchecked.

I refused to believe she was gone for good.

"I love you, Ember," I said. "So does Astor. He almost did something reckless for your sake, too."

"Sounds like him." She blinked hard. "Cori, I won't be able to stay forever. As a ghost, I have a time limit. Either I stay here and end up being drawn into the void, or I go back to the spirit realm on Earth and pass through Death's gates. I don't know how long I have left, but—"

"No," I said. "You're alive. You're just… taking a back seat for a bit."

Ember shook her head. "Cori, it's not worth sacrificing

your own life to save mine, not when we're still in with a chance of stopping her."

I shook my head right back at her. "She already won. She has London's mages *and* the other dragon shifters. If I have to go out in a blaze of glory, so be it."

"When have you ever let the odds stop you before?" Ember said. "Cori, I love you. Let me go."

Tears squeezed from my eyes. "I'm so sorry, Ember. If I destroy her, I'll destroy you, too."

It was a cruel trick of Ignessa's to force me to contemplate sacrificing my sister to save everyone else. If I destroyed the Moonbeam again, she'd be separated from Ember's body, but there had to be a way to finish her off for good. There *had* to.

"Don't worry about me," said Ember. "This realm is on the brink of collapse. There's a reason nobody has lived here in a long time. If Azalea were in control of her own thoughts, she'd have realised that quickly. I can't make her hear me, but maybe you can."

"You think she'll listen to me?" My ghostly hands clenched. "If I go into the city, Ignessa will spot me and she might hurt the others."

"She won't," said Ember. "If her possessing me did one good thing, it stopped her creeping around you as a ghost. She's tied to my body now, so she's limited by what she can see through my eyes."

"Wait, she is?"

"We're not out of the fight yet, Cori." Ember released me, and the void cleared from my vision. Below, my body lay on the path outside the lava pool, sprawled on the precipice near the edge.

I slid back into my body. "Thanks, Ember," I whispered.

"I'll be right beside you," said my sister.

I won't let you go this time. Rising to my feet on the edge of the pit, I found the Moonbeam shard and stepped through it.

I emerged from the portal into the dragon shifters' village. Wrong place. Another step brought me into the dungeon of the mages' guild in Edinburgh. Someone swore, and there was a crashing noise as the mirror fell away behind me.

"Shit!" said a voice. "I didn't know someone would jump out of it."

I squinted into the darkness surrounding me. "Are you *stealing* the mirror?"

"Wait, Cori?" said Morgan. "It *is* Cori, right?"

"Yes." Why he was stealing the mirror, I probably didn't want to know. "Get your sister. I think I'm going to need the Gatekeeper's help. Come through the spirit line —if you can bring the mirror with you, that would be great. Also, don't go into the dragons' city if you want to live."

I hopped back through the mirror before he could reply. This time, I landed in the living room of our house, in front of Will and Kit.

"Damn," said Will. "She's alive."

"Speak for yourself." I caught my balance, my nerves jangling. "Is she here? Ignessa?"

"No, but she's possessing your sister," said Will. "I thought she killed you."

"She pushed me into a volcano. It didn't quite work out for her." Crap. She was *here,* in London? "How long did I miss?"

"A couple of hours," said Will. "I got around half the neighbourhood with the fireproof spell before *she* appeared. It was easy to figure out it wasn't really Ember, but I'm not sure everyone else believed me."

I swore. "Don't tell me Astor went to find her."

"Okay, I won't tell you," said Will. "This place has gone to hell since you left. The mages are neck-deep in crap and flooded with complaints. Nobody knows they're in Ignessa's pocket, so everyone assumes they're just being incompetent at dealing with the problem. The shifters are rioting, and there are fires all over the place—"

"Whoa, slow down," I said. "How'd she get into this realm?"

Kit's brow wrinkled. "I don't know. The mirrors?"

"One mirror is still in the village," I said. "The other should be on its way here. She must have used a Moonbeam piece—and if that's the case, it's lucky she didn't crash-land into our house."

"No shit," said Will. "I hope you have a plan, because I'd have got the hell out of here if it wasn't a dick move to leave my friends to burn."

"Now's not a good time to tell you the dragon shifters' realm is collapsing, then?" I said. "I have to help the others leave, but this place isn't much safer."

"And they're still on Ignessa's side," added Kit.

Dammit. There must be a way to even the odds. I turned around, frustration burning inside me. I'd intended to speak to the necromancers… and to do that, I didn't need to leave the house.

"*Now* what are you doing?" Will said as I ran into the hall, hurtling upstairs to my room. Miracle of miracles, nobody had stolen my necromancy candles.

I scooped them into my arms and ran back downstairs, dropping the candles all over the carpet. "Just testing a theory."

"By summoning ghosts in my house." Will stepped away from the candles.

"It's hardly worse than what's out there." I arranged the candles into a rough circle. "I summon you, Owen of the necromancer guild."

The necromancer's assistant appeared in a puff of smoke. "What the devil?"

"Sorry," I said. "I need your advice."

Owen sighed. "Fine, ask away. I take it the dragon who's causing such havoc outside isn't one of your allies?"

"She's my sister," I said, "and she's possessed by a ghost. I need to perform an exorcism."

You wouldn't think a ghost could turn pale, but Owen proved me wrong. "If she has formed a voluntary bond with this… ghost, there's no undoing it."

I'd bet that was what Lord Sutherland had done. Voluntarily bound himself to one of the gods.

"It wasn't voluntary," I said. "That binding spell I needed the ingredients for didn't just fix the Moonbeam, it bound the fire goddess's soul to Ember's body, too."

He shook his head. "No. It's not possible."

"It is," I said, irked. "The Moonbeam literally brought me back from Death. What did you ask if I was? A spirit binding, or… or a shade?"

"A shade is the soul of a dead person bound to a living body," he said, his voice tremulous. "Any person who died and returned to life would technically fall into the same category—"

"Never mind that," I said. "How do you kill a shade? I mean, re-kill? Just pretend we're talking about a human here."

"Even ordinary shades are more than human," he said. "Binding one's soul to a new body strengthens the spirit, if done right. If done wrong, however, it can lead to the death of both. The proper way to do it involves a ritual—"

"Please, I don't want to know all the details, I just want to know how to get Ignessa out of my sister's body," I said. "She *is* a dead person bound to a living body. Can she be banished?"

"No, but if the connection were broken… if the source of their bond was broken, then there might be a chance."

"Breaking the Moonbeam caused this to begin with."

"Devious," he muttered. "If one soul is stronger than the other, it results in an unbalanced force which eventually consumes the weaker soul."

That sounded unpleasant. "You mean to say my sister is going to disappear?"

"If that goddess remains in control of her body? Very likely. Her soul won't be able to stay attached for long. It's a miracle it still exists at all."

Because it's bound to the Moonbeam. They both are. If I broke it again, Ember might be destroyed for good.

Ignessa had backed me into a corner.

"It is possible to remove a soul from a body," said Owen. "But only for a necromancer, and only if the soul is weaker than the summoner's."

"Meaning me?" If I *summoned* Ignessa... no. She wouldn't stay caged in a summoning circle. But Ember... "I have to try something. Uh, I banish you."

"Hang on—" Owen disappeared mid-sentence, vanishing into the grey.

"I summon—"

Becks meowed a warning, pelting into the room in cat form. A moment later, a rumbling growl echoed over the rooftops, and my heart contracted.

My sister was here.

No. Not her. My enemy, wearing the face of the person I loved most in the world.

I ran to the front door and pushed it open. Plumes of fire lit up the sky, streaking over the rooftops as three reptilian shapes circled one another—Zeph and Thorn, facing off against Ember, and preventing her from reaching the humans below. Jets of fire singed the roofs, and wards shimmered to life on the houses of Magic Avenue.

"Shut the door!" Will bellowed from behind me. "I have faith in those fireproof runes, but don't give Her Fiery Highness another reason to take a shot at us."

The wards are working. Because she wasn't using her goddess's powers—just Ember's.

Maybe she couldn't. If she unleashed her goddess's fire, Ember would burn alive like Lorne had. She was holding back, out of necessity, because it was the only way to hang onto a mortal body. If she lost her temper, though... I needed to set my sister free before it was too late. And that meant exorcising the goddess's spirit.

Another deafening noise came from the street's end, like two metal objects colliding. The dragons' aerial battle didn't cease, and more bolts of fire ignited the sky. Below, a large blocky shape lumbered into view. The automaton.

"Did you even find out who made that thing?" I asked Will.

"No." He stepped up behind me, his arms gleaming with spells. "But I think reinforcements showed up for a reason."

I ran towards the battling dragons, Becks on my heels. "Where's your furry friend, anyway?"

She made a meowing noise which might have meant anything from *none of your business* to *hiding in my room.*

The automaton blocked the way out the avenue, but I kept running, my claws out.

"Don't you dare break another of my toys," bellowed a female voice. "I'm trying to protect the public from that irritating reptile."

Close behind the automaton was a short female figure who walked with a slight limp, clad in black clothing and holding what appeared to be a remote control. Her head was shaved, and scars dotted her face.

"Cori?" Her eyes widened.

"Who are you?"

"I'm disappointed, love," she said. "You can't have been gone for long enough to forget an old friend."

Wait, I knew her… Giselle, Astor's friend and another former Orion League member. Since she was a human without any magical advantages who'd actually aged in the time we'd been gone, I hadn't recognised her at first.

"I take it you're responsible for *that.*" She jabbed a finger at the dragons in the sky. "You know, your sister once promised never to use that Moonbeam to cause trouble again."

"It wasn't really her fault this time."

Giselle was the person who'd stolen the Moonbeam from the Orion League after Lorne had traded it to them. She'd never trusted it, and if I told her how it had brought Ignessa into our world, she'd probably get the automaton to thwack me in the head.

"What's wrong with your sister?" Giselle hit another button and the automaton clanked past, arms swinging. "Don't look so alarmed. It's under my control. Body-guard-for-hire services."

Above, Ember roared, a tongue of fire lashing out and striking the nearby buildings.

"That's not my sister," I said. "She's possessed—and what do you mean, bodyguard-for-hire?"

"I thought she was just throwing a tantrum."

Fire burned inside me, sudden and sharp. *The Moon-beam.* Its presence stirred nearby as though my thoughts had conjured it up, steering me beneath the warring dragons and into the adjacent street.

A figure stood on a rooftop above Tottenham Court Road, visible only because of the dazzling light of the Moonbeam in her hands.

Noll.

Twenty-odd years ago, Noll, who'd once been Lorne's consort, had arrived at our house to beg for our help. We'd helped her start afresh so that her child would never know his father had been a murderous tyrant. Her son would be a teenager now, and if Noll had kept her word, he'd know nothing of the suffering the other dragon shifters had experienced. But despite all that, Ignessa had dragged the two of them into her schemes anyway.

Damn her.

I launched into flight over the rooftops, past the aerial battle and towards Noll, prepared to catch her if Ignessa compelled her to jump.

Landing on the edge, I shifted to human form. "Noll. You were willing to risk death to save your son. Don't you remember?"

Noll's hands trembled on the glowing stone. Then the Moonbeam's light spread around her, revealing the void at the heart of the volcano.

22

"What the—?" I broke off. "You're *opening* the volcano? Ignessa, have you lost your mind?"

Noll stood still, her expression glazed, distant. Behind her, the void murmured with the voices of a thousand trapped souls.

What the hell is Ignessa playing at?

Unless... unless she *wanted* to open the void.

Noll finally spoke, her voice quiet. "If the dragon shifters' realm falls, then London will fall along with it."

"You won't survive either, you know," I said. "Not even you. I thought you wanted to rule."

"Not like this," Noll murmured. "There is no future, only fire."

"You're creeping me out, Ignessa," I said. "You got what you wanted. London is yours for the taking, and you get to fly around breathing fire at your enemies like you did when you were still alive. Isn't that enough?"

Ignessa didn't respond, but Ember's roar grew louder.

Flames danced above the rooftops, but despite their brightness, a sense of abject weariness radiated from Ember's flight.

The goddess had regained some of her strength, but not all of it. Bound to a mortal form, with her real body gone and her power sapped away... it would never be enough for her. She'd use my sister as her vessel until her body gave out and turned to ash, but not even a dragon shifter could sustain a goddess's magic forever. She would never be alive as she'd been before.

The void would claim the dragons' city, leaving her stranded on Earth, a realm with no place for a being such as herself. So she planned to burn it. The void would sweep into London, dragging in everyone, living or dead. Her final *fuck you* to the universe.

"You forgot one thing," said a voice—*Ember's* voice. "That Moonbeam is still a portal."

The void disappeared. Will and Kit burst out of the light, knocking the Moonbeam out of Noll's hands. The bright light reflected in the windows as it tumbled into the street, bouncing on the tarmac. I readied myself to fly down and grab it, but Zeph got there first, soaring to the earth and picking it up. He flew up to land beside me as I pulled a limp Noll away from the edge of the rooftop.

Zeph held out the Moonbeam, turning human. "How do I turn this thing off?"

Noll lunged at him. I grabbed her arm, pulling her back. "Please. I don't want to hurt you, but a lot of people will die if I let you open that portal."

Will raised a hand. The light of a knockout spell went off, and Noll crumpled into a heap. "Better get her out of harm's way."

"Who the bloody hell was that woman with the automaton, anyway?" said Zeph.

"Astor's friend," I said.

"He has friends?" Zeph held up the glowing Moonbeam. "Want me to break this?"

"Not before I get the other dragons out of the city." I turned to Will and Kit. "Did you leave any more Moonbeam pieces in the house? Ignessa just tried open the void in the middle of London."

"She did what?" Will's eyes widened. "You mean we might have fallen into the volcano?"

Ember flew above our heads, shooting a tongue of fire into the nearest building. I took a step back. "Breaking the Moonbeam won't stop it from opening the void. Ignessa's in full-on self-destruct mode."

And if I used my life force to break the Moonbeam the same way Ember had, she'd take over *my* body next. One way or another, London would burn.

My spirit sight clicked on like a light switch, showing grey smoke curling around the rooftops. Dozens of spirits floated in mid-air Moonbeam, invisible to everyone but me. If they went through the portal, *they'd* be trapped in the void, too. Like Lorne's spirit device, but worse, because there would be no reprieve for anyone trapped on the other side. Not until the void opened and sucked everyone living inside it to join the dead.

Ember's body blazed past and rammed into Zeph, tackling him off the roof. I yelled, but he shifted in mid-flight, the Moonbeam slipping from his claws as he grappled with my sister.

Will shifted into gargoyle form and lifted Kit and Noll out of harm's way, leaving me alone on the rooftop.

Shifting into dragon form, I flew over the two grappling dragon shifters, my sister's fire tingling against my scales. *Ember's* fire, not Ignessa's. Ignessa had given up her goddess's fire in the effort to possess my sister. That had weakened her, and I wouldn't get a better chance to bring her down.

Zeph tackled her again in mid-air, and the Moonbeam tumbled into free-fall. I flew to catch it, light blooming in my claws. I landed on my feet, turning human, grasping the burning vortex of fire in both hands.

With the Moonbeam, I could bring every shifter in London under my control. I could open the void and set my parents free. What I couldn't do was remove Ignessa from my sister's body... unless it broke.

Ember and Zeph fought, locked in combat in mid-air. The Moonbeam burned in my hands, and I directed my own fire into it, the same way I had when I'd broken it. White fire engulfed the void, burning as bright as a star, yet it didn't break.

One dragon shifter isn't enough. In order to break the Moonbeam for a second time, someone might have to sacrifice their life the same way Ember had. Unless...

Zeph turned mid-fight, his eyes locking with mine as though sensing my thoughts. *Don't you dare,* his eyes seemed to say.

Ember's claws ripped into his throat.

"NO!"

Zeph fell out of the air, tumbling towards the earth.

A smaller reptilian shape flew below, and Thorn caught Zeph on his back as he collapsed into human form. *Damn. I have to get to him before—*

Pain speared my back, and the Moonbeam slipped

from my hands. Crimson bloomed across my chest as the spear point of a knife pierced me through the middle.

I tilted my head back. Noll's hand gripped the knife, her expression distant, detached.

"Damn," I growled. "You know, I never trusted my sister's decision to help you all those years ago, but I didn't expect the backstabbing to be literal."

She didn't hear me. Ignessa alone deserved my fury, but my lifeblood poured from my chest. Thorn cried out, landing beside me with Zeph's limp body sprawled across his back.

Owen's words echoed through my mind. What had he called me? A shade, someone who'd survived death, and returned. If I'd done it once, I was damned if I died today.

I lurched over to Zeph and Thorn, agony spiking through my body. My hands found Zephs, and I willed the Moonbeam's light to draw us in.

We vanished into the portal, landing in a heap on the living room floor.

Kit exclaimed, jumping to his feet. "Cori!"

I groaned. "Ow."

"She's been stabbed," said Will. "Both of them."

He grabbed a healing spell and applied it to Zeph's throat, while Kit's hands lit up with green energy.

"Bloody hell," said Will, as Kit moved his glowing hands over my bleeding chest. "Did you see where Thorn went? He flew through the portal, too."

"Thought he was here." The dull pain in my chest and back disappeared as Kit's healing magic sealed my wound. "Must have gone back to fight Ember. Zeph, don't you dare die."

He groaned, his eyes opening. Kit's healing magic

spread to his throat and chest, the wounds closing. "Not going to die."

"You'd better not." I turned to Will. "Did you know Giselle's the one controlling that robot?"

"Astor's friend?" Will arched a brow. "Next you'll tell me he's taken up tap dancing."

The light from Kit's hands faded. "You should be fine, but don't do anything too strenuous."

"Like fighting a war?" I sprang to my feet. "Guys, the other realm is on the brink of collapse. We need to get the other dragon shifters out, and then shove Ignessa into the void the instant the realm collapses. Without dying ourselves. And preferably without killing my sister, too."

Zeph's jaw hit the floor. "You want to help her allies?"

"You know they're not in control of their own minds." I looked pleadingly at Will. "The other dragon shifters are Ignessa's hostages. I'll try to get them to the mirror in the village, but I think I'll have to bring them here where I can keep an eye on them and stop Ignessa from using them as bait."

"Oh, for god's sake." Will grabbed the Moonbeam shards. "Fine, but we'll do it outside. I'm not opening the void in my living room. And don't you dare get stuck over there, Cori. We need you."

"I'll try not to." I sucked in a breath. "Guys, I don't think Ignessa wants to rule London any more. She knows she and the dragon shifters' realm are both doomed, so she wants to drag us straight into hell along with her."

"You know, everyone has bad days," Will said. "But destroying the world? No wonder the gods went extinct."

"Tell that to her, not me." I turned to Zeph. "Don't

follow me. Don't shift, either. I need you to help the dragons when I bring them through."

His jaw dropped. "You're shitting me. Cori…"

"Please," I said. "Ignessa might force them back through the mirror into the void again. I can't watch everywhere at once, but trust me when I say I have a plan. Get them into London, protect them if we can, and break the Moonbeam. Oh, and don't let my sister stab you again."

Before anyone could object, I stepped through the Moonbeam shard, and into the dragons' city.

23

I emerged from a pile of shards of stone into the city square. In the same instant, Ember's ghost appeared at my side.

"Ember," I gasped. "I thought you'd disappeared."

"Not yet." Her voice was faint. "I can't stay here for long."

"Hang in there, Ember." I turned on the spot, my spirit sight reaching out and sensing the dragon shifters huddled in the nearby buildings. Not just dragon shifters. I spotted movement in one of the windows and glimpsed several cloaked figures. "There are humans in there."

"They're mages," Ember replied. "I saw the other dragon shifters bring them in. I think they're from Edinburgh."

"Damn her," I said. "I guess she must have been afraid they'd get in her way and didn't have time to brainwash them like she did to the ones in London."

Thanks to the time difference between this realm and ours, she might well have been running London's mage guild for years, planning her takeover. It explained Lord Sutherland staying in power, too. Not that it absolved the mages who'd voted him in, any more than the humans who'd followed the Orion League's creed.

I turned on my spirit sight again—and found myself face to face with Ayla, the prisoner from jail.

"You again," I said. "Did you know the spell that repaired the Moonbeam would bind Ignessa's soul to my sister's body?"

"Of course not," said the ghost. "I've never seen the spell in use. You have bigger problems, Coriander. This realm is collapsing into the void."

"I know it is." I was counting on it. "How long do I have? I'm going to evacuate, and I could use a hand."

I ran towards the town hall, and the door sprang open. Dragon shifters poured out, surrounding me.

"Arrest her," Azalea ordered. "The penalty for escaping jail is death."

"I'm not the one you want to attack," I warned. "Might have escaped your attention, but this place is on the brink of collapsing into the void."

With perfect timing, a plume of fire lit up the sky above the volcano.

Azalea's mouth thinned. "This is our home."

"Even if you don't believe me about Ignessa, you have to leave." My tone turned pleading. "For your children's sakes, if nothing else."

London wouldn't be much safer, but time was running out. I'd just have to hope I had strength enough to stop the fire goddess before she could hurt the other dragons again.

"Listen to her," said Ayla. "This realm is falling apart. The dead are leaving, and soon you will all join them."

Azalea's jaw hit the floor. "Ayla?"

Whoa. The other dragons could *see* her? That must mean the spirit lines were breaking down. If the same was happening on the other side, people in London would think there was a second invasion imminent, and they wouldn't be far wrong.

Azalea turned to the others. "Get the children out first."

Thank god. They believe me. I'd worry about keeping them out of trouble *in* London later. I suspected re-breaking the Moonbeam wouldn't release Ignessa's hold on them, considering she'd managed to control them when she was little more than a spirit, but as long as I got them out of harm's way, I could deal with the rest later. At least Zeph had taken my order to stay behind to heart.

Several of the other dragon shifters ran back into their houses, too, emerging with their children in tow. Azalea ran past with her two children, herding them towards the portal and staying back to help the others. Even under Ignessa's control, their survival instincts had won out.

Not everyone, however.

"You think we'd fall for your lies?" said a male dragon shifter. "This is a trick, a scheme to steal our city."

"You can't think anyone would want to steal this place." I pointed up at the sky, which had turned bruise-grey beneath the torrent of fire spewing from the volcano.

"That's your doing, too." The dragon's hands shifted to claws. "You will regret this."

Fine, then. "Easy way or hard way. Your choice."

He lunged, and I deflected his blow with the side of my

claw. Silently thanking Zeph for making me practise grappling with him in shifted form, I sidestepped and the half-shifted dragon stumbled, off-balance, onto the Moonbeam shards.

White light spread across the ground, and the struggling dragon shifter vanished into the portal.

"You're welcome." Hoping Will and Kit were ready to handle a storm of angry dragon shifters, I left the portal and ran to the nearest house, hammering on the door. "Hey! The volcano's erupting. Azalea's ordered an evacuation!"

Some of them left without questioning, spurred by the fiery sparks in the sky. Others required more persuasion. I was in the middle of arguing with a particularly stubborn one when a flock of miniature dragons descended. For a heart-stopping instant, I thought they meant to attack, but Thorn led the way, screeching at full volume. Eyes blazing, claws splayed, he looked the epitome of the monstrous creature we'd once believed him to be.

And the other dragon shifters still believed he was carrying the virus.

That was it for the stragglers. Forgetting all about me, the dragons fled towards the portal, pursued by a swarm of dragonlings. The eggs must have hatched, and Thorn had brought them here to help us.

As a group of dragon shifters disappeared in a white flash, a human emerged in their place. Astor.

"What are you doing here?" I said. "Come to help out?"

"Wrong turning," he said. "I was trying to get—"

"To Ember? She's possessed and trying to burn London, while Giselle chases people around with a giant robot."

"That was my idea," he said. "I visited her while you were in the volcano. She dug the automaton out of one of the League's hideouts years ago and was using it as a security guard. I figured we needed firepower… not just dragonfire."

"Astor, are you sure you aren't possessed by the spirit of the mad fire goddess?" I ducked my head as another plume of fire ignited the sky, sending several sparks flying above the city. "Now you're here, I need someone to knock some sense into these dragon shifters, and you're the guy for the job."

I ran into the hall of the house where I'd seen the mages imprisoned, finding a locked door inside. I kicked out, but the door didn't budge. I prepared to shift to dragon form, and a sudden spark of lightning made my hair stand on end. The door flew off its hinges, and I found myself looking into the eyes of a group of furious mages.

I raised my hands. "Not an enemy. I'm rescuing you. This place is gonna go up in flames."

A mage stepped forward. "I am Lord Addison," he said. "Coriander, I must apologise for the appalling way you were treated at our hands."

"Apology accepted." What the hell. Life was too short to hold grudges. Very short, at this rate. "If you want to do me a favour, get through that portal and get as many people through there as possible. My friend's living room is on the other side. Oh, and don't arrest anyone. Including my friends."

"Very well." He beckoned to the others to follow him out of the room. Astor and I directed them towards the portal, checking for stragglers.

"They're not under her control?" he asked.

"No. Guess she just wanted them out of the way." Then again, she was only capable of directly controlling dragons or other shifters. With London's mages, she must have used a different method, but that was a question for later.

I ran around, kicking doors in and directing the dragonlings to chase people towards the portal, but several houses remained closed.

"Get *out!*" I screamed, and the dragonlings set up a chorus of shrieks. The square was full of panicking dragon shifters. "We need a bloody fire alarm." I shifted to dragon form and roared, but the sound was lost under the tremors rippling from the volcano. *That's no normal eruption.* Fog masked the whole mountain, the same colour as Death.

The void was coming here. We had less time than I'd thought.

Astor shot the nearest set of closed doors a disgruntled look. "If they want to stay here, we should let them."

I turned human again. "Carry them if you have to. Otherwise, we'll rain down fire on your head, is that clear?"

I didn't wait for an answer. I circled the town and caught up to the portals. Above them, the white light turned to grey smoke. Wait...

"Stop!" I held up a hand. "Hey. Cut that out. We're not finished yet."

A spirit rose from the shattered glass, as solid as a living person, and crashed into me. I reeled backwards, my blood chilling as more ghosts appeared in a flood of greyness. *Crap.* I *wanted* the ghosts to be free from the void, but I needed to help the living before I could even begin to think about the dead.

"Cori!" My mother's ghost appeared, shielding me from the oncoming horde of spirits. My dad appeared at her side, barring the other ghosts from touching me. "Cori—run. Now."

Astor cut me a baffled look. "Who are they?"

"Ghosts." If he could see them, the spirit realm was totally screwed, but there was no help for it. "The portal—"

Astor held up a hand, revealing another slither of Moonbeam shard. "This one's okay."

He dropped the stone, and I willed the portal to open back to London. That was it for the remaining dragon shifters—they wanted out. Pursued by the dragonlings, they pelted into the glowing white. My parents held the ghosts back, keeping the path clear. Once the last of the dragon shifters escaped through the portal, I grabbed Astor's arm and followed.

We landed in the middle of a road in central London. I spotted dragons running left and right while Thorn and his new friends circled above, safely out of range of the portals. A relieved sigh escaped. *We made it out.*

"There you are," said Zeph, who stood beside the portal. "I was about to go after you."

"You wouldn't have got far." Astor stepped to my side. "Everyone's out."

"What's this plan of yours?" said Zeph.

"Get the fire goddess away from Ember and shove her into the void." I looked up at the sky, but the confusion of dragon shifters and dragonlings in flight made it impossible to spot my sister. "I realise it's a long shot."

Giselle's automaton lumbered around the corner, and the woman herself followed. "Cori, did you know your sister's a ghost?"

"Yes. Wait, since when do you have the spirit sight?"

"Since a week ago."

Humans were waking up with magical powers, the magical forces of authority were losing their grip... oh, yeah, and there was a giant robot on the loose. Nothing out of the ordinary here.

A clawed beast flew out of the portal at Astor's feet, releasing a horrible screech.

"What the bloody hell is that thing?" asked Giselle.

"A monster." I shifted my claws and slashed at the fury's neck, sending the beast into the path of the automaton's flailing hands. "Where did you see Ember? I need to find her."

"Over there." Giselle pointed, and my blood turned to water. The air above Hyde Park shone with rippling currents of energy, and within, a red shape moved. *Ember.* Dammit, what was Ignessa doing? Trying to set the spirit lines ablaze?

I launched into dragon form, ignoring Giselle's exclamation of alarm, and took flight. A blast of fire ripped through the sky, striking a group of furies and knocking them out of the air. Looked like Ignessa didn't want the monsters here any more than the rest of us did.

Wait—that wasn't dragonfire. On the streets below, the mages fought the furies with lightning and fire, ice and air, water and telekinesis. Like the dragon shifters escaping their city, some instincts won out over brainwashing. I flew on, over the park—and skidded to a halt in mid-air at the sight of a bright glow somewhere below. The mirror, held by two human-sized figures.

I descended, landing beside a group of people hurrying out of the spirit line. Ilsa led the way, with Agnes and Everett behind her. The two older witch-mages held the mirror between them, while a young woman ran past, her long dark hair tied back and a long sword gleaming with blue light.

"Sorry we took so long," said Ilsa. "Took a wrong turning. This is Ivy." She indicated the woman with the sword.

"I think I met your sister once," said Ivy. "Granted, she was a dragon at the time, so we didn't get to have a proper chat."

"Nice to meet you," I said. "Uh… what are you doing here?"

"Thought you could use a hand." Ilsa pointed to the mirror, which Agnes and Everett had placed on the ground. "My brother said you needed this."

"I did, but I didn't account for the monsters." I looked up at the sky, but the shape I'd taken for Ember was a giant red-and-black striped fury. "Where are those things coming from?"

"Head's up!" Ivy leapt into the air, her sword aloft. An instant later, a severed head landed at my feet.

I took a step back. "Ilsa, where do you find these people?"

"I didn't find her. Ivy usually just appears where there's trouble."

Ivy flicked blood off her sword and ran after another fury. I, meanwhile, ran towards the mirror.

Agnes turned to me. "Cori, I'm sorry the spell didn't

work out. I should have known the goddess had her own agenda."

"Yeah, she did." To say the least. "Agnes, do you have any last-minute tricks?"

"This." She handed me the gleaming orange pendant. "I rather think you need it more than I do."

My hand clenched around the talisman. "Cheers."

A fury shot out of the mirror, straight into Ivy's sword. Ilsa stepped out of range of the spray of blood, and a ghost appeared in the mirror's light.

Ilsa whipped a book out of her pocket—the book with the raven on the cover I'd seen her holding at the mages' headquarters. "I banish you beyond Death's gates."

The book glowed and the spirit vanished in a bright flash of light. Whoa. "What *is* that?"

"My talisman," said Ilsa. "My Gatekeeper's talisman. I can open Death's gates, but whatever's behind that mirror isn't Death."

"No. It's the void that used to be inside the volcano in the dragons' realm before it broke open." I dragged my gaze from the glowing light on her forehead. "My sister is trapped in the spirit realm. Ember. I summon you, Ember..."

I didn't expect it to work, and I jumped when Ember appeared between Ilsa and me. Her eyes flew wide at the sight of the Gatekeeper. "Do I know you?"

"I'm Ilsa." She looked between us, her brow furrowed. "Why are you outside your body? You aren't dead."

"Ignessa is possessing her body," I said. "The only way to make the fire goddess let her go is to destroy the talisman binding their souls. Then I'll shove Ignessa into the void and close it. But we need help..."

"You mean, destroy that?" Ilsa pointed at a spot above the road.

The Moonbeam hung suspended in the air. Above, a spirit line rippled with energy, bolts radiating out from Hyde Park. The void lay wide open, and spirits floated towards it into the grey.

No. It's too late.

Crackling power surrounding the hovering stone. A gasp caught in my throat. Ignessa had given everything to the Moonbeam, and now it'd taken on a life of its own.

"Cori…" whispered Ember.

"Don't you dare disappear," I said fiercely. "Don't."

"Hold on." Ilsa lowered her book. "The *goddess* is keeping her spirit from returning to her body? I'm sorry, Cori—there's a limit to what I can do even with my Gatekeeper's powers. Most people can't survive the separation."

"Shit." I looked up at the floating form of the Moonbeam. "Ilsa, it's not the Gatekeeper's powers I need. The mirror can absorb dragonfire, and so can the Moonbeam shards. We need to break that thing, and I can't do it alone. Ember?"

"Yes?" Her ghost turned to me, her eyes round.

"Can you tell the other dragon shifters I need their fire?" I asked. "Ilsa, you should stay by the mirror with Agnes and Everett… and I'd advise you to duck."

A roar sounded. Ember's dragon form appeared overhead, wings spread wide, fire scorching the rooftops.

"I can tell them," said Ember's ghost, "but I don't think we need any more fire right now."

I looked at her. "Do you trust me?"

"What kind of question is that?" she said. "Of course I do."

Right. "Okay. I'm sorry about this, but it's going to hurt. A lot. I hit hard."

I shifted into dragon form, took flight, and crashed headlong into Ignessa. Claws and teeth tore at one another as my sister and I grappled in mid-air. Ember was bigger than me, but I had the advantage of more recent practise at shifting than Ignessa. She hadn't turned into dragon form since she'd had a body and had spent too long in the spirit realm to be effective at controlling a dragon shifter.

Not to mention I'd been trained by the best.

I batted her on the side of the head, grabbed her horns and pulled her head down, stopping her from sinking her teeth into my neck. I dug in my claws, steering her downwards, using the wind currents to help. We crashed into one of the already wrecked buildings with a bone-shaking thud.

I heard Ember's voice in the spirit realm. "You just wanted the chance to beat me in a fight, didn't you?"

Maybe a little. A growl slipped between my teeth at the sight of *her,* hovering above Ember's body. Controlling her.

"There's a reason I picked her over you." Ignessa's voice whispered. "You're always going to be second best, Cori."

"*That's* the best you've got?" I said, surprised to hear my human voice speak despite my dragon form. I'd briefly detached, leaving my instincts at the wheel. "You don't get it, do you? Ember and I aren't in a competition. We love one another. The only bond you have is with the

Moonbeam, and for all its power, it's just a shiny rock that can't love you back. It's not even loyal, considering I managed to use it against you."

An enraged shriek escaped the fire goddess, and I returned to my body in time for Ember to unleash her next attack. Fire bathed me all over, more of a relaxing shower than a terrifying torrent. I let the flames wash over my body—and a second blast of flames shot past, aimed at the people on the street below.

"Nobody move!" shouted Agnes's voice above the clamour. She marched forwards, holding the mirror aloft. Ember's fire crashed into the glass, which gleamed as it absorbed the flames.

Time to up my game before the goddess realised my plan.

I flew down in front of the Moonbeam, goading her to follow me. Her flames crashed into the glowing orb, but if anything, the light grew brighter. I needed more firepower.

A bolt of fire shot from the Moonbeam, hitting the mirror dead-on. The glass glowed but didn't break. Agnes staggered, holding the mirror aloft, and Ilsa ran to help her out.

I shifted to human form, landing alongside them. "It's not enough. Can you get all the Moonbeam shards you can over here? I think my friends still have a couple…"

I spotted Zeph helping several young dragon shifters shelter from the Moonbeam, while Astor and Giselle cut down furies alongside the automaton. When one of the mages set his sights on Agnes and the others, I recognised the glint in his eyes that marked him as one of Ignessa's pawns.

I moved to block his path. "Hey. What are you doing?"

"You." His hands crackled with lightning. "You're a wanted criminal, Coriander."

"Now really isn't the time." Static made my hair stand on end. "Word of advice? Get out of here."

Ilsa hit him over the head with her Gatekeeper's book and he crumpled into a heap. "He's with Ignessa?" she said.

"I'm not sure how she's controlling him, but I can guess." I grabbed the semi-conscious mage and pushed up his sleeve, revealing a curling symbol etched in the ink of a tattoo pen. "I knew it. One of those bloody marks." It looked a little like the one on Ilsa's forehead, come to think of it.

"He bound his soul to her?" Ilsa's eyes widened. "Cori —I'd drop him."

Fire singed my arms and I let him fall from my grip. At the same time, his body dissolved into ashes. "Guess that's what happens when you disappoint a goddess."

"Cori, that mark was an Invocation."

"A what?"

"Her name," she said. "The goddess's true name, in the Ancients' own language. No human can speak a god's true name without suffering side effects. She must have really meant business."

I frowned, seeing the glimmer of a mark on her own forehead. "Okay, I need to break the Moonbeam first, and to do that, I need all the shards in one place. Can you tell everyone you see?"

I ran among the others, repeating the instruction. Zeph took my place after handing me one of the shards, and I spotted Will, Kit, Becks and Bracken, too, carrying their own shards towards Agnes and the mirror.

A wave of fire seared the air, and I shifted, using my dragon form to shield the humans below. Ember descended in a furious swoop, battered from our fight but still strong, still intact.

"What are you scheming?" Ignessa hissed. "You cannot draw me into the void without condemning your sister along with me."

I know. That's not my plan.

"The void deserves better than your miserable soul, Ignessa."

Ignessa roared, unleashing a tongue of flame. I grinned, flipped over in the air, and held up the Moonbeam shard.

The flames disappeared into the piece of stone, shot out of the mirror, and crashed right into the Moonbeam. The wave of fire disappeared into the void, but I kept flying, blocking every wave of fire with the shard of stone in my hand. Whenever the flames hit the piece of stone, they emerged from one of the other shards below— reflected back at the Moonbeam. Adding to the raging fire building inside it.

Ignessa's roar rumbled from Ember's throat, and Zeph held up his own shard, catching her next attack. Below, the other dragon shifters flew in circles, but wherever their flames went, someone appeared with a shard of glass. Astor, Will, Kit, Becks... all my friends held their own shards of Moonbeam, absorbing the dragons' fire and sending it right back at the Moonbeam.

Not just them. Thorn led the dragonlings in a group, breathing small jets of fire at every Moonbeam shard he could find. The flames entered one portal and emerged from the next, trapped in a whirlwind of fire. *We must be close to the limit by now.*

I shifted to human form, landing on a nearby roof. Then I shouted up at Ember, "You can't kill me with dragonfire, Ignessa. You weakened yourself when you took my sister hostage."

Ignessa gave another furious roar, and fire burst across my vision, crashing into the last Moonbeam shard in my hand. The shard crumbled to ashes, and light bloomed across my vision.

The Moonbeam exploded for the second time, the shards ricocheting in all directions, and Ignessa gave a mad, desperate laugh.

The goddess flew back out of Ember's body, her ghostly eyes glowing with heat. Ember turned to human form, and her body fell in slow motion, tumbling towards the earth—

And then Astor was there, arms outstretched, ready to catch her. I breathed out, but there was no time to see if her spirit had made it back to join her body. I had to finish off the goddess.

Rather than shifting into dragon form, I floated out of my body and tackled Ignessa's ghostly form. "You won't take my sister again. You *won't.*"

Ghostly hands grasped Ignessa from behind, helping me push her towards the Moonbeam's remains. Above the broken shards, the void gaped, shrinking inch by inch.

Then Ilsa was there, the Gatekeeper's book open in her hands. Behind her lay a set of gates, stretching across the horizon. *The gates of Death.* The ghosts were already heading that way, drawn towards the world beyond death.

A place where they would be free from the void's captivity, forever.

Ignessa broke from my grip with a roar of fury, her spirit blazing with light. "I will not be beaten!"

A wave of spirits descended on her, pushing her towards the shrinking void above the portal. I surged along with them, pushing everything I had into the remains of the Moonbeam, willing the portal to draw her in.

The last remnants of power in the Moonbeam shards engulfed the fire goddess. The light winked out, the void disappearing from sight, along with Ignessa.

She's gone.

The ghosts flowed towards the gates, and I blinked back into my body, trembling on the rooftop, which shook with the weight of a second dragon.

A moment later, I felt familiar arms close around me and leaned back into my sister's embrace, my eyes on the horde of fleeing spirits. Two of them paused, looked back, waved... and were gone.

Ember and I watched the gates close, carrying the ghosts of our parents into the afterlife.

24

Ashes rained from the sky around Ember and me, falling like rain or tears. I wrenched my gaze away from the place where the gates had been open, marvelling at how *real* she was. "You made it back to your body."

She squeezed me tightly. "Cori, I owe it all to you. You saved us."

My parents were gone. My sister was back.

The realm of the dragons was no more.

It hurt to breathe. I held onto my sister like she was the only thing anchoring me to existence. Tears fell down my face, and hers, too.

Below, dragons, dragonlings and humans stood and watched the ashes rain down. The remains of the Moonbeam littered the road like frozen pieces of sky.

"We'd better go and join them."

My sister and I shifted back into dragon form, flying to land beside the others. Zeph dropped his shard of

Moonbeam stone—now grey and dull, powerless. "I'm guessing we need to call off the evacuation?"

"I guess so." I hadn't thought that far ahead. Hadn't dared hope for anything other than survival.

He held out his arms. "Way to go, Cori."

I let his warm embrace envelop me. "Hey, you helped, too. I couldn't have done this without it all of you."

Will and Kit were embracing, with the dragonling flying in circles around their heads. Becks had disappeared, while Giselle's automaton had clattered to a halt, half its metal plates burned to a crisp. Astor strode towards Ember and caught her arm in a protective gesture that implied if anyone got between the two of them, they'd find themselves missing a few limbs.

And the dragons? They'd have to find somewhere to stay. Where, I had no idea. We'd made a complete mess of London in the space of only a few hours. The mages assembled a few feet away, wearing expressions of confusion and anger. Ignessa's influence might have vanished, but if they'd seen Ember breathing fire all over the place, we might be in trouble.

"Is the mirror safe?" I asked Agnes. "Safe to get to the village? I think the others had better get to safety before the mages waylay them."

"I expect so." She approached the nearest group of dragon shifters. "Your village is on the other side of the mirror if you want to leave. I can't promise it's in perfect condition, but everything is where you left it."

Azalea's eyes welled with tears. "Cori... I'm sorry. I..."

"Get your kids through the mirror. I think the mages are about to start arresting people, and I'd rather you not be among them."

"C'mon," said Zeph, beckoning more of the dragons over. "Get everyone through the mirror, okay? The void has gone. The village is on the other side. You're safe."

"Once they're through, I'll go with them," said Agnes. "I left rather a mess to clean up in Edinburgh, too, as it happens."

"Speaking of messes." I glanced over at the mages, who'd formed a bemused huddle. "Some of those mages were the dragon shifters' captives, but others bound themselves to Ignessa. She used… Ilsa called it an Invocation. They have tattoo marks…"

"Oh, they didn't." Agnes shook her head. "Fools. I imagine most of the marks might have disappeared when Ignessa perished in the void, but I'll see what I can do."

"If they didn't, tell them they went on a wild night out and got matching tattoos of the fire goddess's name for the hell of it," I said. "If they don't remember being under her control, that's as good a story as any, right?"

"Do you want them to remember?" she said.

My mouth parted. "What, you can erase their memories?"

Agnes rarely employed her most dangerous magical talent. I'd only seen her use it when she'd returned mine and Ember's memories after taking them away from us as children. Oh, and the time she'd made Lord Sutherland and the mages in Edinburgh forget Ignessa's appearance. If it'd worked once, maybe it would work again.

"I can." Agnes's hands glowed. "I won't take more than a week or two… however much is necessary to remove any confusion."

She marched towards the mages, several of whom

turned in her direction. One started to speak, and then they all crumpled to the ground, unconscious.

"I'll tell them there was a war, but Ignessa scrambled their memories," she said. "It's close enough."

"Yeah." It was not a strong start to Lord Addison's tenure as Edinburgh's new head mage, but it couldn't be helped. "I could do with them forgetting about the dragon shifters altogether. And the mirror."

"My ability doesn't have quite that level of finesse," said Agnes. "If it did, I would not have stolen all your childhood memories before the age of five. It's one of my many regrets."

Ember cleared her throat, and I followed her gaze to the only remaining dragon shifter… Noll. She sat on the pavement's edge, her eyes on the road.

I moved to her side. "Where's your son?"

"She didn't find him," Noll whispered. "I sent him to a safe house before Ignessa arrived."

"One of the addresses we gave you?"

"Yes." Noll pushed to her feet and turned to Agnes. "I couldn't help overhearing. My son doesn't know Ignessa brainwashed me, but if you can take the memory from me, I'd be grateful. I tried my best to keep him away from… Lorne."

"Of course," said Agnes. "That, I can do."

"I'd better head off, too," said Ilsa. "I didn't exactly inform my boss before bringing the mirror through the spirit line. Did you want me to leave it here?"

"If it won't get you into too much trouble." I looked around for the sword-wielding woman, but she'd vanished. "Where did Ivy go?"

"I didn't think to ask," Ilsa replied.

The mages began to stir, and Agnes strode over to them.

"You were under a spell," she said. "Cori saved you. Yes, Cori, and Ember…"

———

"Heroes of London." Ember grinned at me across the living room. "I feel bad for taking the credit, but it's better than everyone knowing Ignessa used my body to set half the city on fire."

It could have been much worse, and we both knew it. Thankfully, Lord Smyth had only emerged from his retirement towards the end of the battle and hadn't seen Ignessa's rampage. He'd invited us to the mages' head-quarters for long enough to promise a hefty reward, and then let us go home.

"We'll have to put that on the next round of dragon plushies," I said. "Or T-shirts this time."

"I vote shoes. With wings," said Will. "Little dragons. Or maybe slippers."

"Assuming we can get the shop back into working order," added Ember. "People might think we're still harbouring dragonlings carrying the virus."

"Nobody knows or cares," Will said confidently. "We're free. Anonymous."

Ember snorted. "Really? After being declared heroes? Anonymity is a thing of the past."

"Ember, you made headlines after you first shifted," I pointed out. "Anyway, I thought the mages might offer us jobs again."

"Bet they're saving that until the confusion dies down,"

said Ember. "Since a large number of people saw me flying around raining fire and destruction down on the city when Ignessa was controlling my body."

"There is that," said Zeph. "I reckon they'll all be convinced it was another red dragon they saw by the end of the week."

"Where's Kit?" said Will, frowning. "He said he was coming back here with the dragonling."

"Is he staying?" Zeph asked. "I know it was kinda hard to make a decision while our lives were under threat, but that dragonling really is too big to keep in the house."

Will glanced around, his expression shadowed. There was nothing I could say to comfort him. Kit had to handle the decision on his own.

As for the rest of us? We had our home back. We had another chance to build a future. And best of all, my sister was back at my side where she belonged.

A thud in the hallway signalled the dragonling's presence, and sure enough, Kit entered the room ahead of him. He didn't look as if he'd heard us, at least, but before anyone could venture a question, Becks walked into the room in her cat form, yawning.

"Thought you left," I told her.

She transformed into her human form. "Left? Where would I go?"

"Anywhere," I said. "We're free. Ignessa is gone."

Which left us all with a big question mark over the rest of our lives.

She shrugged. "I don't know. I mean, what do you do when you've saved the world, but fifteen years have passed, and our entire lives are back to square one? Hell if I know."

"You and Bracken saved those shifters last night," I said. "What you said about what we did not making a difference—it did."

"You bet," said Ember. "Look at Noll and her son. Until Ignessa came knocking, they lived in peace for fifteen years. The other shifters we helped out are doing fine, too. We can reopen the shelter… though we might need a bigger property. One with gargoyle-proof walls, this time."

"Yeah, it's getting a bit crowded in here," said Will.

"Especially if we adopt more dragonlings," said Kit. "Or maybe a cu sidhe…"

"Don't get carried away," said Will, but he was smiling. "We're already collecting strays."

"Oh, Bracken isn't staying here," said Becks. "He found a place down by the river."

"Oh?" I arched a brow. "And will you be seeing him again? Even though you don't like him?"

"Maybe." She sprawled on the sofa. "It's nice to have company when you're terrorising evil shifter thieves. London's underworld will be sorry we're back."

A clamour of voices came from outside.

"What's that noise?" asked Ember.

"The other dragons?" suggested Will.

"That's not a dragon." It sounded like… applause.

Becks pushed back the curtains, revealing a crowd gathering outside. I stared open-mouthed at an audience marching towards our house, led by Keira and her cats. Cheers and whooping sounded, and several people waved when they saw us watching.

"They have champagne," said Ember. "We should join them."

"I think I'll pass." Astor left the room, and I heard his footsteps on the stairs. Ember rolled her eyes after him.

Zeph caught my hand and wrapped both arms around me. "I'm glad you're okay."

"Same here." I kissed him on the mouth, enjoying the feel of his arms around me.

Ember cleared her throat, and I gave her an eye-roll. "Really? You're gonna try the big sister crap on me now?"

"No," she said. "Just wanted to congratulate you two. Also, if you do anything to hurt her, Zeph, you'll have two angry dragons chasing you out of London. More than three, if I ask the others to join in."

"Fair enough," said Zeph.

I looked at Ember. "Aren't you going to ask when it happened?"

"You're my little sister. I always know." She grinned. "Let's go and join the party."

The following morning, we went to see the dragon shifters again. With no working Moonbeam shards, we opted to use the spirit line rather than flying. Becks stayed behind, taking advantage of the mages' distraction to nose around the arena for any signs of foul play. Given that she'd invited Bracken to go with her, I suspected she had a different motive, but I wasn't about to begrudge her for making the most of our hard-won victory. Will was only coming because Kit insisted on bringing the dragonling to visit his friends. Astor also remained behind, after saying such a long goodbye to Ember that she had to catch us up at the park.

"Okay, this isn't so bad." I stepped onto the spirit line, which transformed into a transparent path leading in two directions. "Who needs the mirrors when we can hop all over the country in a few minutes?"

"I give it two weeks before the mages start charging for access," said Zeph. He still didn't look thrilled at the prospect of travelling via spirit line, but we were both recovering from the battle and we'd get to stretch our wings on the other side. I still wasn't keen on the dizzying drop on either side of the transparent path, but if I kept my gaze averted, I could pretend I was flying instead.

"Hey…" Zeph pointed. "There's someone up ahead."

Agnes waited for us beside a sprawling tree whose roots extended along the path.

"Where were you?" I asked. "You disappeared after taking Noll back to her son."

"Taking care of some unfinished business," she said. "Lady Montgomery has requested to see you."

"We were on our way to the dragons' village," I said.

"I thought so," said Agnes. "Everett's already there, helping the villagers. So was I, but I had an inkling you might get yourselves lost."

"You aren't wrong. This path is kinda confusing." I looked up at the tree, which looked oddly human-shaped from some angles. "You can't get to the other realm from here, right?"

"Not anymore," said Agnes. "I don't doubt the mages will try to regulate travel via this route soon enough, but for now it's worth taking advantage. You can get close to the village from here if you don't want to fly from Edinburgh. You have something of a celebrity status there."

"Even though Ignessa vaporised those mages?" I frowned.

"You saved their leader's life," said Agnes. "They're aware of that, though their memories are a tad fuzzy at the moment."

"I'll bet," said Ember. "So—is the village near this spirit line?"

"Close enough for me to bring supplies there," she said. "Best get off the path… it gives me the creeps, to tell you the truth."

"It's not dangerous?" I asked.

"Of course not. I just don't like spirit lines."

Now she'd got me paranoid, too. Despite Ignessa's absence, my spirit sight remained. I spotted a few ghosts drifting around the tree, but they disappeared when we went down a fork in the path. We stepped out into the Highlands, shivering in the sudden blast of cool air.

At once, Thorn bounded over to join the other dragonlings, who gambolled around him with cries of joy. Will and Kit walked over to them, hand in hand, while the rest of us made for the village.

The other dragon shifters were waiting for us, with apologies, thank yous, and promises. We refused all gifts—the dragons needed to focus on rebuilding first, above all else—but with Ignessa gone, the Moonbeam's hold over the other dragon shifters had broken. They had the freedom they'd longed for since before the war, before Lorne.

Azalea beckoned me over. "I'm sorry, Cori. I wouldn't blame you if you didn't want to associate with us again."

"If I didn't, I'd have to shun my sister for nearly setting London ablaze while she was under Ignessa's control," I said. "I forgive you. I know you wouldn't have let Ignessa take control of you on purpose."

"I heard what Lorne did… how he was the one who woke her up." She squeezed her eyes shut. "Is she… is she really gone?"

I dipped my head. "The city is gone, and Ignessa along with it. We can't go back."

"I know." Her mouth pinched. "I suppose we deserve no less."

"Don't say that," said Ember. "You got all your people out of the other realm before it collapsed. You saved their lives."

"I almost cost them everything."

"You didn't. Ignessa did," I said. "This was all her. She even played Lorne. Not that he wasn't a scumbag anyway, but Ignessa took advantage of that."

"Yes. That world was hers, not ours," she said quietly. "This realm… this realm doesn't feel like home either."

"It will." I gave an encouraging smile. "If we can get used to London, you can get used to living here. Or you can find somewhere else. Somewhere your kids can make new friends. It's not like before. The Orion League's gone, and dragon shifters aren't hunted everywhere they go. Noll and her son lived in London without incident for fifteen years, and now Ignessa has gone, there's no need for any of you to be afraid."

Old fears had a habit of hanging on, I knew, but Azalea looked a little happier when we parted.

Outside the village, Kit watched the dragonling flying around with his friends. When he glanced our way, his eyes shimmered with tears.

Will cleared his throat. "Kit, do you want to stay here? With Thorn and the others?"

Kit turned on the spot, a couple of tears falling from his eyes. "What?"

"If you want to stay here," Will said. "I'd be—I mean, I can't promise I'd be okay with it, but I understand—"

Kit flung himself at Will. "I want to stay with you, Will. We can come here and visit him, right?"

"Of course," said Will. "You didn't think I'd want to go forever without seeing His Biteyness again?"

Kit released him. "We could always adopt something smaller, and more house-trained. Like a fire imp."

"What?" Will gave him an alarmed look. "Please no. Three dragons in my house is more than enough firepower."

"Maybe not three for much longer," Ember said.

I turned to her. "What? You and Astor…"

"It's getting crowded in that house," she replied. "We'll have to figure out what to do with the mirror, but if Will and Kit are going to turn the place into a zoo, Astor and I are better off moving to our own place. Once I'm gainfully employed again, that is."

"You'll have room to raise a whole flock of baby dragonlings." Will gave her a wink, and Ember swatted at him.

Agnes made an amused noise. "You're going home now?"

"Want to come with us to Edinburgh?" Ember asked Agnes. "We were going to fly, but we can go via the spirit line instead."

"I'll stay here," said Everett, his eyes twinkling. "Agnes has always wanted to ride on a dragon. She just won't admit it."

Agnes scowled. "I won't go into the necromancer guild. Those blasted mages keep showing up on my doorstep asking for advice too often as it is."

"We're going home, too," said Will, nodding to Kit. "Since we don't have an invite to the necromancer guild. But we'll stay here to watch Agnes flying. That, I won't miss."

I grinned. "I can volunteer."

———

Our group entered Edinburgh's necromancer guild to find Lady Montgomery waiting for us, along with what looked like half the guild.

"Hey," said Ilsa, waving me over. "You're popular here."

More necromancers filled the lobby. Behind Ilsa, a short young woman with a sweep of brown hair stood arm in arm with a handsome man with longish hair and angular features, while Morgan stood next to a tall man with dreadlocks.

"You won't remember me, but we met once when you were in dragon form," the brown-haired woman was saying to Zeph.

"I do remember," said Zeph. "Glad you got out of the dragon shifters' realm in one piece."

Lady Montgomery beckoned me aside. "I wanted to warn you that Lord Addison is looking for you."

"What, to recruit me to the mages?" I said. "Or to ask for my advice, like he keeps doing to Agnes?"

"Not quite," she said. "Your actions drew a great deal of attention from multiple angles, and the Council of Twelve is in need of allies."

"Council of what?" I asked.

"It's a supernatural collective across all regions, set up in the last couple of years to help humanity handle other-worldly threats," said Lady Montgomery. "The Council formed after the first evidence of the Ancients' return appeared, but things have escalated recently, with so many humans developing magical abilities."

"Do they want me because of my spirit sight or because I'm a dragon shifter?" I asked.

"Both," said Lady Montgomery. "I'm supposed to inform you that if you wish to join, feel free to get in touch with me, or with Ivy Lane."

Hmm. I'd think about that one later. I'd had entirely too much publicity already. Granted, being a dragon meant keeping a low profile would always be challenging, but it would be nice to take it easy for a bit. Once I got a new job, that is.

"Everyone wants a piece of me," I remarked as we left the guild's headquarters.

"Now you know how I feel," said Ember. "For the record, I'm saying no. I'll be on call to help out if they need me, but I'm not being anyone's poster dragon."

"Nor me," I said. "I notice they didn't ask for the mirror back, at least."

"They don't want dragons invading their headquarters," said Zeph. "Not now they know how many of us there are."

"Speaking of the mirror..." I turned to Ember. "Will you and Astor be taking it with you when you move out?"

"Oh." She paused. "I don't know. It wouldn't surprise me if London's mages came after it again."

"I think they've learned their lesson." *For once.* I turned to Zeph. He'd been alone for a long time, and while he hadn't become close to the other dragon shifters, perhaps maintaining that contact would help him build friendships with the others. Over time, we would rebuild, without the shadow of the goddess at our backs. "What d'you think?"

Zeph wrapped an arm around my shoulders. "I prefer some dragons to others."

"I bet." Ember gave me a nudge. "Ready to go?"

"Sure." I waved to Agnes and the necromancers who'd walked out into the streets to watch us leave. "Want to give them a show?"

Ember took flight first. Then Zeph and I shifted, and as one, we launched into the air, wings catching the breeze and flying over the city. The world spread out below us, an open map waiting to be explored.

No Orion League. No Lorne.

We'd never forget who we'd lost, but we had a future to build, and ahead, London waited for us with open arms.

The last rays of sunlight caught on our scales as my sister and I flew towards home.

ABOUT THE AUTHOR

Emma is the New York Times and USA Today Bestselling author of the Changeling Chronicles urban fantasy series.

Emma spent her childhood creating imaginary worlds to compensate for a disappointingly average reality, so it was probably inevitable that she ended up writing fantasy novels. When she's not immersed in her own fictional universes, Emma can be found with her head in a book or wandering around the world in search of adventure.

Find out more about Emma's books at
www.emmaladams.com.